WON
NEVER

OTHER BOOKS BY TIM DOWNS

WONDERS NEVER CEASE

TIM DOWNS

THOMAS NELSON
Since 1798

NASHVILLE   DALLAS   MEXICO CITY   RIO DE JANEIRO

Published in Nashville, Tennessee, by Thomas Nelson. Thomas Nelson is a registered trademark of Thomas Nelson, Inc.

Published in association with the literary agency of Alive Communications, Inc. 7680 Goddard Street, Suite 200, Colorado Springs, CO 80920. www.AliveCommunications.com.

Thomas Nelson, Inc., books may be purchased in bulk for educational, business, fund-raising, or sales promotional use. For information, please e-mail SpecialMarkets@ThomasNelson.com.

Publisher's Note: This novel is a work of fiction. Names, characters, places, and incidents are either products of the author's imagination or used fictitiously. All characters are fictional, and any similarity to people living or dead is purely coincidental.

Library of Congress Cataloging-in-Publication Data

Downs, Tim.
  Wonders never cease / Tim Downs.
    p. cm.
  Summary: When a car accident leaves a famous movie star in a coma, nurse Kemp—a medical school dropout—devises an evil plan. Manipulating her medication, he pretends to be an angel giving her messages—then dictates a "spiritual bestseller" he believes will make them both rich. But what will he do if real angels show up?
  ISBN 978-1-59554-309-7 (soft cover)
  I. Title.
PS3604.O954W66 2010
813'.6—dc22   2009053724

Printed in the United States of America

10 11 12 13 RRD 5 4 3 2 1

For my beautiful Joy,
my reason to get out of bed every morning
and my reason to return every night.
And for Cyndee Pelton and Madeleine Gaba-Nebres
at Loma Linda University Children's Hospital,
our very own angels in disguise.

"Man is neither angel nor beast, and it is unfortunately the case that anyone trying to act the angel acts the beast."

—Blaise Pascal, *Pensées*

PROLOGUE

I was six years old when I saw my first angel, and nobody was too thrilled about it. Not my mom, that's for sure—she almost freaked. But she had a lot going on in her life right about then, so it's hard to blame her. Now, Kemp—he thought I'd gone postal, but then he never thought much of me anyway. Maybe that's always the way it is with somebody else's kids. Kemp only wanted my mom, after all. That's all he signed up for; I just came with the deal. But a kid who sees angels—that was more than he bargained for. Maybe I shouldn't blame him either—but I do.

I was attending an Episcopal school in Los Angeles when it happened. Funny thing is, they freaked too. Now, this is an angel we're talking about—I thought I might get extra credit. But no, they found it just as hard to believe as everybody else. Hard to figure, isn't it? At least I thought so.

That's right, California. Believe me, that doesn't help when you're telling a story like this. Los Angeles—isn't that supposed to be the "city of angels"? Not anymore, I guess. Maybe I should tell people it happened in New York or Boston—someplace where people are too smart for things like this to happen. Sorry—these were California angels, and I'm just telling you the way it was.

Now you don't know me and I don't know you, but I know

what you're probably thinking right now—'cause I've told this story a dozen times, and every time it goes pretty much the same way. The minute I say the word "angel," you get a funny look on your face. You wonder if you heard me right; you stop smiling; you start to blink. You cock your head to one side and take a closer look at me, like maybe there's a couple of screws backing out of my forehead and my frontal lobe is about to eject.

It's true what they say, you know: if you talk to God, you're religious; but if you hear from God, you're schizophrenic.

No need to apologize. I've seen that look before and I'm used to it.

It took me about a year to collect all the pieces of this story. A lot of it I saw myself, but parts of it I didn't know about 'til later. I don't have any way to convince you, and frankly I don't care if you believe me or not. All I can do is tell you what happened, and then you have to decide. I don't know, maybe you can't believe unless you see it for yourself. But I know what I saw—and I believe it.

This is how it happened.

1

So tell me. What did you think of the script?"

"I loved it. I devoured it. It was genius."

She was lying. In twenty years of acting, Olivia Hayden had never read an entire screenplay from cover to cover. Liv didn't like to read—it bored her. Whenever the studios sent over a script, she simply passed it on to her agent, Morty Biederman. She always let Morty digest the thing and evaluate her part, then run off the pages containing her dialogue and send them back to her, reducing the 120-page screenplay to a manageable few sheets of Courier 12-point text. Liv always told the tabloids that she didn't like to read because she was dyslexic, because that's what Tom Cruise had told them and it seemed to work for him—and Liv could stand a little more sympathy from the rags these days.

The young director let out a sigh of relief. "I was afraid you might not like it."

"It's brilliant," she said with just the right touch of breathless awe.

When the director glanced down at his feet in modesty, Liv used the opportunity to quickly look him over. *I wonder if this kid has a driver's license?* she thought, shaking her head ever so slightly. The guy couldn't have been more than twenty-five—he probably had his UCLA Film School diploma still rolled up in his back pocket. But hey, the kid had a script and he had a studio backing him, and a part is a part. *Is that a pimple? Man, I'm old enough to be his . . . older sister.*

"You know, I cowrote this script," the director said.

"Astonishing. A multidimensional talent."

Liar. Who did he think he was fooling? Morty had already filled her in. The kid had just stumbled onto a decent story concept, then hired himself a second-string writer to hammer out a treatment and first draft. He probably bought the script outright and then pasted his own name on the cover to negotiate a better deal as a writer-director hyphenate, inflating his salary and granting him casting privileges. That's the only reason Liv was sitting there: if this kid wasn't casting the film she wouldn't even be talking to him. She rarely spoke to a director before a deal was signed, and writers—well, everybody in Hollywood knows that writers are basically pond scum.

2

"I can't tell you how thrilled I was to find out you were available," he said.

"You were lucky," Liv said. "I happen to be between films right now."

Way between. Ten years ago she wouldn't have taken a second glance at a half-baked script like this, but it was a lead role, after all, and good parts were getting hard to find.

"What's the title again?" she asked.

"*Lips of Fury.*"

She winced. "Catchy."

"I think some of the dialogue still needs a little tweaking," he said.

"Don't you dare change a thing. It's perfect the way it is."

Why bother? She never argued about a script before she was on the set anyway. Once production started the clock would be ticking and money would be flowing like water—then she would have leverage and she could rip the script to shreds.

They sat together at the bar at Kate Mantilini's on Wilshire Boulevard, perched on round gray barstools with tall rigid backs that were designed for appearance only—*like everything else in this town*, she thought. It was almost morning, though Kate's typically closed by midnight. That's the way Liv planned it; the director had requested the meeting, but Liv had insisted on choosing the time and place. The ridiculous hour wasn't chosen simply to ensure privacy, though Kate's had its share of celebrity patrons and annoying fans; the hour was intended to remind this kid who she was: she was Olivia Hayden, and Kate Mantilini's or any other eating establishment in Hollywood would stay open just as long as she wanted it to. Liv Hayden was used to getting what she wanted, and the sooner this kid learned that lesson, the easier it would be when it came to negotiations. Not negotiations over money—Morty always handled that. The negotiations she was interested in were the ones that took place on the set: when she wanted to shoot a scene without rehearsals, or when the director was demanding a third take when she preferred to head back to her trailer for a nap. She wanted things the way she wanted them, and she didn't want to have to flirt and pout to get her way each time. She had paid those dues by the time she was thirty; Liv was fast approaching forty-five now, and she didn't have the patience or the energy to play those games anymore.

The director grinned at her. "I'm really looking forward to working with you on this film, Ms. Hayden. I welcome your input—your opinion means a lot to me. I mean, an actor of your—stature."

Stature. The word stung, but Liv kept a smile plastered

3

on her face. *Stature—durability—longevity*—they were all just euphemisms for the same brutal reality: *age*. It was no picnic being a forty-plus box office icon in Hollywood, especially for a woman. Oh, sure, male actors complained about the ravages of time, too, but it was different for men. Less than a week ago she was lunching with Nic Cage at The Ivy when he started whining about hairlines and face-lifts and she shoved his corn chowder into his lap. She reminded him that Brando was the size of a Macy's balloon when they paid him $3.7 million to do Superman—but let an actress pack on an extra twenty and the only role she'll get is doing commercials for Jenny Craig. *It's not the same*, she told him. *Women in Hollywood have to do everything men do, but we're supposed to do it crammed into a size four.*

4

And in Hollywood the cameras were everywhere, circling like buzzards, searching the landscape for sagging appendages or a heretofore unreported nip or tuck. The buzzards could smell death—*career* death—and the instant they detected the onset of death the cameras all went *click, click, click*. The digital cameras didn't even make a sound—you never knew where they were or when they were clicking away. And just when you thought they had finally left you alone, you would find yourself on the cover of a tabloid looking worse than you ever imagined possible, bulging out of some horrid swimsuit you should have had the sense to drop off at Goodwill ten years ago.

Buzzards, that's what they were. No—the cameras were worse than buzzards, because a buzzard can only eat you once, but a bad photograph can eat away at you forever.

"Why don't we talk about the part?" the director suggested.

"Yes, let's do." *It's about time.*

She needed this part, because the only antidote for a bad photograph is a good one. The public doesn't have a short memory; it has amnesia. The minute they walk out of that theater they forget your face, and the last image they see of you is the one they remember. This was a smaller film, a film she wouldn't have touched when she was at the top of her game—but that was then and this is now. At least it was a feature film with a respectable budget and decent distribution, not just some pathetic sub-fifteen-million-dollar trailer that would end up buried on the Lifetime Channel. And the role was a good one—the kind that was getting harder to find. Danielle Blakelock, sleek and seductive twenty-five-year-old microbiologist martial arts expert.

Twenty-five. Ouch.

But she could do it—she could still pull it off. After all, it was the same role she had been playing for twenty years. Different name, different location, same role. Twenty-five—it wasn't such a stretch. If shooting didn't start until summer, she still had time to squeeze in three weeks of green tea diets and detox wraps at Las Ventanas. That would do it. That would put her back in top form—except maybe for the close-ups . . .

"Will we be using a body double?" she asked.

The director frowned. "Why would we need to do that?"

She gave him a wink. "I knew I liked you the minute I saw you." She casually laid her hand on her right thigh and hiked up her skirt a little to show just a bit more leg—then spotted a telltale lacework of faint blue lines and slid it back down again.

"I see this character as essentially tortured," the director said. "I think her driving motivation is to relieve her own guilt by redeeming the soul of someone she loves."

"I couldn't agree more." *Whatever.*

"The opening scene finds her in an alcoholic stupor in the middle of a vacant lot. She opens her eyes and looks around . . . Where is she? How did she get there? How long has she—"

5

"Wait a minute. She's an alcoholic?"

The director paused. "How could you miss that? It's central to her entire character."

Liv made a mental note to strangle Morty. "How long has she been an alcoholic?"

"Twenty, maybe twenty-five years."

"What was she doing, sipping margaritas in her bassinet?"

"Huh?"

"The woman's only twenty-five years old."

"What are you talking about? She's closer to fifty."

Liv's left shoe slipped off the footrest and clacked on the tile floor.

"Did she come across younger in the script? I suppose we could knock off a couple of years, but she has to be at least in her midforties if she's got a twenty-five-year-old daughter."

"Daughter?"

"Danielle."

"I thought we were talking about Danielle."

"No, we're talking about your character—Margaret Blakelock, Danielle's alcoholic mother."

A very long pause followed, during which Liv's eyelids slowly lowered until her eyes were only burning slits.

"*Margaret* Blakelock," she said.

"That's right."

"Not Danielle."

"No, Margaret. Didn't your agent tell you—"

"And may I ask who will be playing Danielle?"

"I haven't cast that part yet. I'm thinking about one of the Olsen twins."

Another long pause.

Without breaking eye contact, Liv reached to her left and picked up a bowl of mixed nuts from the bar. She held the bowl in front of her and slowly sorted through them with her index finger, settling on a filbert of unusual size. She brought the nut to eye level and held it like a dart; she took careful aim, then tossed it at the young director. It bounced off the center of his forehead—*plink*.

The director sat speechless.

Liv reached for another nut—a cashew this time.

"Let me get this straight," she said. "You want to cast me as the alcoholic mother of an Olsen twin—an actress who would make me look like John Madden in a housedress just by standing beside me."

She tossed the nut—*plink*.

"I thought you—I thought I made it clear that—"

"Let *me* make something clear: I am Olivia Hayden. I have made twenty-seven feature films, and most of them turned a profit."

Plink.

"I was starring in films when you were still in training pants. My face is known all over the world, and my name is practically a household word."

Plink.

"I have played a sleek and seductive police officer, a sleek and seductive shuttle astronaut, and a sleek and seductive advertising executive. I can even play a sleek and seductive microbiologist martial arts expert, because I'm a professional and I have that kind of range. But I do *not*—"

Plink.

"I do *not*—"

Plink.

"I do *not* play the bloated fifty-year-old mother of an Olsen twin."

She dumped the remainder of the bowl in his lap, slid

7

off her barstool, and headed for the door without another word.

Liv stood seething in the parking lot while the valet brought her car around. The young man opened the door for her and held it, smiling. She stepped up to the car and then stopped and turned to the valet. "Do you know who I am?" she asked.

The valet's smile vanished. "Uh—BMW M6 ragtop—that's what your claim check says, anyway. Is there some problem with—"

"Get away from my car, moron." She jerked the door out of his hand and ducked inside.

She jammed the pedal to the floor and hit Wilshire Boulevard with the tires already smoking. It was after four o'clock and the streets were all but vacant; she raced down Wilshire without regard for speed limits or stoplights, half hoping that a cop would pull her over just so she could pull a Zsa Zsa and slap the fool broadside. She was dying to slap somebody—she needed it bad. She glanced around at the empty streets. *There's never a cop around when you need one.*

She reached the 405 a few minutes later and headed south with no particular destination in mind. She just wanted to drive, and anywhere would do.

Margaret Blakelock, she thought. *Not Danielle—of course not! No, we need someone younger to play that role, someone without distracting body features—like skin! An Olsen twin—I weigh more than both of them combined! I'd have to face sideways the whole picture!*

She passed a minivan like it was standing still and crossed all eight lanes just to feel the car swerve.

The alcoholic mother, she thought. *How glamorous! I can see it now: As the scene opens I'm lying drunk in some vacant lot. I lift my bloated head and drool runs down my chin . . .*

Cut! Print it! Boy, I hope they pick a nice shooting location—a vacant lot in Jamaica maybe. Morty—he knew about this. I'm gonna kill that guy. You keep an agent for twenty years, and this is what he does to you? He didn't send me the wrong pages—he did it on purpose! He's trying to tell me that I'm getting old—that I'm going to have to start taking different parts. Well, thanks for the press release, Morty, but I already knew that.

She shot under an overpass at ninety miles per hour. The wind swirling behind her BMW blasted the concrete abutment with bits of sand and gravel.

Goldie Hawn was right, there are only three ages for women in Hollywood: Babe, District Attorney, and Driving Miss Daisy. What happened to me? Yesterday I was sleek and seductive—suddenly I'm the alcoholic mother of sleek and seductive. Tomorrow I'll probably be checking myself into Betty Ford.

She glanced in the rearview mirror and to her astonishment found a vehicle trailing behind her barely a car length off her bumper. "Moron!" she shouted at the mirror. *Eight empty lanes and this idiot still wants to tailgate! Welcome to Los Angeles.*

For a split second she considered slamming on her brakes and sending him slamming into her tail end, but she knew that at ninety miles per hour his engine would end up in her lap. She tapped on her brakes instead; the car behind her slowed down a little but still remained a single car length behind.

She hit the gas and accelerated—the car behind her kept pace. She changed lanes twice—so did her pursuer. *Who is this idiot?* she wondered, and suddenly she knew.

Buzzards!

The paparazzi—they must have been waiting for her outside Kate Mantilini's. Don't those people *ever* have enough pictures? Doesn't an editor ever have the decency to say,

"Enough! We've got photos of this chick coming out the wazoo—give her some privacy." Couldn't some sympathetic editor at least remind them, "Look—nobody wants to see this woman walking out of a Walgreens with a bottle of Metamucil. And no more shots of her stuffing her face with french fries either—nobody wants to see that." But no, the buzzards were never satisfied.

She glared into the mirror. Where did this guy think she was going at four o'clock in the morning? What was the big attraction? The way he was driving you'd think he was following her to the Golden Globes!

She lowered her window and screamed into the wind, "Get off my tail, you moron! I'm just an alcoholic mother—you have me confused with someone else!"

But the car stayed right behind her.

And that's when Olivia Hayden got mad.

She was sick to death of feeding these buzzards, and she made up her mind right then and there that this guy was one bird that wasn't going to eat tonight. She would outdrive him if it took her all night; she would take the 405 all the way to Irvine, then jump onto the San Diego Freeway and take it all the way to Tijuana if she had to.

An Olsen twin, she kept repeating to herself, and her hands gripped the steering wheel until her knuckles turned white.

≋

Ramon Munoz reached out the window and smacked the 24-Hour Pizza light that was magnetically attached to the roof of his car. The light flickered once and went out again, and he decided to leave it that way. Hey, it was only for advertising— what did he care? It's not like he was driving a cop car—nobody was yelling, "Pull over! Let the pizza guy through!"

He glanced over at the street address taped to the top of the pizza warmer—someplace in Inglewood. He hoped he didn't get lost again. The drivers were no longer obligated to make their deliveries in thirty minutes or less—too many accidents—but a slow delivery meant a cold pizza, and a cold pizza meant a bad tip. *Why don't they give us GPS units? The owner—he's the man, he's got the money. A nice Garmin or something—that would speed things up.* Still, Ramon managed to make most of his deliveries in the originally promised thirty minutes or less, but not because of satellite technology. He managed it because he was smart.

Take this evening, for example. He had spotted the lone BMW zooming down the 405 and had pulled in close behind it, drafting in its wake. *Shrewd move, Ramon*—it would knock a few minutes off his time and it was good for gas mileage too. Hey—it worked for the NASCAR drivers, so it should work for him.

11

And the BMW obviously wasn't worried about the cops; maybe the driver was somebody important—maybe they had a radar detector. Besides, Ramon got a quick glimpse of the driver when she looked at him in her rearview mirror—the woman was hot. Who were the cops going to pull over, the pizza guy in the '97 Corolla or the *chica guapa* in the bloodred M6? He settled back in his seat and fired up the radio. Ramon knew he had it made.

He just wished the crazy woman would stay in one lane . . .

The two cars went screaming down the 405 bumper to bumper.

2

The instant Natalie Pelton opened the door she knew things were running behind. Leah was still sitting at the table in her pajamas, angrily picking the raisins from her toast and dropping each one on the floor in disgust. Mrs. Rodriguez, still dressed in her flowered housecoat, was standing at the counter smearing peanut butter over two limp slices of bread.

"Good morning, Mrs. Rodriguez. How are we doing today?"

"Me, I'm doing fine," she said, and then with a nod toward the table: "That one's a pistol."

"One of those nights?"

"Is there any other kind?"

Natalie dropped her keys on the counter with a *chink* and walked over to her six-year-old daughter, planting a quick one on the side of her forehead. "Good morning, sweetheart. You're going to be late for school. What's the holdup?"

"Raisins." Leah scowled, wiping off the kiss with the back of her hand and returning to her work. "She knows I hate raisins. She gives 'em to me anyway."

"Don't eat them."

"I'm not."

"Don't drop them on the floor either," Natalie said, squatting down beside the chair and collecting the black dots with one quick swipe of her hand.

"Raisins are good for you," Mrs. Rodriguez scolded. "Raisins are fruit, and you need three servings of fruit every day to stay regular. Dr. Oz says so."

"We can argue about it later," Natalie said. "Right now we need to get you to school, young lady. Get dressed and grab your backpack—let's go."

When Leah disappeared into her bedroom, Natalie turned to Mrs. Rodriguez. "How did things go last night?"

"No problems—no new ones, anyway. She did her homework and she watched one hour of TV. Then she read for a while—that girl loves to read. She was in bed by nine, I was in bed by nine fifteen. I swear, she wears me out. I raised three of my own, but I was younger then. Now I run out of steam."

Natalie paused. "Any more stories?"

"Always stories. Lots of stories. She tells them to her dolls, she tells them to the walls, she sits on the front porch and tells them to the cars passing by. She has quite the imagination. Maybe she'll be a writer or a poet someday. She's gifted, that one—maybe that's why she's so *obstinado*."

Gifted, Natalie thought. *That's not the word the counselor used.*

"How was work?" Mrs. Rodriguez asked.

"It was work," Natalie said.

"A nurse's life is not an easy one."

"I can't complain. It's only three or four nights a week."

"But twelve hours straight, all night long. I don't know how you do it."

She glanced at Leah's bedroom. "Neither do I sometimes."

"But what would life be without work?"

She patted Mrs. Rodriguez on the shoulder. "I think they call it *play*."

The door opened again and a man stepped into the kitchen. He was tall and good-looking, with thick black hair and dark eyes to match. He was dressed in blue nursing scrubs, exactly like Natalie's.

He winked at Mrs. Rodriguez. "Hey, *mamacita*. Did you keep the bed warm for me?" Without another word he walked directly into the second bedroom and closed the door behind him.

Mrs. Rodriguez rolled her eyes. "I hate it when he calls me that."

"He knows," Natalie said. "Sorry."

Natalie turned and followed the man into the bedroom. When she opened the door she found him already sprawled facedown across the bed.

"Kemp, what are you doing?"

"What does it look like I'm doing?" he said without opening his eyes.

"It's your turn to take Leah to school."

"Can't be."

"You know it is. I do it three days a week and you do the other two. Come on, we don't have time for this."

"School holiday," he mumbled. "Give the kid a day off."

"Come on, I'm not kidding. If you don't leave right now you'll be late."

Kemp slowly propped himself up on the edge of the bed. "Why do we have to go through this every day? We don't finish our shifts at UCLA until seven. By that time we're both brain-dead—but then we have to race home just to get the kid off to a school fifteen miles away. This is Culver City, Natalie—they've got the best public schools in West LA. They've even got these clever things called 'buses' now that'll pick her up right in front of the house."

"Kemp, come on."

"It's a waste of time and energy, not to mention money. Think about it, Natalie, ten thousand bucks a year for a private school. Think what we could buy with that."

Think what you *could buy with that.* "I'm not having the public vs. private school debate with you this morning. Are you taking her or not?"

He lay back down on the bed. "School holiday," he said. "Check the calendar; it must be Saint Somebody-or-Other's Day. We don't want to offend the powers that be."

"Fine." She turned on her heel and slammed the bedroom door behind her.

Leah was waiting for her at the kitchen door; she held her backpack open while Mrs. Rodriguez loaded her lunch box.

"Better not be any raisins," Leah grumbled.

"Oh, you scare me," Mrs. Rodriguez said. "Make your own lunch next time."

Leah looked up at her mother. "I thought it was Kemp's turn."

"Kemp had a long night," Natalie said. "You ready?"

"I like Kemp better," she said. "He drives real fast and he never talks."

"We'll have to speak to Kemp about that. Let's go."

"I forgot to tell you," Mrs. Rodriguez said. "My niece—she's moving back to LA."

"Your niece?"

"She has two little ones of her own."

Natalie's eyes widened. "Mrs. Rodriguez—what are you telling me?"

"She's going to need me. I'm sorry, I have to take care of my family."

Natalie closed her eyes. "When?"

"Soon—a couple of days maybe. I would have told you sooner, but I just found out myself. Sorry."

"Mrs. Rodriguez, how am I supposed to replace you in a couple of days? Please—I need at least a couple of weeks."

Mrs. Rodriguez smiled a sheepish apology.

"Is this about money? Because if it is—"

"It's about family," she said. "If it was money I would say so."

"Do you know of anyone? Can you recommend somebody?"

"Let me ask around."

"Please, I'd really appreciate it. Somebody who can sleep over; somebody who's good with kids; somebody who might be patient with the—you know—the stories." The more she described the person she required, the more hopeless she felt. Mrs. Rodriguez had been a godsend, and God didn't seem to be sending her any extra blessings these days.

Natalie walked her daughter to the car in silence. She opened the back door and held it for her.

"I guess no more raisins," Leah said.

"Just get in the car."

She started the engine and pulled out of the driveway. They were already ten minutes late; she hoped she could make up the time on the freeway. *Her timing couldn't be worse*, she thought. *How do I find another Mrs. Rodriguez in just a couple of days? There's no way. Kemp and I will have to fill in—one of us will have to switch to days. Won't that be wonderful—one of us working nights and the other one working days. We can shake hands at the door twice a day! Terrific—we're not even connecting now.*

She felt a familiar knot in the pit of her stomach. *This is how it started before. I can't let it happen again—I just can't.*

"Put your seat belt on," she called to the backseat.

"It is on."

Natalie glanced in the rearview mirror. She could see the loose ends of the seat belt lying on the vinyl.

"Put it on, Leah—I mean it."

"Fine."

Several seconds passed before she heard the buckle click.

She thought about Kemp again—backing out of his responsibilities with Leah whenever it suited him. She wondered how many other single moms faced the same struggle with the men they allowed into their lives. Kemp was fine with Leah—even affectionate sometimes—right up until the moment it inconvenienced him, and then it was always, "She's your kid." Natalie hated that—it made her feel like she was begging: "Please—love my daughter as much as I do." It made her feel weak and powerless, and that was something she despised.

When she merged onto the 405 her heart sank—eight lanes at a virtual standstill. There must have been an accident somewhere; even the 405 wasn't usually this bad. She tried to look up ahead, but the vehicle in front of her was one of those towering SUVs that she always complained about and secretly wished she could afford. She eased out of her lane a little to try to peer between the lines of traffic, but the man in the car to her left laid on his horn and flashed the universal sign of brotherhood.

"He flipped you off," Leah said.

"Yes, honey, he did."

"Kemp always does the same thing back."

"That's something else we'll have to talk to Kemp about." She pulled back into the right lane and into the shadow of the SUV.

17

It made her furious that Kemp had played the "private school" card again. He knew why Leah was in a private school; he knew that so many grade school kids in California were struggling just to learn the difficult English language that it sometimes slowed the classes down. It's not easy to learn science or arithmetic when you don't even have a basic vocabulary, but while those students were learning English, the other kids were learning nothing—or less than they could. That was the reason for St. Stephen's Episcopal; that was why it was worth the ten thousand a year.

That was one of the reasons, anyway. The one that mattered to her more—the one she never mentioned to Kemp—was that there might be teachers there who would be a little more understanding of a child with Leah's . . . uniqueness.

For Kemp it wasn't about quality of education or what was best for Leah—it was just about money. Every time he saw a commercial for the latest luxury car or drove past some new upscale housing development, the subject of private school always came up. It was always about money with Kemp—but that's because Kemp grew up with money and he didn't have money now.

She looked at her watch: It was almost eight thirty and they were now hopelessly late. They had been inching forward for the last thirty minutes, and there was no breakthrough in sight. Natalie stopped entertaining the possibility of a miraculous on-time arrival and began to concoct an excuse instead.

"Once there was a girl with golden wings."

Natalie looked in the rearview mirror. "What did you say, sweetheart?"

"The girl never showed her wings to anyone. She kept them folded under her clothing. The straps of her backpack rubbed them and it hurt, but still she kept them hidden."

18

Natalie turned and looked at her daughter. "Did you see that on TV?"

"But when she was alone she would take off her shirt and stretch out her wings, and the gold was so bright that they would blind anyone who looked at them. That's why she had to hide them. That's why they had to be a secret."

Natalie felt her eyes begin to burn . . .

Suddenly she began to see flashing lights and emergency vehicles lined up to her right along the shoulder of the road. There was a brilliant red fire engine with the LAFD logo emblazoned on the side, and two boxlike EMS trucks from UCLA's trauma center. The traffic slowed down even more as drivers and their passengers rubbernecked to take in every detail of the terrible accident. It was like watching a parade, except that this parade stood still while the viewers passed by. First the fire truck, then the EMS rigs, then two firemen wielding some kind of cutting device, then a gurney with a pair of medics holding either end. They all looked exhausted, as though they had been working for hours.

At last came the parade's grand marshal—the accident vehicle itself. It was a fiery red BMW—or what was left of one. The car was flattened and crushed, as though it had rolled several times. There was no roof on the car, and the windshield was nothing but a bent and empty frame. The vehicle was surrounded by medical and emergency personnel, and to Natalie's horror she realized that the victim was still in the car—a blonde-haired woman slumped back in the driver's seat with her eyes closed tight and her mouth gaping open.

"God help that woman," she whispered.

As Natalie's car drew even with the accident vehicle, the traffic came to a complete stop. Natalie heard the click of a

19

seat belt behind her and turned to find Leah standing in the backseat with her face pressed against the window.

"Leah, sit down!" Natalie said.

Leah continued to stare.

"Sit down and put your seat belt back on! Do it right now!"

But Leah was glued to the glass with eyes as wide as saucers.

"Don't look at that woman!" Natalie shouted.

But Leah wasn't looking at the woman. She was looking at a man standing beside the car. He wasn't dressed like the others—he wasn't wearing a fireman's jacket or a doctor's white coat. He was dressed in simple clothes—like a man passing by who had just stopped to take a closer look. He stood right beside the woman with the blonde hair, but no one seemed to notice him and no one seemed to care. The man stood quietly, peacefully, holding his right hand palm-down just above the woman's head.

Then he turned and looked at Leah.

He looked directly into her eyes.

He smiled at her.

Then he put a finger to his lips and went, *Shhh*.

3

And how are we doing this evening, Mr."—the man took a quick glance at the patient's chart—"Jablonski, is it?"

"Not so good. I'm not sleeping."

"That's a common complaint in a neurological ICU. You'll get used to it." He flipped through the chart and quickly scanned the attached medical records. "Who's your attending?"

"My doctor? I think his name is Smithson or something."

The man looked unimpressed. "Smithson—did his residency at UVA."

"Is that good?"

"It'll do."

"Who're you?"

"My name is Kemp McAvoy. I see from your chart here that your initial diagnosis is CIDP."

"That sounds familiar. What is that, exactly?"

"Chronic inflammatory demyelinating polyneuropathy. It's a disorder of the peripheral nerves caused by damage to the myelin sheathing. Essentially, your body's immune system is attacking the covering that insulates your nerves—they begin to short-circuit like a bundle of stripped wires. Let me try something here. Can you sit up for me?"

The man sat up and dangled his legs over the edge of the

bed. "I hate these gowns. They leave your whole backside open."

"That's the least of your worries, Mr. Jablonski." Kemp tapped the man's knee with a rubber percussion hammer—there was no response. "Hmm."

"What?"

"No reflex—just as I expected. Tell me, have you been experiencing weakness in your legs and arms?"

"That's why I'm here."

"Have they drawn spinal fluid yet to test for elevated protein levels?"

"What? No, I don't think so. Does that hurt?"

"Tell me about the onset of weakness in your legs and arms. Did it happen over a period of months? Or was it more like weeks or days?"

"I don't know . . . over a week or two, I suppose."

"Hmm."

"What? You keep saying that."

"I'm not convinced of the original diagnosis. Considering the fairly rapid presentation of symptoms, a better diagnosis might be Guillain-Barré syndrome."

"What's that?"

"You'll need a lumbar puncture to confirm it, but I'm fairly confident of the diagnosis."

"Is that bad? What's a lumbar puncture?"

Just then the door opened and another man stepped inside. He wore a white lab coat with a UCLA Medical Center ID that said SMITHSON, MD. Dr. Smithson took one look at his patient sitting upright in bed and Kemp holding the percussion hammer beside him and said, "What's going on here?"

Neither man answered.

The neurologist pointed an accusing finger at Kemp. "I'm asking you."

Kemp shrugged. "Just looking in on a colleague's patient while she's on break."

"A *colleague,*" Smithson said. "You mean another nurse."

Mr. Jablonski squinted at Kemp. "You're a *nurse?*"

Smithson swung the door open wide. "I want to talk to you outside—right now." He charged out the door and into the hallway.

Kemp looked at Mr. Jablonski. "It's pronounced *Ghee-yan Bah-ray*—just tell them GBS. Somebody around here should know what it means—even if he went to UVA." Kemp calmly followed the neurologist into the hallway and closed the door behind him.

Smithson was waiting for him. "What do you think you're doing, McAvoy?"

23

"My job," Kemp said.

"What were you doing with my patient's chart?"

"Checking to see if there were any orders. That's what nurses are paid to do."

"I know what nurses are paid to do, and what they're *not* paid to do—like second-guessing a physician's diagnosis and dispensing medical advice. Don't bother denying it—I've heard complaints about you from two other neurologists. I know about you, McAvoy. I've heard the rumors—and judging by the size of your ego, you probably started them. They tell me you went to med school at Johns Hopkins and even started your residency there. Is that right?"

"Yes."

"Well, aren't you the bright boy. What was your specialty?"

"Anesthesiology."

"But I hear you never finished your residency. Is that true?"

"It's true."

"How far did you get?"

Kemp paused. "Third year."

"You were in your final year of residency and you quit to become an RN? That was a shrewd career move. What happened?"

Kemp didn't answer.

"I don't really care what happened," Smithson said. "What I do care about is that you seem to think you're a doctor—and you're not. Maybe you've got an MD and maybe you've got a license, but without that residency you're not board certified, mister. You want to practice medicine? Go right ahead—move out to Bakersfield or Fresno and hang up your shingle there. But without that residency you'll never have hospital privileges and you'll never work in a place like UCLA—except as a nurse. *You're not a doctor here*—got it? So why don't you just check the vital signs and empty the Foleys and leave the practice of medicine to those of us who bothered to finish school?"

Kemp just shrugged.

Smithson wheeled around to storm off but turned back for a final word. "And if I ever catch you second-guessing one of my diagnoses again, I'll have you brought up on ethics charges so fast it'll make your head swim."

Kemp watched until the neurologist disappeared around a corner; when he turned around he found three of his colleagues at the nurses' station diplomatically staring at the floor. "And that," Kemp said loudly, "is the problem with health care in this country today." He turned to the charge nurse. "I'm taking my break now, Shanice. Have someone look in on my patient for me, will you?"

He walked down the hall to the nurses' break room. The room was empty and quiet except for a small television chattering in the corner. Kemp flopped down on a natty plaid sofa and stretched his legs out on a coffee table littered with magazines and paperbacks.

Idiots, he thought. *My talents are wasted here. The average nurse in California has a two-year community college degree, and look at me—four years of med school and three years of residency, and at Hopkins no less. And I'm supposed to be draining catheters while fools like that are building vacation homes in Malibu? I've forgotten more about medicine than he'll ever know. Where's the fairness? Where's the justice?*

He hooked his right toe behind his left heel and pried off his shoe; when the shoe fell to the side it landed on top of a glossy paperback that caught Kemp's eye. He slid the book out from under his shoe and looked at it. The title read *Lattes with God: An Encounter with the Almighty over Caramel Macchiatos.*

He let out a groan and tossed the book aside—but not before noticing a golden seal on the corner of the cover that announced, "Runaway Best Seller—Over 12 Million Copies in Print."

The door quietly opened and Natalie stepped inside. "I heard you were taking your break," she said.

Kemp rolled his eyes. "And what else did you hear from my distinguished colleagues?"

"I heard you got a dressing-down from one of the neurologists. What happened?"

"Same old thing—professional jealousy."

Natalie sat down on the sofa beside him. "You know, Mrs. Rodriguez can only work another couple of days. What are we going to do?"

"Do?"

"About Leah, Kemp. We've both been working nights, and

that's been working out great. We both work seven to seven, and that lets us get home just in time to take her to school—then I can grab a few hours of sleep and pick her up again. I get the afternoons with her and we all get to have dinner together—how good is that? And Mrs. Rodriguez helps out in the evenings and sleeps over. It's been a great fit—but now there isn't going to be a Mrs. Rodriguez anymore. Now what do we do?"

Kemp shrugged. "Find another *mamacita*."

"Maybe it would have helped if you didn't call her that."

"So now I'm the reason she's leaving?"

"I'm just saying, what are we going to do?" She waited for his response, but there was none. At last she said, "You're going to have to switch to days."

"Me? Why me?"

"Because she's my daughter, Kemp—isn't that what you're always telling me? Think about it: When I work nights I get afternoons and dinners with her. If I have to work days I'll never see her—she'll be asleep when I leave for work and ready for bed when I get home. You've got to switch—it's the only way."

Kemp shrugged. "Then I wouldn't get to see her."

Natalie glared at him. "Maybe I should just cut back on my hours—switch to half-time."

"Forget that," Kemp said. "We're barely scraping by right now. How are we supposed to make it on half your salary?"

"It would be worth it."

"Not to me."

"Then switch to days—it's the only way."

"I happen to like nights, Natalie. The pace is slower; there are fewer procedures, fewer interruptions—fewer morons poking their nose in your business. Let's not panic here. Mrs. Rodriguez isn't gone yet—we'll find somebody else."

"How? Where? It could take weeks, and she'll be gone in just a couple of days. You've got to switch to days, Kemp—at least for a little while."

"Forget it."

"Then I've got to cut back. You decide."

Kemp allowed several seconds to pass. "Maybe I should just move out."

"What?"

"It's a fifty-fifty deal, honey. You chip in, I chip in, and together we make it work. Now you're expecting me to work full-time while you cut back? How is that fair? I'd be better off on my own."

She shook her head. "I can't believe you said that."

"Hey, fair is fair."

"It's always about money with you, isn't it?"

Kemp turned to face her. "That's right, Natalie—it's always about money. It's about that moron out there who's making four hundred grand a year while I draw thirty-five bucks an hour plus four bucks more because I work nights. It's about a miserable two-bedroom, one-bath, eleven-hundred-square-foot hovel in Culver City that we shell out twenty-two hundred a month for. It's about the $700,000 it would take to buy that miserable dump—$700,000 that we'll never have because it takes every penny we've got just to scrape by each month. Yeah, it's about money—you bet it is."

"What's eating you tonight? What's the problem?"

"I'll tell you what the problem is—the problem is *this*." He picked up the copy of *Lattes with God* and held it up in front of her face. "Look at this—do you see what it says? *Twelve million copies in print.* Some idiot thinks he sees God because he's overdosing on caffeine, so he scribbles it all down and presto—*twelve million copies*. Do the math, Natalie. A writer makes, what—fifteen, twenty percent of net? So this guy's making maybe a buck or two per book. Multiply that by twelve million and you know what you get? You get *my life*—the life I was supposed to have."

Natalie let out a groan. "Not this again."

"And the thing that absolutely kills me is that people actually read this garbage! This is a nurses' break room in a neurological intensive care unit—that means one of our 'colleagues' out there bought this book and she's been reading it during her breaks."

"Or *his* breaks."

"Whatever."

Just then they heard the sound of the door opening again and they both turned to see an elderly African-American man quietly poke his head into the room and reach for a garbage can just inside the door.

"Maybe *that* explains it," Kemp said. "Hey, you, come in here for a minute."

The old man straightened and took a step into the room. "Me?"

"I think you forgot your book," Kemp said, sailing it across the room so that it landed at the old man's feet.

"His name isn't 'Hey, you,'" Natalie scolded. "That's Emmet, Kemp. You know Emmet—he's worked here for years."

"Oh yeah, Emesis. How you doing, Emesis?"

"*Emmet*," Natalie whispered.

"You left your book here in the nurses' break room, Emesis. Better take it with you."

Emmet stooped down and picked up the book. "Don't believe this belongs to me."

"No? Tell me, what are the custodians reading these days?"

"Don't have much time for it myself," the old man said.

"Can't speak for the others." He held up the book. "Is this what the nurses are reading?"

"No," Natalie said. "Kemp mostly reads *Sports Illustrated*, especially if there happens to be a swimsuit inside. Sorry to bother you, Emmet. It's nice to see you again."

"I'll just leave this with you then," he said, setting the copy of *Lattes* back on the coffee table. "I'll take the rest of the trash with me."

When the old man closed the door, Natalie turned on Kemp. "Why do you always have to be so—"

"Now that's really discouraging," Kemp said.

"What is?"

"It wasn't his book—that means one of our 'peers' is actually reading this drivel. These are supposed to be educated people, Natalie—they should know better." He sank back on the sofa. "It can't be that easy to make money. Seven years of graduate education and I'm making thirty-five bucks an hour. I must be missing something." He looked at Natalie again. "It's not fair. I'm brilliant, you know."

"Yes, I know. You've told me."

"I'm serious. Seven years at Johns Hopkins. So what if I didn't finish my residency? I'm as intelligent as anybody around here, and I deserve to be making as much money."

She didn't reply.

"Don't you think I'm brilliant?"

"Kemp—"

"Say it, babe. I need to hear it sometimes."

She hesitated. "You're not really going to move out, are you?"

"Tell me."

"You're brilliant, honey. You should be making as much as anybody here."

"Thank you. At least somebody has some sense around here."

The door opened once again and the charge nurse poked her head inside. "Kemp, you were supposed to take a fifteen-minute break. Would it inconvenience you too much to return to work? They just brought a new patient up from Trauma, and I'm assigning her to you."

"I'll be right there," he said, then held up the paperback. "Hey, Shanice—you forgot your book."

4

*M*ort Biederman rushed off the elevator on the sixth floor of UCLA Medical Center and spotted the sign on the opposite wall. It read Neuro Trauma ICU with an arrow pointing to the right. He hurried down the hallway until it suddenly veered left; through a set of double doors he could see a nurses' station and he headed directly for it. In his left hand he was gripping a forty-dollar bouquet of roses with a few sprigs of baby's breath that he had just purchased from a vending machine in the lobby. *Good thing it took credit cards*, he thought. *I wonder if the gift shop will give me a receipt—this is deductible.*

The double doors slid open for him, and as he entered he called out to no one in particular, "I'm looking for Olivia Hayden!"

"Hold your voice down, sir," a nurse behind the desk called back. "You're in an ICU."

Biederman stepped up to the nurses' station. "Who are you?"

"Uh-uh. Question is, who are you?"

He took a business card from his jacket pocket and slid it across the counter.

The charge nurse ignored the card. "How 'bout you just tell me."

"I'm Morton Biederman," he said. "Liv Hayden—what room is she in?"

"That all depends. What relation are you to Ms. Hayden?"

"Why?"

"We have strict visitation policies, Mr. Biederman—blood relatives only."

"I'm her agent, for crying out loud. I own ten percent of her—if that's not blood, I don't know what is."

"I'm sorry. You need to be a husband, a brother, or a son— that's what we call 'blood' around here. Immediate family only."

"Look—Olivia has no family, no children. She's been married four times, and four times it didn't work out. The first husband, Larry, he was basically a parasite. He got the house on Melrose next to Jack Nicholson and also the residuals from three of her pictures—I figure that's about eight percent of her. The second husband, Antonio, he thought he could take her to the cleaners, but his lawyer was in over his head and Antonio lost big-time in court—he got maybe one percent. Now the third husband, Travis, I figure he got about seven percent, and Stan—Stan was the last one—I figure him at about nine percent. Now me, I own ten percent of her free and clear—that gives me controlling interest."

"Mr. Biederman—"

"I love her like a father, but I pray to God no kid of mine ever turns out like her. I love her like a husband, but she's got some real issues with men. I'm like a son to her, though the woman doesn't have a maternal bone in her entire body."

"Mr. Biederman—"

"Fifty percent of her I can't stand, forty percent of her I respect and admire, and ten percent of her I worship and adore. Now doesn't that sound like family to you?"

"Mr. Biederman, please."

"What I'm saying is, I'm the closest thing to family she's got. And I want her to have the best, do you understand? A private room, the best doctors. Money is no object—she has insurance."

"This is UCLA, Mr. Biederman—believe it or not, Ms. Hayden is not our first celebrity. We understand her special privacy needs. She was assigned to a private room."

Biederman looked impressed. "UCLA Medical Center is the number-three-ranked hospital in the entire United States. Do you know how I know this?"

"Because of the gigantic banner on the side of the building?"

"No—because of people like you. Now, may I please see my family?"

Shanice looked at him dully. "I will allow you to sit with Ms. Hayden for a few minutes—but only until I check with her doctor to make sure it's all right. Do you understand? This way, please."

She led him down the hallway to an isolated room at the far left. Most of the doors they passed were made entirely of glass with only a thin curtain blocking the view of the patient's bed. Not this room; it had a solid wooden door that was obviously designed with prying eyes—and cameras—in mind.

She opened the door for him. "Sit there," she said, pointing to a chair. "And don't touch anything. I'll page her doctor."

"Can she hear me?"

"There's no way to know for sure, Mr. Biederman. Go ahead and talk to her if you want to—we do." She quietly shut the door behind him.

Biederman approached the bed and looked down at the figure lying motionless under the single sheet. Her blonde hair lay matted against her head; there were purple and red bruises under both eyes but no other signs of structural damage. Her nose didn't seem to be broken. *Good thing*, he thought. *That was an expensive nose.* Her arms lay extended on top of the sheet; they were covered with bruises as well. A bluish plastic tube projected from under a bandage on the back of her left hand, winding back along the bedrail until it branched into two other tubes—one attached to a dangling sack of clear fluid, and the other attached to a boxlike device that held a large syringe. There were monitors everywhere displaying undulating sine waves and flashing numbers. Biederman wasn't sure what any of it meant, but he figured it was at least a good sign that the waves weren't flat and the numbers were all above zero.

He sat down in the chair across from the bed.

"So, Liv, how's it going?"

There was no answer.

"I just heard about the accident an hour ago—I don't think the hospital knew who to contact. They said they went through the numbers on your cell phone. Good thing you keep your agent on speed dial."

Biederman watched for signs of movement or recognition; there were none.

"Got a call from that director this morning," he went on. "Looks like *Lips of Fury* isn't going to pan out. Look, about that—I just wanted you to consider the part, okay? You know, like an outfit in a clothing store—I just wanted you to try it on to see how it felt. I knew if I told you up front you would have turned it down flat."

He looked at her lying perfectly still, almost as if she were stuffed and on display in some museum. *She might as well be*, he thought. *Twenty years . . . that's a pretty good run in a business like this—hey, that's a terrific run. For most of those years she was at the top of the food chain and everybody else was lunch. But that was then and this is now, and neither one of us is getting any younger—or richer.*

There was a quiet knock on the door and then it opened. "Mr. Biederman?"

Biederman stood up and shook hands with the physician.

"I'm Dr. Smithson—the neurologist in charge of Ms. Hayden's care. I understand you're Ms. Hayden's agent."

"How is she? What can you tell me?"

"Ms. Hayden was involved in an automobile accident on the 405 early this morning. Her car was smashed up pretty bad; it took them a couple of hours just to cut her free. The EMTs who brought her in said she must have been going very fast."

"Sounds like her," Biederman said.

"Apparently she lost control."

"That sounds like her too."

"She's lucky to be alive, Mr. Biederman. Fortunately, UCLA is a level 1 trauma center. They transferred her up here as soon as she was stabilized. They say her car rolled several times; whenever that happens there's a high risk of injury to the brain, neck, and spinal cord. Ms. Hayden was extremely fortunate. We've done a full body scan and an MRI on her head and neck, and aside from abrasions and contusions she seems to have no significant injuries."

"Then what's she doing in an ICU?"

"When a car rolls over, a body gets thrown violently from side to side—the head is snapped like a whip and the brain actually bounces against the inside of the skull. When that happens the brain can swell; it's what we call *intracranial hypertension*. Fluid accumulates in the brain, and the skull can't allow the brain to expand, so the brain becomes compressed—then

35

brain tissue begins to die, resulting in permanent brain damage or even death."

"Is that what's happening?"

"No—that's what *can* happen, and that's why I'd like to keep her here for a few days. I want to keep her immobilized to give her brain a chance to rest and heal—just as a precautionary measure. We'll do that by inducing a coma."

"A *coma?*"

"Don't worry—it's a common procedure and it's not as bad as it sounds. See that little box with the syringe inside? That's an infusion pump. It's giving her a steady dose of a drug called *propofol*—it's a short-acting anesthetic agent that will make sure she remains unconscious until the risk of swelling has passed. That's all we're doing, really—making sure she stays asleep so she doesn't move."

36

"How long will she have to be in here?"

"About a week—just to be sure. Believe me, this is the best place for her right now." The neurologist crossed to the side of the bed and looked down at his patient. "Liv Hayden," he said. "She hasn't made a picture for a while, has she?"

"None worth remembering. Her accountant's still trying to forget."

"She looks the same as always. A timeless beauty, I suppose."

Timeless beauty, Biederman thought. *Now there's a contradiction in terms.* "By the way, what's that thing on her forehead?"

"This?" The neurologist pointed to a white plastic strap that circled her forehead like a headband; in the center was a rectangle the size of a large Band-Aid bearing two round circles. "That's called a BIS sensor. It registers her brain activity—it tells us her level of consciousness. It's connected to that monitor over there—see the number on the front? The number ranges from 0 to 99. A fully conscious person is a 99; we'll try to keep her at about 60—that lets us know she's fully sedated."

"Is it okay if I sit with her for a while?"

"She's in good hands here if you've got other clients to take care of."

"She *is* my client," Biederman said.

The neurologist smiled down at her. "You know, I can remember seeing her first picture—*Six Weeks of Thursdays*. I was a big fan of hers."

"I'll tell her you said so. It'll mean a lot to her."

"Yeah—I was in middle school at the time."

Biederman paused. "I'll leave that part out."

37

5

Now this is more like it, Kemp thought.

Most of his patients in the ICU were older and in a lot worse shape—and not nearly as pleasant to look at. But this woman—she was a knockout. In fact, aside from the bruising around her eyes and some minor fluid retention, she was drop-dead gorgeous. Kemp rechecked her chart to verify her age: forty-four, it said. He whistled in admiration. *Definitely the deep end of the gene pool.* He leaned over the bed and studied her face more closely. He could just barely detect a telltale line hidden along the bottom of each eyebrow and a similar line carefully tucked away under the curve of her jaw. *This is very nice work*, he thought. *Very expensive—either she's got a sugar daddy or this woman's got money.*

Just then there was the sound of a toilet flushing and the door to the restroom opened. Mort Biederman stepped out and found Kemp bent over his client's bed.

Kemp straightened. "Who are you?"

"Mort Biederman. Who're you?"

"I'm a nurse."

"Oh. Thought you might be a doctor."

"Yeah, me too. We ask visitors not to use the patients' restrooms, Mr. Biederman—it increases the risk of infection."

"Sorry. You know what they say: you only rent coffee."

"So I've heard. Are you family?"

"I'm her agent. I own ten percent of her—just enough to get me visitation rights and an ulcer."

"Her agent?" Kemp looked at the chart again. "*Olivia Hayden*—I thought that name sounded familiar. Is this *the* Liv Hayden?"

"How many are there? I made the name up myself."

"Son of a gun—Liv Hayden, in the flesh." He glanced at Biederman. "Is she married?"

"From time to time. Why?"

"Just curious."

"Forget it, kiddo, she's way out of your league. Besides, she's buried four husbands already."

"They all died?"

"Who said died? She just buried them. So you're a nurse?"

"I think we've covered that."

"How many patients you got? Because I want Olivia to have your full attention."

"This is an ICU, Mr. Biederman. At UCLA it's usually two patients per nurse, but for high-visibility patients like your client it's one-to-one. I've been assigned to Ms. Hayden, and I'll be her night nurse until she leaves the hospital."

"The doctor tells me they'll keep her in a coma."

"That's what her chart says."

"So if she's in a coma, what is it you do?"

"I check her vital signs. I turn her over every two hours to keep her from getting bedsores. I empty her catheter and adjust her IV fluids. I chart her BIS readings."

"That's it? Cushy job."

"Only I don't get ten percent."

"Believe me, ten percent is not what it used to be."

Kemp sneered. "I'll take ten percent of Liv Hayden any day. The woman must be worth millions."

"Worth millions, sure. She just doesn't make millions—not anymore."

"You're kidding."

"This is Hollywood, kid. By the time she was thirty she was already making top dollar, but producers get tired of paying top dollar. There's always some up-and-comer who'll do the role for half. Besides, the public wants to see new faces, younger faces—younger bodies."

Kemp looked down at the bed. "Hers still looks good to me."

"The camera doesn't lie—neither does the box office. Producers and directors, that's another story."

Kemp took a look at his watch.

"I get the hint," Biederman said. "I'll be back to check on her tomorrow. You take real good care of her now, you hear? And if she needs anything at all, you call me." He took out a business card and handed it to Kemp.

Kemp dropped the card into his pocket. "Don't worry. She's in good hands."

When Biederman left, Kemp turned back to the bed again. "So you're Liv Hayden," he said. "Pleased to meet you, Ms. Hayden. My name is Kemp—Kemp McAvoy. I'll be your night nurse while you're with us here at UCLA, so we'll be getting to know each other quite well. By the time you leave, I suspect we'll be very good friends."

He took her pulse and blood pressure and recorded them in her chart.

"Your agent was just here," he said. "Mr. Biederman—a nice enough fellow, though I'd think you'd get tired of finding his hand in your purse all the time. He says he owns ten percent of you—though I have a hard time believing that any man owns a piece of a woman like you."

He gave her a wink and checked her BIS reading; the digital display read 61.

"This? Oh, this is what we call a BIS monitor—that stands for 'bispectral index.' It continually analyzes your electro-encephalograms to assess your level of consciousness. See, when you're awake your cerebral cortex is very active, but that changes under sedation. It all has to do with the metabolic ratio of glucose in the brain. Trust me, it's very complicated; I won't bore you with the details."

He made a notation in the chart along with the current time.

"Well, yes, now that you mention it, I suppose I do sound awfully intelligent for a nurse. That's a long story, but I can give you the *Reader's Digest* version. See, I was planning to be a doctor—an anesthesiologist in fact. My father is a very success-ful anesthesiologist, did I mention that? Right here in Beverly Hills—he might have even been the one who put you under when you went in for that chin tuck. I was following in the old man's footsteps, you see. I aced my MCATs and got accepted to Johns Hopkins no less. I finished med school and started my residency there—that's right, at Hopkins too. I know, it's impressive, isn't it? And I almost finished my residency, but there was this silly disagreement over a minor ethical viola-tion. You know what happened? They kicked me out. That's right—seven years of medical education, and suddenly they tell me that I'm not going to be an anesthesiologist after all. Seven years of my life down the toilet—I don't mind telling you, Liv, that hurt.

"So I moved back to LA. I know—'Why LA? Why not take a job where no one knows you?' Simple—I've got family here, and I was a little strapped for cash at the time. You'd think Dad would have been glad to have his beloved son home again. I mean, it's not like he couldn't afford me—he's not exactly living on food stamps there in Bel Air. But no, my old man's got this thing about 'making it on your own.' So what was I supposed to do after seven years of medical school, wait tables and detail cars? I don't think so. So I went down to the local community college and enrolled in a nursing program. I finished in less than a year. All I needed was the clinical nursing courses—'Bedpans 101' and things of that sort—just enough to fulfill the requirements and qualify me to take the boards.

"So here I am—Kemp McAvoy, MD, RN, arguably the most overqualified nurse in America. I have to tell you, the job is a little demeaning, but it's as close to medicine as I can get right now—until I figure out something else, that is. And I will too—wait and see. I'll make it happen right here in LA, just like I always said I would.

"But enough about me; let's talk about you. Your agent says that you're a washed-up has-been—is that true? Personally, Liv, I have a hard time believing it. I think you're quite beautiful, even if you have had a little work done. No, I don't blame you for that—that's just routine maintenance. It's a competitive world out there, and a woman has to look her best if she wants to keep a man's attention."

There was a soft knock at the door and a nurse poked her head into the room. "Kemp, I'm taking my break now. Can you keep an eye on 616 for me?"

"I'm just getting a patient settled in," he said. "Can't you ask Natalie to do it? She's probably not doing anything."

When the door closed Kemp turned back to his patient again. "See, that's what I have to put up with all the time. Can you believe it? They expect me to do all the trivial things that ordinary nurses do—but I'm not exactly an ordinary nurse, now am I?"

He checked her Foley, then drained it and recorded the fluid level.

"Mr. Biederman thinks you're out of my league. What do you think? Personally, I think he's underestimating me and overestimating you. I mean, if you're a has-been and I'm an almost-was, doesn't that put us in roughly the same category?"

Having completed his check-in, he set the chart aside and pulled up the chair that rested against the wall. He sat down next to her bed and relaxed, folding his hands across his chest.

"Seriously, Liv, I think you and I have a lot in common. You used to be on top of the world, and I was definitely headed there. Now look at you—a shadow of the woman you used to be—and look at me, stuck in this degrading job. I think I understand you, Liv, and I think if you had the chance you might understand me. Who knows? Under different circumstances we might have really hit it off. I mean, we both have talent, we both have ambition, and to be quite honest, women don't find me unattractive."

Kemp heard a sound behind him and turned to see Emmet emptying the trash can just to the left of the door.

Kemp looked him over. "How long have you been standing there?"

"Not long. Why?"

"Never mind. Come in here for a minute."

Emmet hesitated, but finally stepped into the room and shut the door.

"You want to see a really beautiful woman?"

Emmet frowned. "Is this appropriate, Mr. Kemp?"

"C'mon, we're not peeking under the sheets. I just thought

you might like to see a world-class beauty up close. Nothing wrong with that, is there?"

Emmet looked doubtful but stepped closer to the bed.

"This is Olivia Hayden, the famous movie star," Kemp said. "Recognize her?"

Emmet shook his head sadly. "Poor thing. What happened to her?"

"Rolled her car or something. Women—they always want more car than they can handle—more man too."

"Is she hurt real bad?"

"She'll recover—they're just keeping her in a coma as a precautionary measure. Now I ask you: Is that a beautiful woman or what?"

Emmet nodded. "But there's a sadness about her somehow."

"That's just the propofol."

"I wonder if she's happy."

"Are you kidding? She's a movie star. She's got millions of adoring fans and they all buy tickets."

"Still."

"You're probably right," Kemp said. "I'll bet what she really longs for is to be a janitor working nights at UCLA—then she might finally be fulfilled."

Emmet shrugged. "You never know."

"Get back to work, will you?"

"You asked me in."

"Now I'm asking you out. Good-bye."

When Emmet left, Kemp sat down in the chair again. "It looks like I'm the only one who understands you," he said. "Can't say I'm surprised—you're probably the only one around here who could understand me. We need to help each other out, Liv. We need to figure out a way to get both our stars back on course."

6

Kemp looked down the rolling fairway at the glistening oval 455 yards away. The hole was a long two-shotter and he'd need a strong drive to set up his approach to the green. He took out his driver and approached the tee.

"Watch those bunkers on the right."

Kemp rolled his eyes. "Yeah, Dad, I can see them. How many times have we played this course?"

"I'm just saying—with that slice of yours and all. You never did break that habit."

"I can't play golf all day. Some people have to work for a living."

"Whose fault is that?"

It was a near perfect day for golf, and the North Course at the Los Angeles Country Club was a near perfect place to play. The 13th hole was one of Kemp's favorites, with its jewel-like green and sculpted bunkers surrounded by a dense screen of spruce and pine. With nothing but rolling hills visible in the distance, you could almost forget you were in Los Angeles; on a day like this, you could almost forget you were on earth. The sun, the breeze, a round of golf on one of the most exclusive courses in the nation—life didn't get much better than this. It would have been almost perfect—if it wasn't for the company.

"See that stand of trees behind the green?" his father asked.

"The Playboy Mansion is right behind it," Kemp said, "and Hugh Hefner once applied for membership at the country club but they turned him down."

"Have I told you that story before?"

"Every time we teed off since I was twelve. Are we going to talk or are we going to play?"

Kemp shook his head. It was just another one of his father's not-so-subtle reminders of how exclusive the Los Angeles Country Club was. The old man had spent ten years on a waiting list before he was finally granted membership, and he was sickeningly proud of it. Kemp had always hoped that he would someday become a member himself—after he completed his residency and fellowship and set up his practice here in LA. He used to dream about it—not just about the golf, but about the time when he could play here without his condescending old man talking his ear off all day long. But Kemp knew it would never happen unless his current situation changed dramatically. The Los Angeles Country Club was private and exclusive, and you didn't play unless you were a member or a guest—and if they looked down their noses at old Hugh Hefner, they weren't exactly going to welcome a nurse from UCLA.

"Twenty bucks says you end up in the bunker," his father prodded.

"No thanks."

"What's the matter, son? No guts, no glory."

Kemp teed up and pretended to ignore him. It wasn't just a friendly bet—it was a pointed reminder that Kemp didn't have twenty bucks to burn. Nothing the old man did was friendly, and nothing was without a point. It was the sort of veiled insult that his father seemed to find clever; Kemp found it annoying and rude.

"Twenty bucks says you're in the sand in two strokes."

Twenty bucks says I punch you in the face. "Don't waste your money. I'll be on the green in two."

"Then put your money where your mouth is. C'mon— nobody bets on a man who won't bet on himself."

That was a veiled reminder too—and Kemp knew what it meant. "Okay, you're on. Get out your wallet, old man."

He sized up the ball and took his swing. The ball left the head of the titanium driver with a hollow *ping* and rocketed down the fairway high and long. Kemp watched the ball, willing it to go straight—but halfway down the fairway it began to veer sharply to the right. The ball rolled to a stop two hundred yards from the green with a yawning bunker directly in front of it.

His father grinned. "I can smell that money now."

"Don't count on it," Kemp said. "That's an easy iron shot."

"Easy for some people—but you're no Tiger."

They grabbed their bags and began the long walk.

"Still too cheap to rent a cart," Kemp said. "What would it set you back, twenty, twenty-five bucks?"

"It's not the money," his father replied. "I can make that up on a bet with a sucker like you. You appreciate things when you work for them, son. It's true in golf; it's true in life."

You appreciate things when you work for them—how many times had Kemp heard that one growing up? It was one of his father's favorite sayings. It represented his entire philosophy of parenting; it was his golden compass in life, and it had almost ruined Kemp's.

Halfway across the fairway his father asked, "So what's on your mind?"

47

"What do you mean?"

"I'm not stupid, son. You never take me up on golf anymore unless there's something you want. What is it this time?"

Kemp considered denying it, but it wasn't worth the energy just to protect the old man's feelings. "I was wondering if we could arrange a loan."

"A loan or a handout?"

"That depends on what kind of mood you're in."

"You know how I feel about handouts."

"A loan, then."

"What's it for?"

Kemp stopped and set down his bag. "There's a place in Santa Monica we've got our eye on—a place near the beach."

"We?"

"Me and Natalie."

"Oh, right—your 'girlfriend.'" He enunciated the word slowly and crisply.

"We're still renting in Culver City—twenty-two hundred a month. There's no rent control in LA so it's just going to get worse, and we're not building any equity. We can't get a down payment together on our salaries."

"I don't see why not. All it takes is discipline and planning. Your mother and I—"

"I know," Kemp said. "You skimped and saved and pulled yourselves up by your own bootstraps until you had a vacation home at Lake Arrowhead."

"You mock me and then you ask me for money?"

"I'm not mocking you, Dad—I've just heard it all before, okay?"

"I'm not sure you've heard it at all."

"Please—not this again."

"What do you expect me to say? It's the same thing you've

always done—you look for shortcuts. You say, 'We can't get a down payment together.' Sure you can. Other people do it— why can't you? What you mean is, 'I don't want to wait for that place in Santa Monica—I want it now.' So here you are, looking for a shortcut."

"I had a little setback, remember?"

"You call that a 'little setback'? Getting kicked out of the medical profession in your final year of residency? Ruining your career before it even started?"

"It was my career to ruin," Kemp said.

"I know—I made sure of that. I made you pay your own way through college and medical school, because if you didn't work for it you wouldn't appreciate it. But you still looked for shortcuts all along the way—on your grades, with your money. You got into the habit of taking shortcuts and it caught up with you."

"Look—I need money, not a lecture on responsibility."

"Apparently you do, because here you are again."

"Just forget it. I'm sorry I brought it up."

"I told you residency would be tough. I told you the hours would be long and you'd have to pace yourself. But no, that took too much discipline. You had to take another shortcut— but that was one shortcut too many, wasn't it, Bobby?"

Kemp lowered his voice to a growl. "The name is *Kemp.*"

"Sorry, I keep forgetting. Most sons keep the name they were born with."

"Well, I needed a change."

"Changing your name won't change the man you are on the inside."

"Thanks for another useless platitude."

"Does Natalie know?"

"Know what?"

49

"That you had to move back to California and change your name just to get a job in the medical profession? That the reason you never became an anesthesiologist is because you got caught abusing fentanyl?"

"Hey—would you mind keeping your voice down? That's a little personal."

"It's personal for me too. I thought my son was following in my footsteps, then one day I turn around and nobody's there. I thought I'd be turning my practice over to you someday; instead I'm trying to explain to my friends why you suddenly got the urge to go into nursing instead."

"I'm really sorry for your loss, Dad."

"I can't even keep your name straight. *Kemp McAvoy*—where did you come up with that one?"

50

"What difference does it make? Nobody would have hired Bobby Foscoe—not on the East Coast anyway. Word gets around."

His father slowly shook his head. "Maybe it's a good thing you did change your name. I'm not sure you ever were a Foscoe—not really."

"Don't give me that 'I'm made of sterner stuff' garbage—I'm sick of it."

"Face it, Bobby. You're weak—you always were."

"I'm weak and you're strong—you think that explains everything, don't you?"

"You know the numbers just like I do: About two percent of anesthesiology residents get caught with their hand in the cookie jar, and that percentage hasn't changed in years. You're a member of the Two Percent Club, son. How do you explain it?"

"You know, I saw a study in the *American Journal of Psychiatry* the other day. It seems they tested the air in some hospital operating rooms, and guess what they found?

Fentanyl residue. They're saying secondhand environmental exposure might put anesthesiologists at greater risk of substance abuse."

"The air in the operating rooms."

"That's right, Dad."

"The same air I've been breathing for thirty years."

Kemp didn't respond.

"That's the problem with you, Bobby—you're always looking for an excuse. Shortcuts and excuses—I guess that's what two-percenters do."

Kemp grabbed his golf bag and slung it over his shoulder.

"Where you going?"

"Back to the clubhouse."

"We've still got six holes to finish."

Kemp took a twenty-dollar bill from his wallet and handed it to his dad.

"What's this for?"

"Our bet."

"You haven't taken your second shot yet."

"What's the point, Dad? What are my chances—two percent?"

"C'mon, don't get sore—"

Kemp glared at his father. "You know what I hate about playing golf with you? You think the hundred and eight bucks you shell out for my greens fee entitles you to criticize and insult me all morning. Well, forget it, old man. I don't need your money—I'll find a way to get my own, and when I do I'll tell you where you can put yours."

Kemp turned and charged off toward the clubhouse.

7

"Kemp, we need to talk."

Kemp let out a begrudging sigh, then raised the remote to shoulder level and muted the TV. He was still dressed in his pajama bottoms and a T-shirt though it was almost noon. "It's Sunday," he said. "Can we make this quick?"

"No, we can't." Natalie sat down on the end of the sofa and held up an envelope with a ragged edge.

"What's that?"

"A note from St. Stephen's. They're requesting a parent-teacher's conference."

Kemp groaned. "What'd she do now?"

Natalie took a deep breath. "She told another story."

"I can't believe these people," Kemp said. "Aren't they supposed to be encouraging her creativity? So she tells a tall tale from time to time—so what? Everybody stretches the truth sometimes. I'll bet you hear some whoppers from the school board when they're doing their annual fund-raiser."

"Leah saw an angel."

Kemp's eyebrows arched like a cat's back. "I beg your pardon?"

"An angel—she says she saw one the other day while we were driving on the 405."

"We could use a few angels on the 405. Some of those idiots drive like—"

"It's not a joke, Kemp."

"What do you expect, Natalie? It's an Episcopal school. They talk about angels, so now she's making up stories about angels. If we'd put her in a public school the way I wanted, maybe she'd be a little more down-to-earth."

"They don't think she's making it up."

Kemp blinked. "They believe she saw an angel?"

"They think *she* believes it—that's why they're concerned."

"C'mon, it's just a story. The kid tells stories all the time."

"They know that, Kemp. Give them a little credit, will you? They know Leah and they've heard her stories before—this one sounded different somehow. Her teacher wants to meet with us Tuesday morning."

"I'll be asleep Tuesday morning. I have a shift the night before."

"What's wrong—working too hard with your little movie star? I never saw you show so much interest in a patient before."

"Give me a break."

"They want to see us both, Kemp."

"You said this was a parent-teacher conference. Did they say anything about boyfriends? Domestic partners? Significant others?"

"Kemp, don't you dare—"

"What's the big deal, anyway? What's so different about this story? What does she say she saw?"

Natalie glared at him. "If you're really interested, why don't you ask her yourself?"

"Okay, I will." He turned and shouted to the back of the house, "Hey, Leah, come here for a minute!"

53

"You be gentle with her," Natalie warned. "Remember what the counselor said."

"I remember—she's 'externalizing her grief'—and I still say it's a crock. Give me a break, Natalie. So you got a divorce—so what? Lots of people do. It happens to kids all the time."

"She was young," Natalie said, "and it wasn't pretty. There was a lot of anger, and yelling, and—other things. She saw things that a little girl should never have to see."

Leah appeared from around the corner and stood in front of them. "What? I was playing."

"Sit down here, sweetheart," Natalie said. "Kemp wants to talk to you."

Leah sat down on the sofa between them and looked at Kemp. "What?"

"Your mom says you saw something unusual the other day—while the two of you were driving on the freeway."

"So?"

"What did you see?"

"An angel. Can I go now?"

"Wait a minute. Where did you see this angel?"

"On the side of the road."

"She was just standing there?"

"He."

"Okay, he. What was he doing?"

"He was standing beside a smashed-up car. There was a woman in the car, and she looked like this." She tipped her head back, closed her eyes, and let her mouth hang open a little. "The angel was standing beside her, holding his hand like this." Once again she demonstrated, extending her hand palm-down.

"How do you know he was an angel?"

"I just know."

"But how?"

She frowned. "I just know."

Natalie stroked her hair. "We're not doubting you, sweetheart; we're just trying to understand. What did the angel look like? How was he dressed?"

She shrugged. "Like a man. Like anybody."

"He wasn't wearing a white robe? He didn't have wings or a halo, like the angels you see in picture books?"

She shook her head.

Kemp looked at her doubtfully. "Then what makes you think he was an angel?"

She looked down at her feet.

"Go ahead, honey," Natalie said. "We'll listen."

"But you won't believe me."

"Try me," Kemp said.

She looked up at him. "When we drove by, he looked right at me and he went like this." She put her index finger to her lips and went, *Shhh*.

There was a moment of silence before Kemp said, "You gotta be kidding."

Leah scowled. "See? I told you."

"Look, Leah, it was an automobile accident. There were probably people all over the place—cops and medics and rescue workers, right? This guy was probably just one of them. Maybe he was just telling you and your mom to move along—or maybe he was looking over your shoulder at somebody behind you."

Leah shook her head.

"Now tell the truth," Kemp said. "You don't really have any reason to think this guy was an angel, do you? You just made him an angel for your story—a story to tell to your class at St. Stephen's."

55

Leah said nothing.

"C'mon," Kemp said. "If you tell the truth, your mom will take you to the park."

"Kemp!"

"I told you you wouldn't believe me," Leah grumbled. "Can I go now?"

"No," Natalie said, staring furiously at Kemp. "I'm going to take you to the park—like I promised. I think we could both stand to get out of this house for a while."

When the girls finally left and the door slammed shut behind them, Kemp raised the remote and unmuted the TV. A news update on KTTV Fox 11 was airing a segment on the tragic automobile accident involving movie star Liv Hayden.

Kemp leaned forward and turned up the volume.

"The accident occurred early Thursday morning on the 405 just south of the Santa Monica Freeway," the announcer said. "Hayden was apparently driving at high speed when she lost control of her vehicle and flipped several times. Rescue teams and emergency personnel arrived on the scene shortly thereafter, only to find the car so badly demolished that it took rescue workers hours to free Hayden from the vehicle. Hayden was immediately transported to nearby UCLA Medical Center, where she remains in intensive care. Ms. Hayden's publicist declined to comment on the extent of her injuries. However, her agent, Morton Biederman, had this to say to Fox 11 . . ."

Biederman, Kemp thought. *This oughta be good.*

The scene switched to show a forlorn-looking man in sunglasses with a half dozen microphones shoved in his face. "This is a tragic day for movie fans everywhere," Biederman said. "Olivia Hayden is at death's door. I was able to visit her briefly at UCLA last night and I was devastated by what I saw. She's fighting for her life right now, but I've known Olivia for twenty years and she has the heart of a true champion. If anyone can come back from this, she can. Please, I'm asking for everyone's thoughts and prayers on her behalf."

Kemp shook his head in disdain. *"At death's door"—what a joke. In a few days they'll shut off the propofol and she'll wake up with a headache and a pair of black eyes—big deal. The old shyster's just setting her up to look like a miraculous recovery, that's all. "I'm asking for everyone's thoughts and prayers"—that's a good one. What he's asking is for everyone to run out and buy her DVDs.*

He raised the remote again and began to press the button mechanically, surfing through the channels until a familiar image caught his eye. He stopped and looked; it was the cover of the book he had seen in the nurses' break room just the night before.

"*Lattes with God,*" a reporter gushed, "the phenomenal runaway best seller that has now sold more than twelve million copies worldwide. The question is, will God have a second cup of coffee?"

The scene shifted to show a well-dressed young man opening the door to an impressive granite-front office building; the man made a quick nod to the camera as he entered.

"Wes Kalamar is young to be the president and CEO of an entire publishing company," the reporter said. "But then, Vision Press is a very young publishing house. Though it has only a handful of little-known titles to its credit, Vision Press has made a name for itself in the publishing industry through the release of a single book: the mega best seller *Lattes with God*. Kalamar picked up the book after it was rejected by a dozen more-established publishers—and he's glad he did. Profits from the book have allowed Vision Press to expand its staff and to relocate its offices here in posh Beverly Hills."

The scene changed again to an interior office setting. The young man, Wes Kalamar, was now seated casually in a sleek blue-and-gray office chair with gleaming silver accents. His feet were propped up on a sprawling mahogany desk shaped like an artist's palette.

"*Lattes with God* definitely taught us a lesson," Kalamar said thoughtfully. "It taught us that there's a hunger out there for spiritual guidance, and I think Vision Press is strategically positioned to satisfy that hunger. *Lattes with God* was just our first step. Wait 'til you see what we do next."

The segment closed with a wrap-up by the reporter standing in front of the offices of Vision Press. "*Lattes with God* was without a doubt a publishing phenomenon," he said, "but a phenomenon is notoriously difficult to reproduce. The question is, what *will* Vision Press do next? What will be the next *Lattes with God*—and will Wes Kalamar be the one to find it?"

Kemp switched off the TV and sat staring at the blank screen. His mind was spinning like a flywheel.

He thought about Liv Hayden lying in a coma back at UCLA.

He thought about Mort Biederman and his dwindling ten percent.

He thought about Wes Kalamar and the question the reporter asked him: "What will be the next *Lattes with God*?"

Twelve million copies. Twelve million copies . . .

Kemp McAvoy had an idea.

8

*N*atalie looked around the classroom for a place to sit, but the only adult-sized piece of furniture in the room was the teacher's own chair. It seemed like a bad idea to sit there; the last thing she wanted to do was start off the meeting with a turf war. She looked at the students' desks and considered trying to squeeze herself into one of them, but she imagined what she would look like staring up at the teacher with her knees tucked up under her chin. She didn't like that idea either—she felt enough like a child already, called into the teacher's office for a lecture. She finally decided just to stand and wait for the teacher to offer her a place to sit.

She thought about Kemp again and felt a twinge of anger. He should have come with her. He should have known how important this was to her. He didn't have to play the father; he didn't have to say a word. He just should have come—he shouldn't have left her to do this by herself. *He should have known.*

She looked down at herself and smoothed the front of her blouse. She had come directly from work and briefly considered wearing her nurse's scrubs, but decided instead to go for a less professional and more parental look. She hoped it was a wise decision.

The door suddenly opened and the window glass rattled in the brittle wooden frame. Natalie jumped.

"I'm sorry," a man said, standing in the doorway. "Did I startle you?"

"No. Well, a little."

The man entered the room dragging a wooden chair behind him; the legs made a dull scraping sound on the linoleum floor. He extended his hand. "I'm Matthew Callahan," he said, smiling pleasantly. "Just call me Matt. I'm Leah's teacher."

Natalie returned the smile. She could see why Leah liked this man. *What's not to like?* she thought. He was younger than a lot of teachers, probably about her own age. He looked like a definite California native, with thick wavy hair that could never look combed and skin that had spent too much time at the beach. There was a faint purplish patch down the center of his nose where the old skin was sloughing off and new tissue was about to break through. His eyes were blue and friendly and his smile was genuine. Natalie's instinct was to glance down at his ring hand, but she reminded herself that this was business.

"You're Natalie Pelton," he said. "Leah talks about you all the time."

"Uh-oh."

He smiled again. "Don't worry; it's all good. Thanks for coming in so early in the morning. It seems to be the best time to do these things."

"I just got off work," she said. "I would have been dropping Leah off anyway."

"You work nights?"

Natalie hesitated. "Yes, at UCLA Medical Center."

"You're a doctor?"

That was generous. "No, I'm a nurse."

He gestured to the classroom. "I'm afraid we don't have much in the way of adult seating. If I cram myself into one of the kids' desks I'll never get out again—that's why I bring my own chair. Why don't you take this one and I'll just do this." He leaned up against one end of the teacher's desk and waited for her to be seated.

"Thank you," she said. She found herself staring up at him slightly, but it didn't seem to matter—there was nothing intimidating about his manner.

"You obviously got my note," he said, "so you know what this is all about."

Natalie nodded.

"That Leah's quite a storyteller," he said.

"Yes, she is."

"I think it's terrific."

"You do?"

"Absolutely. Some of these kids have no imagination at all—too much Xbox and PlayStation, I suppose. But Leah, she's really out there. She's telling stories all the time—you pick the topic, she's got a story about it. It's a real gift. I hope she develops it."

Natalie said nothing.

"I know. You're probably thinking, 'If you like her stories, then what's the problem?'"

"Well—yes."

"A couple of days ago we were doing 'See & Say'—that's what they used to call 'Show & Tell' back when we were in school. Leah told a story about seeing an angel on the way to school that morning."

"Is that a problem?"

"A *story* about an angel wouldn't be a problem at all. The problem is, she didn't tell it as a story—she told it as a real event. I've heard dozens of Leah's stories, Ms. Pelton—"

"Natalie."

61

"*Natalie*. I've heard dozens of Leah's stories, and they're always recognizable as stories. They usually start out, 'Once upon a time.' This one started with, 'This morning on the way to school.'"

"Maybe she was just trying to make it seem more real."

"Is that what you think?"

Natalie barely shrugged.

Matt leaned a little closer. "Your daughter is extremely bright," he said, "but she also has a tendency to be moody—angry—withdrawn. I was hoping you could help me understand her a little better."

Natalie took a deep breath; this was the part she was hoping to avoid. "Her father and I divorced when she was four. It was—difficult for her." She offered nothing more, hoping that would be enough to satisfy him.

"Does she still see her father?"

"No. That wouldn't be a good idea."

"Has Leah ever seen a counselor?"

"Yes, she has. The counselor thinks she makes up stories as a way of dealing with her emotions."

"Sounds reasonable," Matt said. "It sounds healthy too—it's a lot better than keeping it all bottled up inside."

"Thanks for understanding."

"I'm not concerned about Leah's stories," Matt said. "I just want to be sure that she can separate the real world from fantasy."

Natalie raised one eyebrow. "Are you saying angels are fantasy?"

Matt grinned. "Not necessarily—but I haven't seen one on the 405 lately either. You need to understand something, Natalie: It's a different atmosphere in the classroom today. Everybody thinks about Columbine and Virginia Tech; everybody's trying to figure out how to spot the next crackpot before he pulls out a gun and starts shooting."

Natalie frowned. "Leah doesn't own a gun."

"I'm not talking about Leah—I'm talking about an atmosphere of fear and concern. Schools are paying closer attention to the psychological health of their students these days. That's one of the reasons I asked you here today."

"Leah's 'psychological health' is just fine."

"I hope you'll try to look at this in a positive light. It's one of the benefits of a private school. We have smaller classes; we can pay more attention to individual kids. If Leah were in a big public school, maybe nobody would have noticed."

"What is it you want?" Natalie asked. "I can tell Leah to stop telling stories—"

"That's the last thing I want you to do," Matt said. "I just want to make sure that Leah has a healthy grip on reality."

"So what do you want me to do?"

"I'd like you to make an appointment with our school counselor."

"I told you—Leah's already seen a counselor."

"This is different. This is just to make sure that somebody here at St. Stephen's is tracking with Leah emotionally."

Natalie glared at him. "Tell me the truth, Matt. Are you really asking Leah to see a counselor for her sake? Or is it so that if Leah turns out to be the next crackpot, St. Stephen's can say they did everything they could?"

"Natalie, please—"

"I tell you what," Natalie said, standing up and straightening herself. "I'll make sure Leah tells her stories at home. You just teach her math and English and let me worry about her 'psychological health'—okay?" She turned and started for the door.

63

"I'm afraid it's not an option," Matt said.

Natalie turned. "What?"

"If Leah wants to continue here at St. Stephen's, she has to be evaluated by the school's counselor. Please try not to be offended, Natalie—it's school policy. It's only a precaution, and it's for Leah's own good."

Natalie felt her face growing red. She stared at him for a moment, then turned away again. "Thank you for your time, Mr. Callahan. I'll make an appointment with the school counselor on the way out."

9

The young woman dropped the stack of papers on the mahogany desk. "Here's that manuscript, Wes. We need the copyedits by Wednesday."

Wes Kalamar looked up. "Why are you giving them to me?"

"Because you're the copy editor now."

"Me? What happened to Furkin?"

"You let him go last month."

"Then what about Dunderson?"

"The month before. We went over this in our last 'reorganization' meeting, remember? You're handling acquisitions, editing, production, and marketing. I'm doing scheduling, author relations, and publicity—in addition to being your personal assistant, I might add."

Wes looked at the formidable stack of paper. "Can't you do it?"

"Wes, I've got an associate degree in massage therapy—suddenly I'm a proofreader? I can't even spell 'proofreader.' Besides, I've got four jobs already. Which reminds me—if I'm doing four jobs, how come I only get one paycheck?"

"C'mon, Annie, this is a lousy time to hit me for a raise. You know how it is right now. Things are a little tight."

"A little tight? We've only got six people left, Wes, and

Elliot just threatened to quit unless I give him a fifty-minute shiatsu."

"Look, we're just having a bad quarter, that's all. Things will turn around—we've got a strong lineup for fall."

Annie looked at him over the top of her glasses. "Have you actually read any of our books?"

"Well—"

"Honeycutt—our old acquisitions editor? I think he was on drugs. We've got a book called *The Bulimic Diet*. Who wants to read that, Wes? Who should? We've got a children's book called *Things Rich Kids Have*. Is that what you want your kids to be reading?"

"I don't have kids," he said.

"Maybe that's the problem. We've got self-help books that will put you in therapy. We've got marriage books that could get you strangled. We've got travel books to places no one wants to go. Face it, Wes, we're not just having a bad quarter—we're having a bad career."

"We've still got *Lattes with God*."

"Which has already gone from hardcover to trade paper to mass-market paperback. You can buy *Lattes* on the remainders table at Borders for three bucks; you can buy it used on Amazon for a buck forty-nine. We've also got the audiobook, the study guide, and the *Lattes with God Reflections Journal*. How much milk can you get from one cow?"

Wes grabbed a pen. "That would make a great title for a business book."

"Forget the business book. Listen to me: We need another *big* book. The ship is sinking and we're handing out floaties—the plane is going down and we're reaching for pillows. How many metaphors do you need? We just got lucky with *Lattes*, Wes, but it's going to take more than luck to keep this ship afloat."

"I know," Wes said, "and I'm working on it."

"Well, you'd better work fast," she said. "By this time next month you'll be the janitor and I'll be on unemployment." She shoved the manuscript across the desk to him. "We need it by Wednesday so it can go to typesetting."

Wes looked at the cover page: *Shout It Out! Resolving Disagreements the Quick & Easy Way.* "Is this as bad as I think it is?"

"Worse," she said, turning for the door. "Enjoy."

Wes slumped back in his chair and looked around the office. It was a truly great office—the office he had always dreamed of. The floor-to-ceiling windows with the glimpse of the homes dotting the Hollywood Hills; the Italian designer furniture; the fabulous Noguchi coffee table and the Eames leather chairs that were softer than a baby's bottom. It was the office he had always wanted—but maybe he had signed the lease just a little too soon. He felt terrible about having to let most of his employees go—but not terrible enough to downsize to a more affordable office. But why should he? He was a creative, after all, and creatives needed creative surroundings to create.

He stood up and looked at his office chair. Fifty-six hundred dollars for a chair—maybe that was a bit steep. But it was an Interstuhl Silver, after all—the chair Al Pacino used in *Ocean's Thirteen.* All the metal parts were actually made of silver—how cool was that? He could never part with his Silver. How was he supposed to create without it? The chair was like a cosmic antenna—he could practically feel creative energy channeling into him through those silver arms . . .

He shook his head. *I don't need to downsize the office,* he thought. *I need to upsize the business—that's the positive approach! Annie's right—we need another big book. But where am I going to find it?*

He sat down on his cosmic antenna and began to think—but before the creative energy had time to reach him, there was a knock at the door.

Annie leaned in. "Someone to see you."

"Who?"

"An author—says he's got something that will make *Lattes* look like decaf."

"I'm the publisher—I don't meet with authors."

"You're also the acquisitions editor."

"Tell him to send me a book proposal."

"He's here now. I'm sending him in—or you can empty your own trash." She pushed the door open and stepped aside.

A young man walked into the room and smiled confidently. "Hi there," he said. "My name is Kemp McAvoy."

Wes reluctantly extended his hand. "Wes Kalamar. I'm the publisher here at Vision Press."

"Yes, I know," Kemp said. "As seen on TV." Without waiting to be invited he sat down in a leather armchair and swung a leg over one of the arms. He was dressed in khakis with a square-cut Malibu sport shirt and a pair of Teva sandals dangling from his feet.

"Nice chair you've got there," Kemp said. "Is that an Interstuhl?"

"Not many people recognize that," Wes said.

Kemp shrugged. "I have a taste for nice things."

"I understand you're a writer, Mr. McAvoy."

"Me? No. Actually, I'm a nurse. I work over at UCLA Medical Center."

"You've got a story concept, then?"

"Not really. You could say I have a concept, but not for a story."

"Then why are you here?"

Kemp reached into his back pocket and pulled out a mass-market paperback edition of *Lattes with God*. "I actually spent good money for this," he said. "I can't believe I shelled out seven ninety-nine for this drivel, but I thought I should become familiar with it." He flipped through a few pages. "Listen to this: 'No one in the bustling Starbucks could see that the Creator himself was seated across from me, smiling with satisfaction as I delighted in one of his finest creations.' Tell me, does God like those little biscotti?"

Wes frowned. "Mr. McAvoy, *Lattes with God* was the best-selling book in the world last year—it outsold everything except the Bible."

"How ironic," Kemp said. "I wonder where *Lattes with God* will be a few millennia from now?"

"Mr. McAvoy, may I be blunt?"

"It's your office."

"I'm a busy man. Any fool can find a few things wrong with a book—"

"Especially a book like this one."

"—so I'm not interested in your critique of *Lattes* unless you've got something better. Do you? If not, get your legs off my Italian leather and let me get back to work."

Kemp smiled. "As a matter of fact, I do have something better—a lot better."

"Well?"

"The way I see it, there's one problem with this book that outweighs all the others."

"And that is?"

"It's last year's book—and as I understand it, you're looking for next year's book. Does that pretty well summarize your present dilemma?"

"That's every publisher's dilemma. So?"

Kemp swung his legs around and leaned forward, resting his forearms on his thighs. "What if I told you that Liv Hayden is about to have a near-death experience—a series of conversations with an angelic being. Would you be interested in publishing a story like that?"

"Liv Hayden the movie star?"

"That's right."

"I heard about her on the news. Wasn't she in some kind of accident? Isn't she in a coma right now over at UCLA?"

"Right again."

"And you say she's had a near-death experience?"

"Not yet—but she's about to."

Wes just stared.

Kemp leaned back and smiled. "I work in the Neuro Trauma Intensive Care Unit at UCLA. I'm a nurse—Liv Hayden is my patient. As a precautionary measure, Ms. Hayden will be kept in a medically induced coma for the next several days. Her injuries are minor; this is only a precaution. Her coma is being induced by a drug called propofol, injected into her veins at a constant rate. It would be a very simple matter to reduce the amount of propofol she's receiving and bring her to a semi-conscious state—a suggestive state, you might say, where she could see and hear and would remember very clearly everything told to her during that period of time."

"What are you talking about?"

"I'm talking about the next *Lattes with God*, Mr. Kalamar. Liv Hayden is a world-famous celebrity. Her face, her name, they're everywhere—she's got her own line of cosmetics with Estée Lauder. Imagine it—one week from today she awakens from her coma and suddenly remembers something: while she was at death's door an angel appeared to her and gave her a series of messages from God that must be shared with the entire world. She wants to write a book about her experience; she needs a publisher, so she signs an exclusive agreement with none other than Vision Press. Think of the publicity—Liv Hayden's famous name plastered across the cover, Liv Hayden's perfect face gracing the back of the book, Liv Hayden herself on *Regis & Kelly* and *The View*. It would be like *Lattes with God* on steroids."

"Wait a minute," Wes said. "Am I understanding you correctly? Are we talking about *manufacturing* a near-death experience?"

"It would be technically simple to do. Propofol is a short-acting drug—it's rapidly distributed into peripheral tissues. I could bring her from a deep coma to a semiconscious state in less than an hour, and return her there just as quickly. No one would ever know."

"This is insane."

"Is it? I work nights at UCLA; there are fewer doctors on duty, fewer procedures, fewer interruptions. Ms. Hayden is a famous celebrity, so she has a private room—a room with a solid door so no one can see in. Ms. Hayden is my patient—my only patient—and I spend hours alone with her every night. I could easily adjust her medication without anyone ever knowing."

"But—what about the near-death experience itself? The message from God? Where would that come from?"

"I told you—from an angel."

"What angel?"

Kemp grinned. "Ta daa!"

"You? *You're* the angel?"

"I hate typecasting, don't you? It's simple—when Ms. Hayden reaches her semiconscious state, I simply slip on a white lab coat and set up a bright examination light behind

71

me. Instant halo! Her vision should be a little blurry, so the effect will be perfect."

Wes began to slowly walk around the room. "Is this really possible?"

"It's not only possible, it's doable. Trust me—I have considerable technical expertise in this area."

"But what if something went wrong? What if we injured her?"

"She's injured now. She's only in a coma to keep her from moving and to give her time to rest. She's wearing a device that allows us to monitor her precise level of consciousness; I'll simply bring her to a level where she can see and hear but still not move. What's the danger?"

Now Wes was pacing back and forth like a duck in a shooting gallery.

"What do you think, Mr. Kalamar?"

"I don't know. I need time to think about this."

"Unfortunately, time is the one thing we don't have. Ms. Hayden will only be kept in a coma for the next few days. Once they bring her out of it, the opportunity will be gone forever. If you want in, you have to decide now. If you don't want in, believe me—I'll find a publisher who does."

Wes stopped and looked at him. "This 'message from God'—what would it be?"

"Who cares?" Kemp said, tossing his copy of *Lattes with God* on the desk. "How hard can it be to come up with nonsense like this?"

Wes just stood there, blinking.

"Who wrote *Lattes with God*, anyway?" Kemp asked. "I don't know and I don't care. But imagine this on the cover: *by Liv Hayden*."

Wes gazed at his Interstuhl Silver . . . It was starting to look like a bargain.

"Twelve million copies would just be the first printing," Kemp said. "With Hayden on the cover you'd sell twenty million for sure."

Twenty million copies, Wes thought. *Now that's what I call a big book.*

"Well, Mr. Kalamar? Are you in or not?"

Wes suddenly stopped. "Wait a minute—what's in this for you? What's your fee for manufacturing this near-death experience?"

"I'm not interested in a fee," Kemp said. "What exactly is the publisher's cut, anyway—about eighty percent of the net profit? Let's see . . . a twenty-five-dollar hardcover, twenty million copies, eighty percent after discounts and expenses . . . That's a lot of money, Mr. Kalamar—plenty for all three of us."

"Three?"

"There's one small problem with my plan," Kemp said. "When Ms. Hayden wakes up from her coma, who will make sure that she writes a book about her experience? And how can we guarantee that she'll choose Vision Press as her publisher?"

Wes had no answer.

"I happen to know Ms. Hayden's agent," Kemp said. "Morton Biederman—he's just the man for the job."

"Is he in on this?"

"Not yet, but he soon will be. I want a three-way split, Mr. Kalamar—you, me, and Biederman—one-third each of Vision Press's profits."

"Thirds! That's unheard of."

"It's only fair. If you think about it, I'm bearing all the risk here. No one but me even has to know that you and Biederman are involved. Let's not get greedy here, Kalamar—like I said, there's plenty for all three of us."

Wes barely heard him—he was too busy doing the math.

Kemp smiled. "So what's it going to be, Mr. Kalamar? *Lattes Part Two*, *Three*, and *Four*—or *by Liv Hayden*? A cold cup of coffee with God, or a movie star's date with an angel? Just how much vision does Vision Press have, anyway? Take your time; think it over; and while you're thinking, I'll be looking up the phone number for Random House."

10

*N*atalie sat in the counselor's office with Leah seated in the chair beside her. She wriggled a little, trying to find a more comfortable position, but it was no use; the institutional chairs were wooden with rigid backs, the kind that force you to sit with correct posture—the kind you can sit in for an hour and never feel relaxed. Leah's legs didn't quite reach the floor, and she swung them back and forth like a silent metronome. Natalie reached over without a word and laid one hand on her thigh.

For fifteen minutes they had waited in silence while St. Stephen's counselor studied a manila file folder containing Leah's school records. With every passing minute Natalie became more frustrated. *She's only six*, she thought. *How long can her record be? Maybe he's just a slow reader.* She glanced over at Leah and saw a familiar dark scowl on her face. Natalie flashed a quick smile at her daughter, hoping she might take the hint and brighten her demeanor. It didn't work.

By now Natalie had studied every inch of the tiny office's walls; they were covered with neatly framed diplomas and certificates, all testifying to the knowledge and expertise of one Charles Armantrout. Only one of the documents represented any true accomplishment—a diploma from Chico State conveying a BS in psychology. The rest seemed to be mostly certificates of attendance for different seminars and work-shops; Natalie couldn't imagine why anyone would think they were worth framing.

Armantrout finally closed the folder and looked up. He was a thin man with a long and angular face that seemed perfectly suited for looks of boredom and disdain. He was completely bald on top, though the hair on the sides of his head bushed out in tight curls of gray. The shape of his skull was almost conical, and Natalie couldn't help thinking that his head looked like a rocket lifting off through clouds of smoke. A pair of black half-frames rested on the tip of his nose and accentuated a pair of tedious eyes.

Armantrout suddenly flashed a smile at Leah, causing Natalie to blink. The smile didn't seem to fit his face; it looked practiced and artificial, like the smiles politicians wear when they're tired of posing for pictures. "So you're Leah," he said.

Leah made a roll of her eyes that said, "Are you just figuring that out?"

"I'd like to ask a few questions if you don't mind," Armantrout said.

Leah replied with a bored shrug, and Natalie wished she could kick her without being spotted.

"How long have you been seeing angels?"

"I only saw one," Leah said. "It's not like they're everywhere."

"Do you see any now?"

"Do you?"

"Why just the other day, Leah? Why do you suppose you saw the angel then?"

Leah glared at him. "'Cause that's when he was there."

Armantrout nodded and scribbled something on a legal pad. He looked up again and asked, "Leah, what is it like for you at home?"

"Excuse me," Natalie said. "What exactly are you asking?"

Armantrout ignored her. "Leah, do you feel loved? Accepted? Would you say that you feel—safe?"

"Hold it a minute," Natalie said. "Leah, would you mind stepping out in the hallway for a moment? I'd like a chance to speak to Mr. Armantrout alone."

When Leah left the room, Natalie turned to the counselor. "What are you doing?"

"I'm just trying to understand Leah better."

"You ask my daughter if she feels loved in front of me? Don't you think that's putting her on the spot a little? What's she supposed to tell you?"

"Are you afraid of what she might say?"

Natalie narrowed her eyes. "Look—my daughter *feels loved*, okay? Nobody loves her daughter more than I do."

"And your husband?"

"I'm not married."

"Divorced?"

"Yes."

"Was the divorce amicable?"

Natalie glared at him. "Do you know what a divorce is?"

"What was the experience like for your daughter?"

Natalie paused. She didn't mind the questions as much as his manner of asking them; he casually tossed them off as though he were reading from a grocery list. "It was difficult for her, okay?"

"Tell me, had Leah formed an attachment bond with her father?"

An "attachment bond"? "As much as he would let her."

"And after the divorce, did she experience a sense of loss? Of upheaval?"

"Her parents split up. We moved. He disappeared. What do you think?"

"And what about now? Do you live alone?"

Natalie gritted her teeth. "Would you mind telling me where you're going with all this?"

"I'm simply trying to understand Leah's home environment, that's all."

"I have a boyfriend," she said. "We live together."

"And how long has this relationship been going on? How long have you shared a household?"

"We met at work not long after the divorce. We've been living together for almost a year."

"Would you say Leah has bonded with this man?"

Natalie stopped. "Look, these are very personal questions—*too* personal. I don't see why you need to know all this."

"Ms. Pelton, your daughter claims to have seen an angel. Doesn't that concern you?"

"My daughter has a very vivid imagination."

"But this is more than just an imaginative story. Leah insists that she has actually seen an angel. She seems quite convinced."

"I just don't see the harm," Natalie said.

"Your daughter has apparently suffered a psychotic episode."

"Whoa," she said. "A *psychotic episode*? What in the world are you talking about?"

Armantrout turned and took a dictionary from his bookshelf. "Let me read you something: '*Psychosis*: a severe mental disorder, with or without organic damage, characterized by derangement of personality and loss of contact with reality and causing deterioration of normal social functioning.'"

"*Derangement of personality*?" Natalie said incredulously. "You have to be joking."

"Let me draw your attention to the phrase 'loss of contact with reality.' That's what concerns me here. I'm also concerned by the phrase 'causing deterioration of normal social function-ing.' Leah is possibly in the early stages of psychosis; we need to determine whether her condition is likely to deteriorate, and whether she could become a danger to others."

"A *danger*? I don't understand you people. It's not like she saw the devil or something. Leah thinks she saw an angel—one of the good guys, remember? Isn't this an Episcopal school?"

Armantrout smiled. "We're not all so medieval around here, Ms. Pelton. Some of us are trained in the sciences. There has to be a naturalistic explanation for what your daughter saw, and that explanation is probably psychological or emo-tional in nature. I don't mean to pry into your personal life, but it's quite possible that Leah's home environment has triggered this episode."

"How do you figure that?"

"Leah has suffered a trauma: the breakup of her family; the absence of her father; the loss of the safe and secure world of her early childhood. She suddenly finds herself living in a new place with a man she doesn't even know. Tell me, Ms. Pelton, does Leah feel safe around your boyfriend?"

"What? Of course she does!"

"It's quite possible that Leah is projecting an angelic being as a kind of defense mechanism. An angel is a powerful mythi-cal being—strong, protective, someone that Leah hopes can watch over her and keep her safe from harm."

Natalie stood up. "I've had enough of this."

"Ms. Pelton, please—"

"Tell me something, Mr. Armantrout. Are you actually a licensed psychologist, or is this just an armchair diagnosis? Because I don't appreciate your making accusations about Leah's 'home environment' or suggesting that she doesn't feel safe. My daughter is safe and secure—and loved. I don't know what she saw or why she thinks it was an angel, but if you think this is a *psychotic episode* then I think *you're* psychotic."

Armantrout held up both hands. "We're all simply trying to understand Leah."

"No, that's what *you're* trying to do. I'm just trying to satisfy this school's ridiculous requirements so my daughter can go back to class where she belongs."

Armantrout picked up his pen. "I'm recommending that Leah have a full psychiatric evaluation."

"What? Are you out of your mind?"

"And possibly an MRI."

"An MRI? What in the world for?"

Armantrout referred again to the open dictionary. "'*Psychosis*: a severe mental disorder, with or without organic damage . . .' There are abnormalities in the brain that have been known to produce hallucinations, Ms. Pelton. An MRI would rule out the possibility of any organic damage. I think it would be a good precaution."

Natalie was so furious that her hands were trembling, but she did her best to control her rage. "Okay," she said evenly. "First I talked to the teacher and now I've seen the school counselor—I've done what everyone's asked of me. Thank you for your suggestions, Mr. Armantrout; I'll consider them. Is there anything else, or can Leah go back to class now?"

Armantrout looked at her. "I think it's safe for Leah to return to class—but we'll have to keep an eye on her, Ms. Pelton. After all, we owe it to the other children."

11

"You gotta be kidding," Biederman said.

Kemp smiled. "Do I sound like I'm kidding?"

Biederman turned and looked at Wes Kalamar. "You're a respectable businessman. Do you think this thing is possible?"

"I know how it sounds," Kalamar said. "I thought the same thing myself at first, but I think Kemp might be onto something here."

The three men sat in upholstered chairs arranged in a horseshoe configuration in the West Lobby of Century Plaza Towers, the twin forty-four-story skyscrapers that provide premium office space to those in the investment, technology, and entertainment industries—including talent agents like Mort Biederman. The lobby was bustling with people, walking and talking and chatting on cell phones, their shoes clicking loudly on the Mesabi granite floor—providing the perfect sound mask for a delicate discussion.

"Let me get this straight," Biederman said. "At night, while nobody's looking, you bring Olivia out of her coma—"

"Halfway out," Kemp corrected. "Just enough to bring her to a semiconscious state."

"Okay, halfway out—then you dress up like an angel and you give her a message from God. Right so far?"

Kemp nodded.

"Then when the doctors bring her out of the coma for good, Olivia thinks she just had an out-of-body experience."

"A near-death experience."

"Whatever. And you say she'll remember it. She'll actually believe it."

"Why wouldn't she? It will seem perfectly real to her—because it *was* real."

"No offense, my friend, but you don't look like any angel I've ever seen—not that I've seen any."

Kemp shrugged. "A blinding light, fuzzy vision, a slight buzz from the propofol—her mind will fill in the rest."

"And my part would be to encourage her to write a book about her experience." He nodded to Wes. "A book that his company will publish."

Kalamar leaned closer. "She doesn't even have to write the thing—I can write it. Shoot, I can write the book in advance because we already know what the 'message' is going to be. We'll do some interviews with her—make her think she's dictating the whole thing—but we can have the book practically ready to go. We can get it to press in no time. How good is that?"

"You sound like a man in a hurry," Biederman said.

"Who isn't in a hurry to make money?"

Biederman nodded. "You have a point. And when the book comes out, we split thirds—is that the basic deal?"

"That's the offer."

"So?" Kemp said. "What do you think, Mr. Biederman?"

Biederman stared at each of the men in turn. "I'll tell you what I think, gentlemen. Olivia Hayden is like a daughter to me—the daughter I never had. I think the two of you are asking me to take advantage of her—to exploit her terrible misfortune for profit. I'm sorry, gentlemen, that's something I cannot do—not for a measly third."

Kemp shook his head. "Forget it, Biederman. Straight thirds—that's the deal, take it or leave it. You've got the smallest part of this operation, and you stand to take a bigger cut than either one of us. You're her agent—if you broker this deal with Kalamar, won't you take a percentage of Hayden's earnings too? And as for exploiting 'poor Olivia,' who are you kidding? Let's not forget the twenty percent she'll walk away with—that's worth millions. Aren't you her agent? Isn't it your job to find profitable deals for her? Can you think of a deal more profitable than this one? Think it over, Biederman—in this deal everybody wins and nobody loses."

Biederman paused. "And absolutely no danger to Olivia?"

"I'm a nurse and a trained anesthesiologist," Kemp said.

"If you're an anesthesiologist, how come you're a nurse?"

"Long story," Kemp said. "The point is, she'll be in a hospital and I'll be with her from seven p.m. to seven a.m. every night. Ordinarily I only work three or four nights in a row, but I can work something out with the other night nurses. I can arrange to be her nurse every night the entire time she's there. There'll be no danger to your client."

Biederman finally nodded. "Okay. We split thirds of the publisher's earnings."

"*Net* earnings," Kalamar corrected. "After production and promotional expenses."

"Which will be itemized—in writing."

"Of course."

"And what about foreign language editions? Book clubs? Subsidiary and affiliate editions? What about—"

"I hate to interrupt you *businessmen*," Kemp said, "but we can work out all these details later. We've got something a lot more important to take care of right now, and we need to do it fast."

"What's that?"

"Hayden will only be in that coma for the next few days. We need to get this thing rolling immediately—even tonight—but I need something to say. What's this 'message from God' going to be?"

"He's right," Kalamar said. "We need a story."

Biederman shook his head. "What we need is a script."

"Who's going to write it?"

The three men looked at one another.

"I should do it," Kalamar said. "I work with stories every day."

Biederman looked at him doubtfully. "And every busboy in LA has a screenplay."

"I'm serious. You show me a publisher and I'll show you a frustrated writer."

"Frustration I got—we need good material. Besides, a story is not what we need here."

"Why not?"

"Because McAvoy can't just open a book and read it to her: 'Once upon a time there was an angel.' He has to talk to her—he needs dialogue—he needs a script."

"I don't have time to memorize a script," Kemp said.

"You don't have to. You can prop it up in front of you. Just keep it off-camera—Liv does it all the time. Little notes, little reminders. Did you see *Ashes of Desire*? Big love scene with Johnny Depp and Liv kept forgetting her line: 'What is love, but a peculiar form of blindness?' Even I can remember it, but she kept drawing a blank. She finally had to stick a Post-it on his forehead."

"I still say we need a story," Kalamar said. "It needs structure—a lead, an objective, a confrontation, a knockout ending. It needs transcendence."

Biederman groaned. "What it needs is a decent setup and a third act that doesn't put the audience to sleep. I should write it. I've been reviewing scripts for Olivia for twenty years."

"How many scripts have you *written*?" Kalamar asked.

"How many books have you written?"

"Hold it," Kemp interrupted. "We all need to write it—together."

Both men looked at him. "What do you know about writing?"

"Nothing—but I don't want you two 'frustrated writers' cranking out Shakespeare when you're not the one who has to repeat it. I'm the guy who has to deliver this 'message,' so I should get a say in what I'm delivering. Besides, it doesn't really matter what the message is."

"What do you mean?"

"C'mon, look at *Lattes with God*—it's complete nonsense. People who buy this kind of claptrap obviously have no rational capacity anyway. I could say just about anything I want."

"Like what?" Kalamar asked.

"Anything. I'm saying it doesn't matter."

"You're wrong, McAvoy—it does matter. This has to be a book, and believe it or not, people won't shell out twenty-five bucks just to hear an angel stuttering. Olivia Hayden's name and face might help on the cover, but there still has to be something inside. It's still a book."

"And a movie," Biederman said.

The two men turned to him.

"You two haven't thought of that yet? That was the problem with *Lattes*, Kalamar—it had no film potential. A conversation in a coffee shop—who wants to watch that for two hours? A movie needs interesting characters, exotic settings, maybe a car chase or two—if we think ahead we can work all that in. Film rights—that's another cash cow we can take to the butcher."

The three men all stared across the lobby in silence.

"We need to get going on this right away," Kemp said.

"All three of us?" Kalamar said. "How do we do that?"

"In Hollywood, writers work in teams all the time," Biederman said. "With three minds working together we should be able to hammer this out in no time. We'll do it the way they do for television—one episode at a time. We'll hole up right here—we'll take a suite across the street at the Century Plaza. We'll eat here, we'll sleep here if we have to. Every day we'll crank out an episode, and every night McAvoy will deliver it."

"That's good," Kalamar said. "I'll run back to the office and grab some supplies—paper, a laptop and a printer, stuff like that."

"I'll reserve the suite and check out room service," Biederman said. "We'll meet back here in one hour."

Kemp didn't move.

"Is there a problem, McAvoy?"

"My girlfriend."

"What about her?"

"I work nights; I sleep days. How do I explain what I'm doing for the next few days?"

"So explain. What's the matter, doesn't she trust you?"

"I'm not sure she'd go along with this. It's a little . . . outside her box."

"How does she feel about a couple million bucks? That should be 'inside her box.' Look, tell her whatever you have to. Or don't tell her anything—just show up with some roses and a Maserati in a couple of months. I guarantee she'll get over it."

Kemp slowly rose to his feet. "You're right," he said. "Okay, one hour. And bring your halos, fellas—we need to think like an angel."

12

"Are you all settled in here?" Natalie asked. "Have you got everything you need?"

"I guess so," Leah grumbled.

Natalie looked around the nurses' break room. "You've got your homework; you can do it on the coffee table right here. I'll put your snack in the refrigerator over there—see it? When your homework is finished you can read or you can watch your Hannah Montana DVD—just keep the volume down because it's a hospital, okay? And when it's time for bed I'll come back and tuck you in. We'll roll out your sleeping bag right here on the sofa."

"Do I have to go to school tomorrow?"

"Of course you do—it's Wednesday. When I get off work in the morning, we'll swing by the house and you can clean up and change your clothes. How's that?"

"Great," she said. "Now we live in a hospital."

"We're not moving in, Leah. This is just for a few nights—just until we can find someone to replace Mrs. Rodriguez." She leaned down and kissed her daughter on the forehead. "Kemp will come by and visit you too."

"Oh, goodie."

Natalie walked to the door. "Thanks for being flexible,

sweetheart. Remember to keep the noise down in here—people are trying to sleep."

Natalie quietly shut the door and taped a hand-lettered Please Do Not Disturb sign above the knob.

She walked to the nurses' station and found the charge nurse. "Thanks, Shanice—I really appreciate this."

"As long as it's only for a few days," Shanice said.

"Just until I find a new caregiver, I promise. There was nothing else I could do. I can't switch to days—I'd never see her."

"What about Kemp? He could switch."

"He—won't. Kemp is . . . well, Kemp is Kemp."

Shanice nodded. "Say no more."

Natalie was grateful that Shanice understood, but it bothered her that Kemp's inflexible attitude required so little explanation. Shanice knew Kemp—all the nurses did. They knew that he could be charming and that he was always nice to look at—'easy on the eyes,' Shanice liked to say. But they also knew that Kemp could be selfish and arrogant and vain. Natalie knew it too—and it was becoming more apparent all the time. She wondered why she didn't see it at first. Maybe she did; maybe she just didn't want to admit it to herself. Maybe she was just especially needy when Kemp came along—but that was more than a year ago. She needed something else from him now, and she was beginning to wonder if what she really needed just wasn't there.

=⊨=

Leah completed her homework in record time. It wasn't that she was hurrying; the material just wasn't difficult for her. Besides, she would rather read her own books than the stupid ones the school provided—boring books that were supposed to introduce her to nouns and verbs she had mastered a long time ago. Leah had been reading since she was four, and she now read at a grade level three years beyond her own. While her classmates were still sounding out basic vocabulary, Leah was craving stories—the more complex and imaginative the better. She opened her backpack and took out a dog-eared copy of *The Magician's Nephew* and began to read.

But she wasn't used to reading in such a quiet environment, and the silence quickly became a distraction. She kept looking up at the door, wondering where her mother was right now, imagining her walking down the hall toward the nurses' room and reaching for the doorknob at that very moment—but the door didn't open.

Leah tossed her book aside and walked to the door. She opened it a crack and looked out. The hallway was empty and she could see the doorways to the patients' rooms lining the opposite wall. Some were open and some were closed. She wondered what was going on in each of those rooms; she wondered which one her mother was in right now. She mentally reviewed her mother's instructions: *Do your homework and keep the noise down.* She never said Leah had to stay in the nurses' room—what harm would it do to take a look around? If anyone asked she would simply say she was looking for her mother—and just in case she found her mother, she began to construct an excuse. *I couldn't figure out how to work the DVD player*—that should do it.

She slipped out into the hallway and closed the door behind her. She began to slowly work her way down the hallway to her left, hugging the wall as she went, stopping across from each doorway to peer inside. The first patient's room was dimly lit, but through the glass in the door she could see a man lying in bed. A blue curtain concealed most of him; only his legs were visible. She could see his hospital gown that ended just below his knees and his woolly white socks that sagged over at the toes. She could even see the dark curly hair on his legs and it was fascinating to her; it was just like the hairy leg on the Pirates of the Caribbean ride at Disneyland. She imagined what the rest of the man might look like—that he might be an actual pirate, with an eye patch over one eye and a green-and-yellow parrot lying on the pillow beside his head. She snickered and covered her mouth.

She moved down to the next room and found the door open just a few inches. This time the figure in the bed was nothing but a lump under the covers, but she could see a man standing at the foot of the bed, waving his hands and talking angrily. Every minute or so he would suddenly stop like a wind-up toy running down—then a few seconds later he would just as suddenly start up again. Leah imagined a nurse inserting a giant metal key into his back and winding him up until his spring was so tight that his head popped off and landed on the bed.

Each of the rooms was different. Some were brightly lit and some were dark except for the flickering blue light from a wall-mounted TV; some were crowded with family members and others were as empty as tombs; some rooms seemed to be happy places—even in a hospital—and some seemed lonely, sad, and still.

When Leah came to the seventh room, she was surprised to find the door wide open and the curtain pulled back from the bed. She could plainly see the figure under the covers—an old man with pale skin and his eyes peacefully closed. There was a woman standing beside the bed, standing so close that she could have reached out and stroked the old man's hair. But she wasn't stroking his hair—she was standing perfectly still and holding her hand palm-down just above his head. Leah stared wide-eyed at the woman; a moment later the woman suddenly looked up directly into Leah's eyes. She smiled at Leah, then raised one finger to her lips and went, *Shhh.*

"And who might you be?"

Leah jumped. Standing behind her was an old black man in a gray custodian's uniform. She didn't answer his question; she just pointed at the door.

"You belong in there? You best get back in there then—your folks might be wondering where you disappeared to."

"An angel," she whispered.

"How's that?"

"I just saw an angel."

The old man blinked. "You saw an angel? Whereabouts?"

Leah pointed at the door again and looked; now the door was closed and the curtain was drawn around the bed.

"In there," she said. "There was an angel standing beside the bed. She was going like this." She held out her hand palm-down.

"Like that? What for?"

"I don't know. I think maybe it helps."

"What did this angel look like?"

"It was a woman this time."

"This time? You're in the habit of seeing angels, then?"

Leah frowned. "You don't believe me, do you?"

"'Course I do."

"You do?"

"We get angels around here all the time."

"Really?"

"You bet. Doctors like to think they do most of the work around here, but I'm not so sure. I've seen people walk right out of here who were never supposed to, and nobody was more surprised than the doctors. 'Course, they don't say so, 'cause doctors are supposed to know everything."

"My mom is a nurse here."

"You don't say! What's her name?"

"Natalie. Natalie Pelton."

The old man smiled. "I know Natalie Pelton. She's a very nice woman, your mother. And who might you be?"

"Leah."

"Hello, Leah. I'm Emmet."

He extended his hand and Leah took it; it was wrinkled but it felt soft, like an old glove.

"My mom's boyfriend works here too."

"And who would that be?"

"His name is Kemp."

Emmet nodded once. "Yep—know him too."

"What's that thing?" Leah asked, pointing to the device that Emmet held in front of him—a gleaming chrome machine with a circular bottom.

"This? It's a floor polisher. People walk up and down this hallway all day. They get the thing all scuffed up, and I come in at night and make it shiny again. Want to see how it works?"

"Okay."

Emmet jiggled the handle but nothing happened. "Seems to be broken. Hold your hand out like that angel did."

When she did, he flipped the switch and the machine began to softly purr.

"You're making fun," she said.

Emmet smiled. "Can't think of a better thing to make."

"Leah! What are you doing out here?"

Leah turned to find her mother standing behind her with her hands on her hips. "I was just talking to—"

"You can't be bothering the people who work here, Leah.

This man has important things to do. I'm sorry, Emmet, Leah was supposed to stay in the nurses' break room."

"You never said I couldn't come out," Leah grumbled.

"Well, I'm saying it now. Now go back to the nurses' room and stay there until I come to tuck you in. Understand?"

Leah turned away without a word. Natalie and Emmet watched as Leah sulked all the way down the hall.

"Delightful young lady," Emmet said.

"I'm sorry if she was bothering you," Natalie said.

"Not at all. I was the one who spoke first."

"What was she doing out here?"

"Just stretching her legs, I imagine. Young legs just have to move—remember?"

"Just barely. Mine are always looking for a place to sit down."

"Mine too. How old is your daughter?"

"Six."

"Wonderful age—an age full of wonder."

"Do you have children, Emmet?"

"Never had that privilege."

"Would you like one?"

Emmet didn't reply, and there was a brief but awkward pause.

"Sorry," Natalie said. "That was a bad joke. I love Leah to death; she's just having some problems at school right now."

"A bright girl like that?"

"It isn't her grades," Natalie said. "It's—something else."

"I suppose it's always something."

"I suppose." She looked at Emmet sheepishly. "Emmet, I'd like to apologize."

"For what?"

"For the other night. For Kemp. He can be so . . ."

93

"There's something about being young," Emmet said. "Sometimes a young man gets to thinkin' he's all that and a bag o' chips, but age has a way of changing things. I knew a lot of things when I was younger; I know a lot less these days. One thing I do know, though: that's a wonderful little girl you've got there."

Natalie smiled appreciatively. "Thanks, Emmet—I needed to hear that. We're a little worried about Leah right now. She's been . . . imagining things. We're hoping it's just a phase she's going through."

"I wouldn't worry about it," Emmet said. "Things have a way of workin' together for good—you wait and see."

13

*W*es Kalamar lugged two boxes of office supplies over from Vision Press that included legal pads, sticky notes, multicolored pushpins, paper clips, correction tape, and fluorescent scented accent markers in six fruit colors. He also brought a telescoping aluminum tripod with a 30 x 40 inch easel pad to facilitate group participation. The suite had a western exposure overlooking 200 Avenue of the Stars and the Century Plaza Towers beyond. Wes set up the tripod and angled it so it would catch the afternoon sun. There was a table in the center of the room; in front of each chair he placed a crisp new legal pad and a ballpoint pen that wrote in four colors. He noticed that the top sheet on one of the legal pads was crimped at the bottom-right corner. He carefully removed the sheet and left a fresh one showing on top.

Mort Biederman concentrated on the refreshments. From the Starbucks in the lobby he bought a Coffee Traveler of Café Estima and was careful to include a variety of flavored creamers, sweeteners, insulated cups, and tiny wooden stirring sticks. From the room service menu he ordered a deli tray and a seasonal fruit sampler, though Kemp and Wes both voted for the Spicy Wings Fiesta with assorted dipping sauces. Biederman vetoed both of them: "We've got thinking to do," he said. "You need blood circulating for that." He also ordered an entire case of bottled Agua Spring drinking water, in the event that sudden dehydration threatened any of them.

Kemp's contribution was to stretch out on a sofa with his feet propped up on a pillow and do his best to look pensive until he began to doze off.

Biederman stood over him and said, "Hey, Angel, are we keeping you up? How 'bout you get with the program?"

"You guys work days," he mumbled. "I work nights—I should be sleeping right now."

"You are."

Kemp sat up and rubbed his face. "All right, let's get to work. Where do we begin?"

"The beginning is a good place," Biederman said.

"Okay, what's the first thing our angel says? Liv Hayden is coming out of her coma; her mind begins to clear; she sees someone standing over her—a man bathed in blinding white light—an angel! The angel opens his mouth, and he says to her—what?"

"'How's the head?'" Biederman suggested.

Kemp looked at him. "*How's the head? Is* that the best you can come up with?"

"I didn't hear anything from you."

"Biederman, this is supposed to be an angel. Would an angel travel halfway across the cosmos just to tell her to take a couple Tylenol?"

"How would I know? I never met an angel."

"Well, use your imagination."

"I'm trying. What have you got?"

"Kemp's right," Wes said. "This is a majestic being and he needs to lead off with something majestic. His first words should be extraordinary, unexpected, inspirational—"

"Who's arguing?" Biederman said. "So what's the opening line?"

"What we need is something big—something visionary—something almost poetic. The angel opens his mouth and he says to her . . ."

Two hours later the deli tray had been completely demolished, though both the fruit sampler and the crisp legal pads had been left untouched. The coffee was making all three of them irritable—a side effect of caffeine commonly mistaken for productivity. Biederman, the oldest of the men, had to excuse himself to use the bathroom every fifteen minutes.

"What's with you?" Kemp complained. "You must have a bladder the size of a peanut."

"Call me when you're fifty and we'll compare notes," Biederman said.

"How are we supposed to get a train of thought going when you keep taking bathroom breaks? Tomorrow I'm bringing a catheter."

"While you're at it, bring a brain. My bladder is larger."

"Guys," Wes said. "Let's try to focus here. What have we got so far? Somebody read it back to me."

"Read what?" Biederman said. "We got nothing."

Kemp shook his head in disgust. "Do I have to do everything? I thought you two would be creative geniuses—all I'd have to do was polish the dialogue a little."

Wes picked up a felt-tip pen and stepped up to the easel. "Why don't we try a little 'word association' to get our creative juices flowing. When I say the word 'angel,' what's the first thing that comes to your mind? Go ahead—call out anything."

"Harp," Kemp offered. "Clouds. Wings. Halo."

"Boxing," Biederman said.

Both men stared at him.

Biederman shrugged. "Olivia was at Kate Mantilini's before

the accident. Kate Mantilini was the first female boxing promoter. There's a boxer named Angel Rivera."

Kemp slumped back on the sofa. "And they think Liv Hayden is in a coma. This isn't *Six Degrees of Separation*, Biederman, we're trying to write a book here."

"What did you come up with, McAvoy? Harp, clouds, halo—what are we supposed to do with that? Chubby baby, chicken wings, bow and arrow—is that any better?"

"Forget word association," Wes said. "Let's try role-playing instead. Let's put ourselves into the part and see what we come up with. Kemp, lie down on the sofa again."

"What for?"

"It's what you do best," Biederman grumbled.

"You're Liv Hayden," Wes explained. "Biederman, I want you to come here and stand over him—you're the angel."

They both did as instructed.

"Now think like an angel," Wes said to Biederman. "This woman is dangling by a thread between life and death. You have only a few moments with her, and there's something you must tell her—something she needs to hear. What is it? What is that message?"

Biederman looked down at Kemp. "Sweetheart, look at you—you've really let yourself go."

"Get out of the way, Biederman." Wes shoved him aside and took his place. He looked down at Kemp. "I have a message for you," he said, "a message from the Creator of the universe. This is the most important message you will ever receive, and I want you to go back and share it with the whole world. I want you to talk about it, and write about it, and after you write it down, I want you to publish it. This is the most important message in the world, and everyone, everywhere, needs to hear it."

He stopped and stared off into space.

"Well?" Kemp said. "What's the message?"

Wes sank down in a chair. "I have absolutely no idea."

"We're getting nowhere," Kemp grumbled. "We've been at this for hours and we don't even have an opening line yet—we'll be here forever at this rate. Maybe I should just write it myself."

"Not a chance," Wes said. "I have to publish this thing."

"And I have to sell the film rights," Biederman said. "Sorry, boys, we're stuck with each other."

Another hour passed . . .

"Forget the opening line," Wes said suddenly. "It's bogging us down. Any author will tell you the opening line of a book is the hardest one to write. What we need is a basic story line—we can go back and write the opening later."

"Okay," Kemp said. "Then what's the story?"

99

"We need a story with conflict—tension—something to hook the audience and draw them in."

"I like it," Biederman said. "Keep going."

"How about this? The angel tells Hayden there's a cosmic conflict brewing somewhere in the universe, a conflict to determine which path people will follow—the old way or the new way. You know, sort of a *Star Wars* thing: 'A long time ago in a galaxy far, far away . . .'"

Biederman frowned. "I thought it was 'A long, long time ago in a galaxy far away.'"

"No, it's far, far."

"Are you sure about that?"

"Look it up if you don't believe me."

"Hey," Kemp said. "If you two Jedi knights don't mind, I'd like to get some sleep. Keep going, Wes."

"Anyway, the angel says this conflict has been going on

for centuries—maybe millennia. And what is this conflict about?"

Kemp shrugged.

"Truth—deep knowledge—*this message*. Will people learn the truth and be set free to live lives of freedom and joy, or will they remain slaves to the old way of thinking? This is an ancient message, the angel tells her, one that people have known about for centuries, but it's been forgotten, buried, suppressed."

"'Suppressed' is good," Biederman said. "People like 'suppressed.'"

"Who suppressed it?"

"Beats me. The church—Republicans—sub-prime mortgage lenders. We can just leave a blank there and fill it in later. Of course, some people have always known about this deep knowledge—smart people, successful people, rich people."

"And only smart people *can* know it," Biederman added. "That's a nice touch—a little snob appeal never hurts."

"This is good," Wes said. "I think we're onto something here."

"This is just an outline," Kemp said. "I have to meet with Hayden tonight—I need something to *say*. 'There's a cosmic conflict brewing in the universe.' Terrific—that'll take me, what, five seconds? Then what do I say? What's the actual message?"

Wes shook his head. "I don't know yet."

Kemp swung his legs around and sat up. "Guys, we've got to do a whole lot better than this. Liv Hayden's only going to be in that coma for the next few days. Every night we miss means one less installment in our 'message,' and that means one less chapter in our book. We can't afford to get writer's block on our first day—we need to come up with some material." He stood up and began to collect his things.

"Where are you going?" Biederman asked.

"I work nights, remember? I need a couple hours of sleep before my shift begins."

"Maybe he's right," Wes said. "We could all use some sleep."

"Oh, no you don't—you two aren't going anywhere. You geniuses are going to stay right here until you come up with something, even if it takes you all night. By this time tomorrow we need a full-blown message."

"But what about tonight? What are you going to tell Hayden?"

"I'll just give her the 'cosmic conflict' bit—after that I'll just have to wing it."

"Can you remember it all?"

"Let's see . . . cosmic conflict, ancient knowledge, suppressed by Republicans, only snobs get it. Wow—an astonishing feat of memory."

"Don't write us into a corner," Wes said. "Don't give her any specifics yet—keep it vague."

"I don't have much choice, do I? Look, I get off at seven in the morning—I'll be back after that. Try to have something for me by then, will you?" He glared at Biederman. "Something *coherent*."

At the door he turned back and looked at them. "The clock is ticking, guys—I'm counting on you. Remember: no message, no money."

101

14

*N*atalie took the laminated number from the glove compartment and placed it on the dashboard where the carpool monitor could see it. *Two hundred twelve*—that was the number St. Stephen's had randomly assigned to Leah, and that was the number the monitor would call out to find Leah among the beehive of children swarming in front of the school.

The line of cars inched forward again and Natalie moved along with them. Just six more cars to go and she could grab Leah and get out of there—back home for a quick dinner before they headed out to UCLA again. Natalie hated the idea of her daughter spending another night camped out in the nurses' break room, but she had no choice. Between work and sleep and the annoying teacher-counselor meetings here at St. Stephen's, she hadn't had a minute to search for a replacement for Mrs. Rodriguez. UCLA would just have to do for now—but she hoped it wouldn't be for long.

It could go a lot faster if Kemp would pitch in, she thought. *If he won't attend the teacher-counselor meetings, he could at least help search for a new caregiver.* But Kemp wasn't much good at certain things—like thinking of someone else besides himself. Right now she hoped that's all he was thinking of. He didn't come straight home after work this morning; he didn't stumble into bed until several hours later, and he offered no apology or explanation when he did. When Natalie left to pick up Leah from school, Kemp was still sound asleep. She wondered where he had been all day and why he seemed so tired; the thought made her feel a little uneasy.

She glanced up ahead in the carpool line and spotted Matt Callahan standing with his class. When he turned and looked in her direction she quickly looked down at the floorboards, hoping to avoid eye contact. Ordinarily she didn't mind seeing Leah's teacher—none of the moms did. If you had to be stuck in a carpool line for thirty minutes there were worse things to look at than Matt Callahan—you almost didn't mind waiting. But things felt different to Natalie after their parent-teacher meeting; now all she wanted to do was grab her daughter and get out of there.

She heard a sudden rap on her window that startled her. She looked up to find Matt Callahan's face smiling down at her. She just stared up at him until he made a little rolling motion with his index finger. She took the hint and lowered her window.

"Hi, Natalie. I saw your car."

"Hi, Mr. Callahan."

Matt frowned. "Are you still mad at me?"

"I'm just here to pick up Leah."

"About that," he said. "I wanted to apologize."

"For what?"

"For the way our meeting ended the other day."

"You were just doing your job. We can't have kids like Leah climbing up in some bell tower with a sniper rifle."

"Now I know you're mad," Matt said. "I never said anything like that. All I said was—"

"I need to pull up." Natalie pointed to the empty space in front of her and eased the car forward.

Matt walked along beside her car. "I think Leah is a great kid—I told you that before and I want you to hear it again. Like you said, I was only doing my job. It's nothing personal."

"Leah is my daughter. It's always personal." She started to raise the window again, but Matt reached out and put his hand on the edge.

"You can roll the window up if you want to," he said, "but I'm just going to stand here and stare at you if you do. You'll look pretty stupid in front of all these parents."

"So will you."

"I'm a teacher. I always look stupid to parents—but look who I'm telling."

Natalie didn't respond.

"Of course, you can always pull out of the carpool line and drive away if you want to—that's one way to get rid of me. But then you'd just have to turn around and come back for Leah. Wouldn't it be easier to just listen to me for a minute while you're here?"

Natalie rolled her eyes and lowered the window again.

"I wanted to apologize for something else," he said.

"What?"

"I read the report from your meeting with the school counselor. Mr. Armantrout forwarded me a copy. How did you think it went?"

"Terrific," Natalie said. "He thinks Leah had a 'psychotic episode'—those were his exact words. He wants Leah to see a psychiatrist; he wants her to have an MRI. An MRI, Matt—he thinks something could be wrong with her brain."

Matt looked at her sympathetically. "I know. I read his recommendations. I think he was overreacting—Armantrout has a tendency to do that."

Natalie pulled forward again without giving him notice.

Matt stepped up to the window again. "I was only doing my job," he said. "I'm required to pass on any emotional or psychological concerns to the school counselor, and he's required to report back to me. You don't have to take his suggestions, Natalie. I don't think Leah needs to see a psychiatrist."

"Thanks for the vote of confidence."

"But I do want to keep an eye on her. I don't know what Leah saw the other day; hopefully, it was just a onetime occurrence. But if I have any other concerns about Leah, I want to be able to talk to you about it. Can I do that?"

"You're the teacher. You can do anything you want."

"But will you listen?"

Natalie took the number from the dashboard and held it up to the window. "Number two-twelve—would you send her over, please? I have to get to work."

Matt stepped back from the window. "I'm not the bad guy here, Natalie. Believe it or not, I'm on your side." He looked over the top of the car at the crowd of children. "Two-twelve! Leah Pelton, your ride's here!"

As Leah opened the rear door and slung her backpack onto the seat, Matt leaned down to the driver's window once more. "I think I'll go around behind you," he said to Natalie. "I'm not sure it's safe to walk in front of your car right now."

Natalie raised her window and drove off with no reply.

"So how was school?" Natalie called to the backseat.

Leah shrugged.

Natalie glanced in the rearview mirror. "How do you like Mr. Callahan?"

"He's cool."

Cool, Natalie thought. *That's a rave review coming from her.* "What makes Mr. Callahan cool?"

"He just is."

Natalie let a few minutes pass before she said, "Sweetheart, do you mind if I ask you something?"

Another shrug.

"Do you ever miss your dad?"

"Maybe."

"Maybe yes, or maybe no?"

"Just maybe."

She paused. "When you're at home—where we live now—do you feel safe?"

"I guess so."

"Would you tell me if you didn't? Because I would want to know—I always want you to feel safe. If anyone ever tries to hurt you, I want you to promise you'll tell me—okay?"

"Okay."

"Promise?"

"*Okay*, Mom."

Natalie decided to leave it at that. "Can I ask another question?"

Leah let out a beleaguered sigh. "What?"

"The other day—when you saw that angel—how did it make you feel?"

"Feel?"

"I mean, did you feel funny in any way? Dizzy? Light-headed?"

"I just saw an angel, that's all. I didn't feel anything."

"No headache or anything like that?"

"No."

"So it was just like looking at anything else?"

"It was just an angel," she said.

Just an angel, Natalie thought. *Just your run-of-the-mill psychotic episode.*

They drove the rest of the way home in silence.

When Natalie opened the door she found Kemp seated at the kitchen table with a cup of coffee and the Orange County edition of the *Los Angeles Times*. His thick black hair was disheveled and he had a five o'clock shadow.

"Hey," he said without looking up.

Natalie stepped aside to let Leah pass. "Go and get your things together," she told her. "Dinner's in half an hour. Don't forget your clothes for tomorrow."

When Leah left the room she turned to Kemp. "You were out late."

"Yeah," he said. "I had some things to do."

"It's not like you to give up sleep. Mind if I ask where you were?"

"I told you—I had things to do. Do I need to file a flight plan?"

"It would be nice if you called," she said, "just so I don't worry."

"Did you worry?"

"I . . . wondered."

"I figured you'd probably be asleep—no sense disturbing you."

"Thanks," she said. "How thoughtful of you."

He looked up from his paper. "While we're on the subject, I might as well tell you I'm going to be late the next few days too."

"More 'things to do'?"

"Yeah, something like that."

Natalie glared at him. "I don't suppose it's occurred to you, Kemp, but we've got a few 'things to do' around here, and you're not helping out. We need to find a replacement for Mrs. Rodriguez as soon as possible, and I don't have time to do it. Why can't you help? I haven't had a minute lately. I've had all these teacher's meetings—what's your excuse? I'm having to drag Leah over to UCLA every night. The poor thing has to sleep in the nurses' room. She shouldn't have to do that."

"What's the big deal? She's right there where you can keep an eye on her."

"I don't want to 'keep an eye on her.' I want her to be able to sleep in her own bed, and I want you to help make that happen."

"Not this week. I'm busy."

"Busy doing what?"

"That's none of your business."

"It is too my business. These 'things to do'—are they more important than Leah? More important than me?"

"They're important to me," he said. "They're important to all of us."

"Why?"

"Sorry," Kemp said. "You'll just have to trust me. Now can we have dinner? If you don't mind, I have to get to work."

15

"ow you doing in here?" Emmet asked.

"Okay," Leah said.

"You get lonely sometimes?"

She shook her head. "I don't mind being alone."

"Me neither," Emmet said. "Gives a soul time to think. People today, it's like they can't stand quiet—always got to have something plugged in their ears or shoved up against their heads."

"Some of the nurses stop and visit me," Leah said.

"Well, who wouldn't want to? I had to stand in line just to see you myself."

Leah grinned.

"Brought you something from the cafeteria," Emmet said. "Here you go." He reached into his shirt pocket and handed her a Little Debbie chocolate cupcake wrapped in clear plastic. "You know what that is, don't you?"

"A cupcake."

"It only looks like a cupcake. Truth is, it's medicine. Doctors here hand out all kinds of nasty pills, but that'll cure most anything that ails you. It's a proven fact—give it a try."

"I'm not sick," she said.

"And if you eat those you never will be."

Leah tore the plastic with her teeth and took out the cupcake. "Some people think I'm sick."

"Now why in the world would they think that?"

"Because I see angels." She took a bite and looked up at him. "Do you think I'm sick?"

Emmet shook his head. "I think there are people who see things other people can't see, that's all. I call that a gift."

"Do you see angels?"

"I see what's in front of me—some people don't." He watched her for a moment. "How's that cupcake?"

"Really good."

"You feel better now, don't you?"

She nodded.

"What'd I tell you? Cures most everything." He patted her on the leg and stood up. "I best get back to work now. I'll tell your next visitor they can come in." He walked to the door and looked back. "What about Mr. Kemp? Has he been by to see you this evening?"

"He's busy," Leah said. "Mom says he has a movie star."

"I'm sure he'll stop by when he can. After all, lots of people know movie stars; how many people know a girl who sees angels?"

≡≡

Kemp checked the BIS monitor again; in less than thirty minutes the digital display had inched its way up from 60 to 78. In another few minutes Liv Hayden would reach a semiconscious state, and he needed to be ready when she did.

He opened the door a crack and peeked into the hallway; it was empty. That was the benefit of being a movie star like Liv Hayden: Celebrity status got you a private room at the end of a hallway where none of the other hospital staff were likely to drop by unannounced—especially at this hour of the night. He should have at least an hour alone with her, and that was all he needed.

He slipped on a white lab coat and buttoned it all the way to the collar, then rolled an examination lamp up to the bed and swiveled the arm so that the light would be positioned just above and behind his head. He flipped the switch and flooded the bed in brilliant white light, then positioned his face directly in front of the light, creating a near-total eclipse. He imagined what the scene would look like to Hayden: his handsome face shrouded in mysterious shadow, surrounded by a majestic nimbus of light. The effect should be impressive; he found himself wishing he could see it himself.

The monitor now read 82, and Kemp could detect a slight flutter beginning in Hayden's eyelids. He quickly adjusted the infusion pump to stabilize the propofol drip; the last thing he wanted was his patient regaining full consciousness and sitting upright in bed. She was just about there—in a semiconscious, trancelike state—and in another few seconds she would open her eyes and meet her celestial guide . . .

Hayden suddenly opened her eyes, then just as suddenly squeezed them shut against the blinding light. When she eased them open again they were only narrow slits, staring up at the mysterious figure hovering over her.

Kemp bent down and studied her eyes . . . her pupils were constricting in response to the light exactly as they should. He waved his hand in front of her face and detected a slight flinch. *Kemp, you genius, you.* He had reduced her dosage of propofol almost perfectly—Olivia Hayden was now in a semiconscious state.

Uh-oh.

When it suddenly dawned on him that the curtain was up

and Hayden's mental camera was rolling, Kemp straightened so abruptly that he almost banged his head against the examination light. In his preoccupation with the technical details he had forgotten to think of anything to say. It was like a childhood nightmare: he was the star of the show, it was opening night, but he had forgotten his lines.

His mind raced, but all he could come up with was: "Greetings, earthling!"

Idiot! he shouted to himself. *This isn't* Star Trek*! You're an angel, remember?* His immediate instinct was to smack himself on the forehead, but it didn't seem the sort of thing an angelic being would do. He took a moment to compose himself. He needed to pull himself together before his "message from above" turned into "The Three Stooges in Orbit."

He cleared his throat.

"You're probably wondering who I am. I am a messenger, Liv, a messenger sent from a distant dimension to tell you something very important—something that I want you to share with the whole world, preferably in the form of a book. In fact, definitely a book—in hardcover."

Careful, he thought. *Don't get ahead of yourself—just stick to the basics.*

"I have been called by many names in many times and places. Many have attempted to describe the things I am going to tell you, but they all got it wrong. I am here to correct their mistakes—to tell you how things really are and how the universe really works."

How the universe works? Those two morons had better come up with something or I'm really overpromising here.

"Oh—by the way, the message I bring you is the last and most important of all. In other words, this message renders all previous messages null and void. Are we clear on that?"

So much for the competition.

"There is a great change taking place in the universe," he went on. "A new awareness, a new consciousness, a new way of thinking—and you have been chosen to communicate this new way to the world. You may wonder, 'Why me? Why have I been chosen for this task?' The reason is that you are special; your mind is receptive to new ideas; you are spiritually attuned. Plus, you've held up very well for a woman your age, and that doesn't hurt either."

Hayden's eyes slowly widened as they adjusted to the light. Her pupils were tiny pinpoints—a side effect of the propofol. She never blinked; she just continued to stare up at the heavenly messenger and soak up the words like a sponge.

"Your presence here in this hospital is no accident, Liv. It's all part of a great cosmic plan. There are no accidents. Well—your automobile accident was an accident, but that's different. I think you know what I mean."

Stop rambling, you fool. Wrap it up.

"I will appear to you each night about this time and I will reveal my thoughts to you. We will become very close, Liv. You will come to know my voice better than you know your own, until my voice is your voice and my thoughts are your—"

There was a knock on the door.

Kemp whirled around. He fumbled for the switch on the examination light and gave the light a shove, sending it rolling across the room. He ripped open his lab coat and wrestled it off, sending buttons flying like shrapnel, then wadded the coat into a ball and kicked it under the bed. He was just about to reach for the infusion pump when there was a second knock, louder and more insistent than before. There was no time to adjust the propofol; one knock could be ignored, but not two.

He hurried to the door and opened it as casually as possible.

Natalie looked at him. "Did you say good night to Leah?"

Kemp's heart started beating again. "What?"

"When I went to the break room to tuck her in, she said you hadn't been in to see her tonight."

"I'm working, Natalie. Do you mind?"

Natalie looked past him into the room. "I heard talking in here."

"I was talking to Ms. Hayden," he said. "It's standard practice with comatose patients. You know that."

"We talk to the ones we're trying to bring out of a coma, not the ones we're trying to keep in. What are you doing in here, sharing your heart with your new movie star friend?"

"I resent the implication and the interruption. Is there anything else?"

"You might try talking to your daughter once in a while—she's actually conscious."

Kemp was about to say, "She's not my daughter"—but he knew that would only prolong the argument. Instead he diplomatically replied, "You're right. I should have stopped in to tell her good night. I got distracted and I forgot. Let's not make a big deal out of it."

"It's a big deal to her, Kemp."

"Maybe."

"Even if it's not, it's a big deal to me."

"Okay, point taken. If she's here tomorrow night I'll stop and see her then."

"Where else would she be? I can't find a caregiver in the next twenty-four hours—not by myself, anyway."

Kemp didn't respond.

"Are you still going to be home late?"

"I told you—I have things to do."

She looked at the figure lying on the bed. "Like talking to movie stars?"

Kemp shut the door halfway. "I tell you what—let's talk about work when we're at work and home when we're at home. Right now I'm working—I have a patient, and if I remember correctly, so do you. That may not mean much to you, Natalie, but it does to me. Perhaps an extra five years of education gives one a different attitude toward the practice of medicine. Now if you don't mind, my patient requires my attention. Please don't interrupt me again unless it's work-related."

He closed the door in her face.

He walked back to the bed and looked down at Liv Hayden. Her eyes were still half open, staring up into empty space. He adjusted the infusion pump and watched as the number on the BIS monitor began to tick down and her eyes slowly closed again.

"Sorry to leave you hanging," Kemp said. "People like you and me have a lot of demands on us, don't we? If you don't mind, I think I'll take my lunch break now; you seem to be dozing off anyway. Let's pick it up where we left off tomorrow night, shall we? By then I might even have something to say."

115

16

"Mind if I join you?"

Kemp looked up from his *LA Times* to see Emmet sliding his cafeteria tray onto the table across from him. Kemp looked at him in disdain. "Don't the janitors have their own tables?"

"The cafeteria's a democracy," Emmet said. "That's what I like about the place. I'm not allowed in the physicians' lounge, and I don't belong in the nurses' break room unless I'm collecting the trash. But in the cafeteria a man can sit wherever he wants. I can sit right next to a doctor if I want to. I can even sit across from you."

"Then why did you ask if I mind?"

"Just a courtesy," he said. "Pass the salt, please."

Kemp slid the shaker across the table. "Speaking of courtesy, would you mind not talking to me? I'm trying to read here."

"That's a waste of an opportunity," Emmet said. "You can read the paper anytime you want. Here in the cafeteria you get a chance to meet people—to learn from somebody different than you."

"Smarter than you?"

"Maybe; maybe not. I find you can learn from most anybody if you keep an open mind."

"So this is how janitors spend their breaks—mingling with the hoi polloi."

"Wrong word," Emmet said. "'Hoi polloi'—that's Greek, I believe. Most people think it means 'the high and mighty,' but it really means 'the common man.' See there? You learned something new already."

"Did you learn that from one of the doctors?"

Emmet smiled. "I don't seem to learn much from doctors—truth is, I learn a lot more from the staff. The cafeteria crew, for example—very bright people. Doctors, they seem to have a kind of tunnel vision—ever notice that? They know a lot about science and medicine, but they don't always know much about life. Take you, for instance."

"Me?"

"You've got a little girl upstairs who needs to be loved, but you're so caught up in your own life right now that you're lookin' right through her. Big mistake, friend."

"I'm not your friend," Kemp said, "and she's not my daughter."

"Does it matter? You're the man in her life right now. Natalie's a good woman. She worries about her little girl the way all mothers do, and let me tell you something: the way to any mother's heart is through her child."

"Did the cafeteria crew give you that little gem of wisdom?"

"No, but they all know it's true. Funny thing—a man who's paid eight dollars an hour to scrape grease off a plastic tray knows something you don't."

"I'll tell you what else is funny: a man your age who doesn't know when to mind his own business."

Emmet shrugged. "Well, you can't blame a man for trying."

"Can't I?"

"One more thing," Emmet said, "since I'm out on a limb already: she's not real, you know."

117

"Excuse me?"

"That movie star patient of yours—the one you're spending all that time with? She's not real, Mr. Kemp—and when she wakes up in a few days, I guarantee she won't give you the time of day. She'll look down her nose at you the same way you're lookin' at me right now."

Now Kemp smiled. "You never know. You might be surprised."

"Don't kid yourself. Natalie and Leah—they're real, and they're right in front of you if you'll only look. I think you need to remember that."

Kemp looked at his watch. "I'll tell you what I think, Emesis. I think I'm on a fifteen-minute break and you just wasted five. It's a big cafeteria—how about celebrating democracy somewhere else?"

Emmet picked up his tray and left without another word.

Kemp buried his face in his newspaper, but a moment later he heard the chair beside him slowly slide out from the table. Without looking up he said, "I thought I told you to get lost."

A much deeper voice replied, "I don't think so—Bobby."

Kemp looked up. The man who sat down beside him was enormous, and the legs of his plastic cafeteria chair bowed slightly under his weight. He was dressed in baggy khakis and an ugly Hawaiian print shirt festooned with badly rendered beach scenes and palm trees. The shirt's pointed collar stretched open across his barrel-like chest, and a tuft of curly black hair bushed out from underneath. His neck was wider than his ears, and his bald head narrowed to a gleaming grapefruit-sized dome; he seemed to taper from the waist up, creating a strange foreshortening effect that made him look towering even when he was sitting down. He wore a simple gold ring in one of his ears and sported no facial hair except for a coal-black soul patch under his rubbery lower lip.

When Kemp saw the man, his face went white.

Tino Gambatti began to take items from his tray one at a time and arrange them neatly on the table in front of him. "It is Bobby, right? Bobby Foscoe from Baltimore? Bobby Foscoe, that whiz-bang medical student from Johns Hopkins I last met in a lounge at Trump Plaza in Atlantic City?"

Kemp almost choked. "Tino," was all he managed to get out.

The man slid a bowl of lime green Jell-O in front of him and picked up a plastic spoon; it looked like a toy in his chubby fingers. "I'm impressed, Bobby. It's been a long time. But then I suppose doctors have good memories—even doctors who don't turn out to be doctors after all."

"What are you doing here, Tino?"

He paused to take a spoonful of Jell-O. "I'm here on business. You'll have to excuse my appearance. It's California, after all—I was trying to blend in."

"If this is about the money—"

"Funny you should mention that. As I recall, you borrowed some money from me once. Correct me if I'm wrong."

Kemp swallowed hard.

"How much was that again? Refresh my memory."

"A hundred thousand."

Tino nodded. "That number sounds vaguely familiar. Remind me again—I don't have your memory—what were the terms of our agreement?"

"Two years," Kemp said. "Fifty percent interest."

"Two years," Tino repeated. "Enough time to let you finish up at Hopkins and set up a nice little practice somewhere. Enough time to let you start putting people to sleep and raking in an easy half million a year. Two years to come up with a measly hundred and fifty grand—that should have been easy for a bright boy like you."

"I—I screwed up. They didn't let me finish."

"Yes, I heard about that, and if I was your mother I might even care. But since I'm your business partner, I could care less. I just want my money, Bobby."

"Sure, Tino, no problem. But—I don't have it right now."

Tino turned and looked at him for the first time. "What's the matter, Bobby? You look a little pale. Maybe you should get out more—take a little sun."

Kemp didn't answer.

"Let me explain something to you—something you maybe didn't understand when we made our little agreement. See, I'm a businessman; I'm in the loan business. I loan money to people like you, and people like you pay me back—with interest. That's how I make my living. Only I'm not like a regular bank—I'm more like a convenience store. You need groceries, you go to the grocery store; you want quick and easy, you stop off at 7-Eleven—but you expect to pay more. Me, I'm the same way. You want a conventional loan, you go to Bank of America—only as I recall, you were already up to your eyeballs in debt and your old man wouldn't cosign another loan for you. But you couldn't wait to start living the good life, could you? You wanted that hundred thousand right away, and you didn't want any questions asked. That's why you came to me, and we worked out a deal. Remember?"

"Of course I remember."

"I wasn't so sure. You seemed to forget all about our agreement. You left town, Bobby; you moved to California; you even changed your name. What is it now? Kemp something-or-other? You know, I went to a lot of trouble to track you down. What was I supposed to think?"

"I needed some time, that's all."

"Eight years? That's a lot of time."

"I'll get you your money, Tino. I just need a little more time."

"More time? Eight years is not enough?"

"I'll get the money, okay? I've got a deal I'm working on right now. I just need a couple of months. Just be patient—don't do anything crazy, okay?"

"What do you think I'm going to do? You insult me. I'm a businessman, remember? Dead men don't repay their loans, and all I want is my money—with interest. That's another thing, Bobby—the interest has compounded a little."

"What?"

"Our deal was fifty percent on two years. It's been eight years—plus my time and trouble tracking you down. I'm afraid a hundred and fifty won't do it anymore. It's half a million now."

Kemp's mouth dropped open. "Are you out of your mind? Where am I supposed to get that kind of money?"

"That's your problem."

"You can't just change the terms of the agreement!"

"You did."

"But—it's impossible! There's no way."

"What about your old man? I hear he's pretty well off. Maybe he's had a change of heart."

"Never. He wouldn't even consider it."

"Have you asked him? Sincerely, I mean. I'll bet you haven't."

"Believe me, I've asked."

"Maybe he hasn't been properly motivated."

"Now wait a minute—"

"Look, Bobby, we need to put our heads together and

come up with some creative repayment options. See, at this point I'm exactly like a bank. When one of my clients defaults on a loan, I have to find a way to recover my losses. We need to review your assets, your income, your other obligations, and see what we can do. We have to work something out, Bobby, because if we can't I'll have to foreclose."

"I don't own a house."

Tino looked at him without expression. "Who's talking about a house?"

Kemp's throat went dry. "Look—I have a girlfriend. She has a daughter."

"Has your girlfriend got any money?"

"No. She's as broke as I am."

"So?"

"Don't hurt them, okay? That would devastate me. I couldn't bear it. I'd blame myself forever."

Tino almost smiled. "You think I would hurt your girlfriend as a way to punish you? What kind of man do you think I am? I would never have thought of such a thing—but you did. Shame on you, Bobby—this is between you and me."

Tino was sitting so close that their legs were almost touching. When Kemp tried to slide his chair farther away, Tino said to him, "Don't even think about it."

"We're the only ones at the table," Kemp said. "People are looking."

"Get used to it. You're into me for half a million dollars, and I'm not leaving until I get it back. No more running, Bobby. I'm going to stay so close to you that when I fart you'll say 'Excuse me.'"

"But where am I going to get half a million dollars?"

Tino shrugged. "Tell me about this deal you're working on."

17

$\mathcal{M}$att Callahan sat in the back of the classroom and pretended to listen as each of his students stepped up in front of the blackboard and shared about a favorite family member, the soccer team, or some recent experience that he or she thought the class might find unusual or interesting. Matt graded papers as he listened, throwing in a question or comment from time to time to let the class know he was still tuned in. "See & Say" wasn't a graded activity anyway—it was just a weekly opportunity for the kids to develop their verbal skills and gain confidence speaking before a group. A little boy with sandy hair was just wrapping up his presentation.

"So my brother and me, we launched the rocket and the cat went way up in the air just like we planned, only the cat came down safe and sound because we put a parachute on him before we shot him off. It was cool."

"Thank you, Larry, that was quite a story," Matt called from the back. "Tell me, this cat of yours—is it full grown?"

"Yeah. Sure."

"How much does it weigh?"

"Um . . ."

"If it's full grown, it must weigh a few pounds at least. This rocket you used—did you buy it at a hobby shop?

Because most of the model rockets I've seen, they only have a few ounces of thrust. I wonder how that rocket managed to lift that cat?"

Larry stopped to ponder this point.

"Tell me, Larry, did you and your brother really put a cat into orbit, or were you just entertaining us with a tall tale?"

Larry grinned sheepishly.

"Class, let's thank Larry for a very imaginative story."

The students reluctantly applauded.

"Only next time, Larry, let's stick to a real event for See & Say and save the imaginary stories for Creative Writing—okay? Who's next?"

Leah raised her hand.

"Leah Pelton, the floor is yours. What do you want to tell us about today?"

Leah walked to the blackboard and turned to face the class. "I saw an angel," she said.

Matt put down his papers. "Leah—you already told us this story."

She shook her head. "That was a different angel. I saw another one."

Larry's hand shot up. "How come she gets to tell about angels, but I can't launch my cat into space?"

Leah glared at him. "Because that's just stupid, that's why. You just made that up, but I really saw an angel."

"Liar!"

"Am not!"

"Are too!"

"Everybody calm down," Matt said, rising from his chair. "Now Leah, you just heard me tell Larry that See & Say is for real events. You understand that, don't you?"

"Sure I do."

"Then you're not just making this up. Right?"

"Right."

Matt paused. "Okay, then go ahead. Tell us what happened."

Leah looked at her classmates. "My mom is a nurse at UCLA. Right now I have to sleep there at night, 'cause Mrs. Rodriguez—that was our babysitter? She can't stay with me at night anymore. I'm supposed to stay in the nurses' room, but I get bored in there—so the other night I went up and down the hallway and looked in all the rooms."

"Did you see any dead people?" one of the boys asked.

Leah narrowed her eyes at him. "No—that's not what happened. In one of the rooms there was an old man who looked real sick. There was this beautiful woman standing beside his bed, and she was holding her hand out over his head—like this." She held her right hand out, palm-down.

She smiled at the class as if her story was finished and started to return to her seat.

"Hang on a minute, Leah," Matt said. "I have a couple of questions for you."

"Me too," Larry said.

"Thanks, Larry, I think I can handle this. Leah, what makes you think this woman was an angel?"

"She just was."

"But how do you know?"

"I could tell."

"There are lots of visitors in hospitals, Leah. Did you see any visitors in the other rooms?"

"Sure."

"Then what was different about this woman?"

"She was an angel."

The class began to snicker and Matt gestured for them to quiet down. "Was she dressed differently?"

"No."

"Was she doing anything unusual—anything that might make you think she was different from everyone else?"

"She was holding her hand like this." Leah repeated the palm-down gesture.

"Maybe she was stroking the man's hair. Maybe she was taking his temperature."

Leah began to frown. "She didn't touch him. She just held her hand there."

"Why do you think she was doing that?"

"I think it was making him better."

"Did you see him get better? Did he get up and get out of bed?"

Leah didn't answer.

"Then you really don't have a reason to think this woman was an angel, do you?"

"She just made it up," Larry scoffed.

Leah gave Larry a burning stare. "I did not! There's a nice old man who works at the hospital—he told me they get angels there all the time. He says some people can see things other people can't. He says I have a gift."

Larry sneered. "I saw my cat take off, but nobody else did."

"It's not the same!" Leah shouted.

"Larry, that's enough. Leah, please go back to your seat." Matt looked at Larry. "Leah's right about something, Larry— her story is not the same as yours. You know your cat never left the ground, but Leah actually saw something and she told us what she saw. She thinks she saw an angel—I'm not so sure. But whether she's right or wrong, she was describing a real event—and that's what See & Say is for. Now who's next?"

Matt watched Leah as the next child stepped to the front of the class and began to speak. Leah sat slumped in her chair, staring at her desk and fighting back tears. Matt wondered if he had done the right thing. He couldn't just let the story go—not after he just gave Larry a slap on the wrist for an obvious fabrication. He was hoping that a few pointed questions might cause Leah to give up her story as a hoax, but she seemed as determined as ever to defend it. One thing seemed certain: Leah clearly believed that she had seen an angel—another one.

He took out a blank sheet of paper and began to write:

Natalie,

I told you in the carpool line that if I had any other concerns about Leah I would let you know. This morning she told the class she saw another angel—this time at your hospital. We need to talk, Natalie. Please call me at your earliest convenience.

I'm on your side,
Matt Callahan

127

18

Kemp shoved his key card into the door slot of the Century Plaza suite; when he pulled it out again a green light flashed and the lock made a clicking sound. He glanced down at the carpet beside the door and saw a room service tray littered with ketchup-smeared plates, forgotten vegetables, and translucent french fries left over from the night before. Beside that tray was a breakfast tray, apparently from just this morning—and beside that was an empty pizza box blotched with dark streaks of oil and tomato sauce.

"Your friends have healthy appetites," Tino said.

Kemp shook his head. "If these guys could write half as fast as they can eat, we'd be done by now." He looked at Tino. "Don't say anything, okay? Let me handle it. This is going to be a little bit of a surprise."

Kemp opened the door and the two men stepped inside.

The suite had been trashed. There were sheets of paper from the easel pad plastered all over the walls and crumpled wads of legal paper dotting the floor like yellow snowballs. There seemed to be more socks and shoes than there were feet, and a wrinkled blazer hung on a coat hanger from a chandelier. There were half-eaten slices of pizza abandoned on tissue-thin paper napkins, and empty cups and water bottles were scattered everywhere.

"Hey," Kemp called out. "Where is everybody?"

"What time is it?" Wes called out from behind the sofa.

"It's after eight," Kemp said. "Look at this place. What are you guys, a couple of rock stars?"

"We were trying to stay focused," Wes said.

"Obviously not on neatness. Did you do anything but eat?"

A toilet flushed and Biederman emerged from the bathroom. "McAvoy—how'd it go last—" He stopped.

Wes poked his head up from the sofa and looked.

Standing beside Kemp was an enormous man—a man they had never seen before.

"This is Tino Gambatti," Kemp said. "Tino's from Baltimore—he's an old friend of mine. Tino, this is Mort Biederman—he's the talent agent I told you about. That's Wes Kalamar over there—he's the publisher."

Tino nodded a greeting to each of the men, but neither of them returned it.

Biederman looked at Kemp. "McAvoy, can I talk to you for a minute?"

"*McAvoy*," Tino said. "That's it—I never can remember that name."

"I thought you two were old friends," Wes said.

"I'm an old friend of Bobby Foscoe," Tino said. "Bobby disappeared from Baltimore eight years ago; I'm just getting to know Kemp McAvoy now."

"Who's Bobby Foscoe?"

Tino pointed with his thumb. "He is."

Both men looked at Kemp.

"I need to explain," Kemp said.

"You sure do."

"My real name is Bobby Foscoe, okay? I changed it when I moved back to Los Angeles."

129

"Why?"

"Because Bobby Foscoe got kicked out of medical school," Tino said. "He had to change his name to get a job."

"That's not true," Kemp said. "I finished medical school. I just got kicked out of my residency, that's all—in my last year."

"Kicked out why?" Wes asked.

"It's personal," Kemp grumbled.

"Not if it affects us," Biederman said.

"It doesn't," Tino said. "I assure you, Bobby knows quite a bit about medicine—more than enough to pull off this little project of ours."

Biederman looked at Tino. "*Ours*? Who invited you?"

Tino pointed again. "He did. Well, Bobby didn't actually invite me—you might say I invited myself. He didn't really have a choice."

"I owe him money," Kemp said, staring at the floor. "A lot of it."

"Half a million dollars," Tino said. "Bobby has no other way to repay his debt, so I was forced to consider alternate repayment options."

"You're a loan shark?" Biederman asked.

Tino frowned. "I'm an investor—and I've decided to invest in this project."

"Don't we have something to say about that?" Wes asked.

"Bobby doesn't. He told me about this project of his. It's really quite ingenious. I think it could be very profitable if it's handled well—and I want to make sure it is."

"Thanks," Wes said, "but I think we can handle it."

"Maybe," Tino said. "I want to make sure. You might say I already have half a million dollars invested in this project; I want to make sure I get it back. Bobby's quite capable of pulling off this scheme of his; he's also capable of screwing it up completely. I want to keep that from happening. Bobby's really a very bright boy—he just needs adult supervision."

"We don't need someone looking over our shoulders," Biederman said.

"Oh, I'm not here as an observer—I plan to participate. How else can I make sure things go the way they should?"

"Have you ever written anything?" Wes asked.

"Business plans, mostly."

"Business plans—that'll help a lot."

"Why wouldn't it? Isn't that what the angel is proposing, really—a new way of doing business in the universe? Your angel is presenting a business plan—a concept, an objective, a market analysis, channels of distribution . . ."

"Sounds like you've already given this some thought," Wes said.

"I have—and from what Bobby told me about your first writing session, it sounds like you could use all the help you can get."

"We were just getting our momentum going," Biederman grumbled.

"Then let's not lose it," Tino said. "I suggest we all get to work."

Wes turned to Kemp. "How did the first episode go last night?"

"Just like I told you it would. The system worked like a charm."

"What did you say to Hayden—I mean, what did the 'angel' say?"

"You guys didn't give me much to work with—I had to just make it up as I went along. It was basically just an introduction: 'I'm an angel, you're so special, I've got a message for you, let me get back to you tomorrow.' But I'm going to need more than that tonight—the woman's expecting some details."

"I think we might have a concept," Wes said.

"Well, it's about time." Kemp took a seat on the sofa while Wes and Biederman set up the easel in front of him. Tino sat down right beside Kemp—much to his annoyance.

"Okay," Wes said, "here's what we've got so far. Remember when you were a kid, and you thought the whole universe revolved around you? But your folks were always telling you to grow up—that life wasn't all about you? Well, it turns out they were wrong. It *was* about you."

"Excuse me?" Kemp said.

"Everything is about you. It was always about you. The whole universe revolves around you, and you must embrace that truth."

"It's about Bobby?" Tino asked.

"No—for you it's about you; for me it's about me."

"I'm not following you," Tino said.

"You are the only one in the universe who actually exists. Everyone else is just a figment of your imagination, and when you die the whole universe will cease to exist—at least as far as you're concerned."

"This is what you guys came up with?" Kemp said. "What was on that pizza?"

"Actually, Biederman remembered it from an old *Twilight Zone*—but we think it has definite possibilities. It came to us about four in the morning. We'd been banging our heads on the table for hours and we still weren't getting any-where. Suddenly we realized the problem: we were working backwards."

"Backwards?"

"The problem was, we kept asking, 'What would an angel

want to tell people?' Instead we needed to be asking, 'What would people want to hear from an angel?' That's when it came to us—it was like an epiphany. *It's all about you*—that's the angel's message."

"That's it?" Tino said. "Sounds like a very short book."

"*It's all about you* is just the big idea—the whole thing spins out from there."

"For example."

"Okay—if it's all about you, then what's your chief responsibility in life? *To make sure you're happy.*"

"Think about it," Biederman said. "If everyone would concentrate on making himself happy, it would be a perfect universe. See, everybody says he wants somebody else to be happy, but nobody really cares—at least, not nearly as much as he cares about himself. So why should I waste my time making a halfhearted attempt at pleasing someone else when I would gladly pursue my own happiness with all my heart? If I would just focus on making myself happy—if everybody did that—then everybody would be happy."

"And just forget about other people?"

"Other people are the problem. Don't you see? We're always worrying about how other people are doing, how other people are feeling, but we have no control over that. The only thing you can actually control is your own attitude, so your chief responsibility is to make sure you're happy."

"Think of it this way," Wes explained. "You are like a rock dropped into a pond, and you send ripples out all around you—you affect everyone else. Remember that old saying, 'If Momma ain't happy, ain't nobody happy'? Well, if that's true, then what's the most important thing for Momma to remember? *I need to make sure I'm happy—because if I'm happy, I make everyone else happy.*"

"Who's Momma?" Tino asked.

"Try to stay with us," Biederman said. "If you want other people to be happy, you must first be happy yourself—and to be happy, you must love yourself. So the most important thing in the whole universe is for you to love yourself—more than your wife, more than your kids, more than your friends. You might say, since the most important thing is to love yourself, loving someone else more than yourself is actually unfaithfulness to your first love."

Kemp and Tino just sat there staring at the easel.

"That's what we've got so far," Wes said. "What do you guys think?"

"What do I think?" Kemp said. "I think it's an unbelievable pile of crap."

"Yes, but does it flow?"

"I'll tell you what *I* think," Tino said. "I think it's a very good thing I got involved when I did."

"What does that mean?"

"It means you lack structure—you lack organization."

"And a business plan would sound better?"

"I don't see how it could sound worse."

Kemp got up from the sofa. "There's no sense arguing about it. What difference does it make? I just need something to say, that's all. Most people are basically morons anyway, and a moron will buy just about anything—*Lattes with God* proved that. If you two geniuses think this will make a book—a book that we can *sell*—then count me in. I'll go with what you've got tonight—I don't have much choice, do I? But we're going to need more for tomorrow, so get back to work. Tino's got a few ideas he wants to throw in; maybe the three of you together can come up with something better. Now help me get some notes together—I can't do this from memory."

≡≡

Natalie heard Kemp's key in the lock and she checked the clock: it was 3:30 in the afternoon. She was sitting at the kitchen table with a cup of coffee and an open letter in front of her. The door opened with an almost inaudible squeal.

"Hey babe," Kemp said with a nod, tossing his keys on the counter.

"What a surprise," Natalie said. "I wasn't sure you'd be coming home at all."

"Don't start, okay? I need to hit the sack for a couple of hours."

"Why so exhausted? Things to do?"

"I think we've been over this."

As he passed the table she held up the letter.

"What's that?"

"It's from St. Stephen's. Read it."

Kemp quickly scanned the letter and groaned. "I thought we took care of this."

"You mean you thought *I* took care of it. So did I. I met with Leah's teacher, then I met with the school counselor— that was a real picnic. I took Leah along on the counselor's visit. I thought that might discourage her from coming up with any more stories, but apparently it didn't. Leah says she saw another angel, Kemp. What are we going to do about it?"

"Take her back to the counselor and leave her there this time. Let him see what he can do with her."

"I'm serious. Matt thinks we need to talk."

"Matt?"

She paused. "Leah's teacher. Mr. Callahan."

"So it's 'Matt' now?"

"Excuse me. I'm not the one who's been staying out all night."

"Well, why don't you and 'Matt' get together and work this out? Let me know how it goes." He started for the bedroom.

Natalie followed him. "That's not good enough. You're a part of this whether you like it or not."

"How do you figure that?"

"The counselor—Mr. Armantrout—he thinks Leah might be coming up with these stories because she doesn't feel safe."

Kemp turned and looked at her. "What kind of a crack is that?"

"Leah's life has changed a lot. Her home, her—family."

"You mean me."

"Like I said—you're a part of it."

"You're saying Leah doesn't feel safe around me."

"I didn't say that."

"I've got the perfect solution," Kemp said. "If Leah doesn't feel safe around me, just keep her away from me. Problem solved."

"I want you to go with me tomorrow to talk with Matt and the counselor. Maybe if they met you—"

"Not this week. I'm busy this week—I told you that."

"It has to be this week. This can't wait."

"Then go by yourself."

"What's so special about this week? What have you got going on?"

"I can't tell you—not yet. It's sort of a surprise."

"Surprise me by going to the school with me. That's what I need from you right now—that's what *we* need."

"That's not all we need," Kemp said. "Now if you don't mind, I need to get some sleep."

19

Liv Hayden lay mesmerized by the angelic face hovering above her . . .

"It's all about you, Liv," Kemp said. "Perhaps you've always suspected it—from the time you were only two years old. Maybe you were on the playground one day, and another child had a beautiful ball. You wanted that ball, so you shouted, 'It's mine!' and took it—but your parents made you give it back. They were wrong to do that, Liv. That ball was yours—that ball and all the other balls in the universe. They all belong to you."

Kemp took a quick look at his notes. *Not bad for no rehearsals.* Sure, he was embellishing a little, but he was managing to cover the main points.

"You may wonder, 'If everything belongs to me, then why don't I own everything?' You do, Liv—you just haven't realized it yet. All the seashells in the sea belong to one ocean, but the ocean keeps them scattered on the beaches of the world. In the same way, all the world's possessions really belong to you—they're just scattered in the lives of other people. They've been saving them for you, Liv—they just don't know it yet."

Cross that one off. What's next on the outline? Okay, here we go . . .

"That leads me to the next principle," he said in his most

beatific tone. "There's not enough to go around, so *get yours first*. Some believe the universe is so abundant that everyone can have what they want; try believing that the next time you're waiting in line for a new iPhone. There's not enough to go around, Liv; that's the hard reality of life—not enough iPhones, not enough condos in Pacific Palisades, not enough love. Remember, the most important thing in the world is for you to be happy. If you let others go ahead of you, you postpone your own happiness—but if you're not happy, they're not happy. So if you postpone your own happiness, you postpone their happiness as well. Do you grasp the wisdom of this principle? *Get yours first*. Open your mind to this truth; embrace it. It might seem difficult at first, but hey, if it was easy you wouldn't have needed an angel to explain it to you."

138

Kemp checked his watch; it was three a.m. An hour had already passed and he was overdue for his break. He never missed a break—the other nurses all knew it. He needed to wrap things up before anybody got suspicious.

"We've got time for one more: You must forgive yourself. How can you forgive others if you've never even forgiven yourself? We're all human, Liv—well, I'm not, of course, but other people are. You humans all do things to offend one another from time to time—it's only human. What should you do when you offend your brother? Do this: Look into your brother's eyes and say to him, 'I forgive myself.' When he sees your willingness to forgive even yourself, it will open the floodgates of his own forgiveness."

Somehow that didn't sound quite right. He glanced at his notes again—Biederman's handwriting looked like left-handed chicken scratchings. Oh well, it didn't matter—he got the basic point across. It was all nonsense anyway.

"Don't forget, Liv: Love yourself—that's the most important

thing of all. If everyone concentrated on loving himself, there'd be a lot less bickering in the universe. You must love yourself more than anyone else; you must love yourself first. Others are waiting to love you, Liv; free them to love you by showing them that you love yourself. By loving yourself you prove to them that you are lovable, and thus you open the doors to their love. Don't make them wait, Liv—let them know the doors are open. Pick up the phone—give them a call—tell them, 'Feel free to love me.'"

He checked the reading on Hayden's BIS monitor. She remained semiconscious, but he knew it was best not to keep her there too long—she was a lot less stable in this in-between state. That was enough for one night anyway. Kemp wasn't really sure how much her mind could retain—no sense pushing her too far.

"Well, I should go and let you get some sleep. It's a busy day in the universe, and I've still got other stops to make. Oh yes, I'm an adviser to many worlds—didn't I tell you? This wisdom I'm imparting to you spans all times and places—even other planets. Yes, many intelligent beings from distant galaxies know that—"

Kemp heard the door suddenly open behind him. He whirled around and looked.

Emmet was standing in the doorway with an empty trash can in his hand. He looked at Kemp; he looked at the white lab coat he was wearing; he looked at the examination light positioned above the bed; he looked at Liv Hayden lying on the bed with half-open eyes.

Kemp stood frozen, waiting . . .

Emmet backed out without a word and closed the door behind him.

20

"How did the child seem to you at the time?" Armantrout asked.

Matt shrugged. "What do you mean?"

"When she was recounting this 'second angel'—did she seem agitated? Distracted?"

"No, I wouldn't say that."

"Excited? Euphoric?"

"It was See & Say," Natalie interrupted. "It's like a book report. Did you ever feel 'euphoric' doing a book report? You must have liked school a lot more than I did."

"I'm simply trying to understand the child's emotional state at the time," Armantrout said. He turned to Matt again. "You're certain that Leah understood the nature of the presentation—that the event she described was supposed to be real and not fictional."

"She understood," Matt said. "I reminded her twice."

"Yet she went ahead with the story anyway—and insisted it was true."

"That's right."

"Did you object? Did you reprimand her?"

"No, not exactly."

"Why not?"

Matt glanced over at Natalie. "Because Leah is a tender-hearted girl. I didn't think it would help."

"'Tenderhearted'—what is that exactly?"

"She can be sensitive to criticism and blame. If you embarrass a child like that she can just shut down; that's the last thing I want."

"Why?"

"Because I'm trying to encourage their imaginations, that's why."

"It sounds to me like you may be encouraging them too much. Maybe a reprimand is just what Leah needs to bring her back to reality."

Natalie's teeth began to make a dull grinding sound.

"Did anyone in the class challenge her story?" Armantrout asked.

"There was one boy," Matt said. "He told her she was lying—that she made the whole thing up."

"And how did Leah respond to this criticism?"

Matt paused. "She got angry. She began to withdraw."

"Can you blame her?" Natalie said. "Someone called her a liar—wouldn't you get angry?"

"Someone caught her in a lie," Armantrout corrected. "I think that's different. We need to keep in mind here that the story was patently untrue. Leah insisted that it was true, and when her claim was challenged she became angry."

"There's something else we need to keep in mind here," Natalie said. "None of us know what Leah actually saw."

Armantrout made a thin smile. "Well, we know it wasn't an angel."

"Do we?"

Matt looked at her. "What are you saying, Natalie?"

"I'm just saying that nobody knows. Leah says she saw a

woman holding her hand out over a patient's head, and for some reason she thinks the woman was an angel. If you had been there, Mr. Armantrout, what would you have seen?"

"Not an angel—I can tell you that."

"You would have seen a woman holding her hand out over a patient's head, just like Leah did—only you would have thought it was just a woman."

"I don't see your point, Ms. Pelton."

"Leah wasn't lying about what she saw—you just don't agree with her about what it meant, that's all."

"I'm afraid it's not that simple," Armantrout said. "If we all saw a mouse but Leah insisted it was an elephant, there would be cause for concern. You're quite right, Ms. Pelton, this is not about lying. This is about Leah's ability to distinguish fantasy from reality—and how she responds when challenged."

142

"What does that mean?"

"Mr. Callahan tells us that Leah became angry and withdrawn when a boy challenged her story. Unfortunately, if she's going to keep telling stories about angels, she's going to be challenged quite often. Will she always get angry? How angry? Will her anger response increase over time? Could her anger spill over into violent behavior?"

"Violent behavior? Now wait just a—"

Natalie started to rise from her chair, but Matt reached over and put a hand on her arm. "Hold on a minute," he said to Armantrout. "Aren't we getting ahead of ourselves here?"

"That's what counselors try to do—get ahead of things. Right now Leah's fantasy is probably nothing more than a harmless delusion triggered by exposure to religious mythology. But what about next year, and the year after that? What will happen when she reaches adolescence and her fantasies become fueled by psychosexual drives?"

"This is nuts," Natalie said. "You're treating Leah like some kind of deviant. The girl thinks she saw an angel! Joan of Arc did that and they made her a saint!"

"It's interesting you should mention that," Armantrout said. "A number of contemporary scholars have offered medical explanations for Joan of Arc's visions. Some think they were caused by migraines; others schizophrenia. One historian believes she suffered from bovine tuberculosis caused by drinking unpasteurized milk."

"I don't believe this," Natalie muttered.

"Migraine sufferers are sometimes known to experience 'auras' before the onset of an attack; so are epileptics. Perhaps Leah's visions are akin to that—an indicator of some underlying medical condition."

Matt cut in. "Mr. Armantrout, I don't see what all this has to do with—"

143

"I'm simply saying that we shouldn't rule out a physical examination for Leah. What could it hurt? We need to keep in mind that this is Leah's second imaginary angel sighting in only three days—if she does have some physical condition, it might be getting worse. I mentioned an MRI before; I think you should seriously consider it, Ms. Pelton. You work at UCLA, don't you? You could easily arrange it. At least that way we could know whether we're dealing with a physical or a psychological problem here."

Natalie stood up. "Are we done here?"

"Natalie, wait—"

"Thank you, Mr. Armantrout, Mr. Callahan. I appreciate your concern for my daughter and I'll take your suggestions under advisement. Now if you'll excuse me." She turned on her heel and hurried toward the door.

Matt was right behind her. He waited until they were in

the hallway before he took her by the arm and said, "Natalie, hold on."

She turned and glared at him. "I thought you said you were on my side."

"I am."

"Well, you sure have a funny way of showing it. You could have said a lot more in Leah's defense."

"Nobody was attacking Leah."

"Oh no? 'Fantasies fueled by psychosexual drives'—what do you call that, a commendation?"

"We just want what's best for her."

She pointed back down the hall. "*He* doesn't. He just wants to be a little demigod who gets to poke around in other people's heads."

144

"I agree with you," Matt said. "Armantrout is an idiot—personally I can't stand the guy. But he might have a point, Natalie. The school is going to expect you to do something just to show that you're taking their recommendations seriously. Maybe you should consider that MRI—just as a compromise. I think it might get Armantrout off your back."

"Have you ever had an MRI, Matt?"

"No, I haven't."

"The machine is huge—it fills a whole room. They put you on this rolling table and strap you down so you can't move—that's because the narrow little tunnel they put you in is so claustrophobic that some people panic. They lock your head in a kind of vise that holds it perfectly still, then they slide you into that tunnel and make you wait for fifteen minutes while these massive magnets buzz all around you. It doesn't hurt at all—not one bit—but believe me, the minute you see that machine you think something must be wrong with you."

Natalie's eyes began to fill with tears. "I've made some

big mistakes in my life, Matt, and my biggest fear is that my mistakes have already screwed up my daughter. I want her to have a normal childhood. I want her to think that everything's okay—that *she's* okay—and I want her to be able to see angels without somebody wanting to shove her head into an MRI. To tell you the truth, I'm jealous of Leah. I wish *I* could see an angel right about now—God knows I could use one."

"Natalie—"

"Thanks for caring, Matt. But if you're really on my side, the next time Leah mentions an angel, don't tell anybody. Just call me—okay?"

21

Kemp parked his old Honda Civic in the UCLA Medical Center staff lot; the car sputtered and made one final death kick before it gave up the ghost. He checked his hair in the rearview mirror and took a thermos from the front seat—then he remembered something else. *Can't forget the notes*, he thought, grabbing a leather folder beside him. *I know an angel who needs them.*

Last night's installment had gone off without a hitch—with the slight exception of Emmet's unexpected intrusion. Kemp recalled the blank look on the old man's face as he took in the scene and then quickly backed out of the room. Did the old man have any idea what was going on? He was just a janitor, after all—just a minimum-wage drudge with no knowledge of medical procedure. It probably just looked like some kind of examination to him. *Nothing to worry about*, he told himself.

Kemp was feeling good tonight. After working out a few bugs in a shaky opening night performance, he felt like he was beginning to hit his stride. He had the system down now: each morning the four partners would meet in the Century Plaza suite to hammer out that evening's episode, and each night the angel would faithfully present it to his captive audience. By now Kemp knew precisely how much to adjust the propofol, and exactly how long it would take to move Hayden into and out of her semiconscious state. Last night he remembered to hang a freshly laundered lab coat in the closet—can't have the angel looking frumpy, after all. Tonight he even thought to bring a spare bulb for the examination light just in case of a burnout. *Attention to detail—that's what separates the professionals from the amateurs.*

There were other touches he was adding too. Last night he took the time to speak with each of the other nurses just before beginning his hour-long session to avoid appearing absent any longer than necessary—especially Natalie, to prevent any more awkward interruptions like the first night. He wished there was a lock on the door, but that was something no hospital allowed—can't have stubborn patients locking themselves in their rooms. As soon as the session was over, Kemp readjusted the propofol and immediately took his half-hour break, strategically making contact again with each of the nurses and using the break time to allow Hayden to slowly sink back into her coma.

147

By now the system was a thing of beauty—an elegantly choreographed dance, a perfectly synchronized symphony. He had the whole thing down to a science now, and science was something Kemp was very, very good at.

He was getting pretty good at this angel thing too; he was feeling the part. It had all seemed a little awkward that first night, but by the second night the words came more quickly. He had more confidence; he improvised freely, throwing in a personal comment or insight whenever it seemed like an improvement on the notes. Kemp imagined that this must be what Liv Hayden felt like when she was in the middle of shooting a picture—when she began to inhabit a role to the point that she was no longer pretending to be a character—she *was* the character. *I could get used to this role*, Kemp thought. *It fits me.*

Kemp took the elevator to the sixth floor and headed immediately to Hayden's hospital room, but when he opened the door he saw something he didn't expect—he found Dr. Smithson examining his unconscious patient. Kemp took a quick look at his watch—*awfully late for rounds*, he thought. The neurologists usually left hours ago.

Smithson looked up as he entered the room.

Kemp nodded a cursory greeting. "You're working late."

"I like to be thorough," Smithson said. "So how is our patient doing?"

"You're the doctor."

"So are you," Smithson said. "I'm curious about something, McAvoy. You've managed to let everyone around here know you've got your MD, but I've never actually heard you refer to yourself as *Dr.* McAvoy. Why so modest?"

"It could lead to misunderstandings," Kemp said. "A patient might be tempted to give my opinion more weight than he should. We wouldn't want that to happen, now would we?"

"No, we wouldn't—but there's no reason we can't talk doctor to doctor, is there? So tell me, Doctor: What's your evaluation of Ms. Hayden's condition?"

Kemp shrugged. "You've only kept her comatose as a precautionary measure. Her vitals have been stable—no indications of intracranial hypertension."

"Then you think I should bring her out of it."

"What's the hurry? The only risks in keeping her under are the usual ones for anesthesia: impaired gastrointestinal motility, suppressed immune response, a minor risk of infection or pneumonia. The risks are minimal; I'd give her another few days."

Smithson smiled. "I'm bringing her out of it the day after tomorrow."

"Then why did you ask my opinion?"

"I wanted to see what you'd say. I'm going to start backing off on the propofol late tomorrow." He paused. "Then I plan to give her a dose of Versed."

Kemp did a double take in spite of himself. "Versed? Why?"

"It helps with anxiety. I think it might help with her emotional readjustment, considering the trauma she's been through. Is there some reason I shouldn't?"

"There's just no reason for it. You might use Versed to help jump-start a coma, but not when you're bringing her out of it. The only effect it would have is to—"

Kemp stopped.

"What, Dr. McAvoy? What effect would it have?"

"It's unnecessary medication, that's all. It carries the same risks as all other anesthesia."

"Which you said were minimal."

"Yes, but—"

"I think what you were about to point out is that Versed has an amnesic effect—it erases memory."

"It's just unnecessary, that's all—in fact, it's useless. Versed's amnesic effect is limited; there's no telling what she'll remember and what she won't."

"Is that a problem?"

"Look, you asked my opinion and I'm telling you. All anesthesia involves risk, and prescribing a powerful sedative that may or may not have the intended effect is unprofessional. In fact, it's unethical."

"Thank you for your opinion, Doctor. Now perhaps I could get your opinion on something else." He opened Liv Hayden's chart and took out a folded computer printout. "These are Ms.

149

Hayden's electroencephalograms from the last few days—I was reviewing them just before you came in. There was really no reason to bother, since there haven't been any complications or concerns, but like I said—I like to be thorough." He unfolded the printout and spread it out on the bed. "Notice these sections—here and here. Ms. Hayden's EEGs indicate that she's been in a deep coma since her arrival a week ago—except for these two brief periods of time. According to the time code, each incident occurred in the middle of the night—one last night and one the night before. Each incident occurred while you were on duty."

Kemp looked at the printouts. "Are you saying she regained consciousness?"

"It would have been more like a semiconscious state. Tell me, did you notice anything different about Ms. Hayden during those periods of time?"

"Like what?"

"Any change in her vitals? An increase in blood pressure or pulse rate?"

"Her vitals are all charted. You can check for yourself."

"I already did. Were there any changes in her verbal or motor response? Any spontaneous eye movement?"

"I would have noticed that."

"Yes, I'm sure you would. Just one more question, Dr. McAvoy . . . why exactly did you leave Johns Hopkins?"

Kemp just stared at him.

"You're right, Dr. McAvoy, there's no reason at all to give Ms. Hayden Versed. All it would do is block some of her memory—as any anesthesiologist would know. That's why I suggested it, and when I did you just about had an aneurysm. Why is that? You don't want her to forget anything from her time here, do you? What is it you want her to remember so

desperately? Your phone number? Your address? Your declara-
tions of love?"

"Don't be absurd. That would be unethical and illegal."

"Yes, it would—and I'm wondering if you're the sort of guy
who would go that far."

"Are you accusing me of something?"

"I don't know," Smithson said, "but I'm sure going to find
out. I plan to put in a call to Johns Hopkins on Monday—they
should get back to me in a day or two. I'm going to see if they
can tell me what sort of person you really are. Have a nice
night, McAvoy. If you've got any last messages for your girlfriend here, you'd better deliver them fast. She's coming out of
it on Sunday."

22

Kemp allowed the door to the suite to slam shut behind him and immediately headed for the coffee. It was only their fourth day in the Century Plaza suite but the room was a complete disaster now; it looked like the Gulf Coast the day after Hurricane Katrina. The addition of a partner the size of Tino didn't exactly help things.

The three men stopped writing and looked up.

"Hey," Wes called out. "How'd it go last night?"

"Slick as a proctologist's glove," Kemp said. "What did you expect?"

"Did you make it through all the material?" Tino asked.

"Every line."

"No problems then?"

"No problems." Kemp paused. "But I'm afraid I've got some bad news."

Biederman got up from the sofa. "What bad news? What's going on? What happened?"

Kemp stared into his coffee cup; it looked like a layer of dirt had settled in the bottom. "I talked with Hayden's neurologist last night. He plans to bring her out of her coma on Sunday."

"Sunday? That's tomorrow!"

"What does that mean for us?" Tino asked.

"It means we've only got one more shot at Hayden and that's it. Tonight's our last chance; later today they plan to start backing off on her propofol. I might be able to squeeze in a few extra minutes with her tonight, but that's all. If there's anything else we want our angel to say to her, he'd better say it tonight."

"Only one more shot?" Wes said. "We need more time."

"What have you guys been doing here? I gave you one little job."

"Hey—you try writing a book in less than a week."

"Guys, it's like a children's book. How hard can it be?"

"We need to think of anything else we want in the book," Wes said. "C'mon, everybody, we need to pool our thoughts here."

"That should be shallow water," Kemp mumbled.

Tino put a hand on Kemp's shoulder. "The man said everybody—that means you too, Bobby."

Kemp begrudgingly dragged up an armchair and joined the others around the easel.

Wes rubbed his hands together as if he were warming himself in front of a fire. "All right, who's got something? Anything at all—just toss it out."

Biederman raised his hand.

"We're not in kindergarten, Biederman. Just talk."

"People are always living in the past," he said. "You know, regrets and misgivings and all. 'I could have done this better; I should have done that instead.' I say, forget about it."

"Forget about it?"

"It's a waste of time and energy. What good does it do?"

"What if the regret involves someone else? You know—'I shouldn't have done that to my wife' or something."

"*Forget about it*—I guarantee you she's trying to. What good does it do to keep bringing it up all the time? It's like picking at a scab. Every time I try to apologize to my wife it only makes things worse—so forget about it."

"You know, that's not bad," Tino said. "What does it really mean to forgive someone? It basically means you forget what they did to you."

"Exactly," Biederman said. "So the angel says, 'Speed things up—forget about it now.'"

Wes jotted it on the easel with a felt-tip marker. "Okay—what else?"

"I've got something," Kemp said.

"Good—go for it."

"*You're not as good as you can be, but you've never done anything bad.*"

"How's that again?"

"Take 'dishonesty,' for example—what does that word really mean? It means you failed to be honest, that's all. Evil doesn't really exist—it's just a lack of something good. Dishonesty is a lack of honesty; impatience is a lack of patience. So what are you really doing when you're being dishonest? Nothing—you just could have been more honest, that's all. Since evil doesn't exist, you've never really done anything bad—you just could have been more good."

"I like that," Biederman said. "It's positive. It's upbeat."

"I told you, this is child's play."

"We're not done yet, smart guy. What else have you got?"

"How about this: *Look at the next guy in line.*"

"What does that mean?"

"Nobody's happy the way they are; everybody wants to be like somebody else, but they end up picking unattainable role models. A two-hundred-pound woman thinks, 'I want to look like Liv Hayden!' Fat chance of that. What's she looking at Liv Hayden for? A two-hundred-pound woman should be looking at a hundred-and-ninety-pound woman and thinking, 'I want to be like *her*.' See the idea? Imagine everybody in the world in one long line, and everybody's standing next to somebody who's just a little bit better off than they are. That way all they have to do is *look at the next guy in line*."

Wes took notes as fast as he could. "This is good stuff. Keep going."

"How about this," Biederman volunteered. "*It should have been you.*"

"Go on."

"We said the universe wants to give you every good thing, right? Only sometimes the other guy gets the good thing and you end up with squat. So what went wrong? The universe missed, that's all—it should have been you. It's like you take your kid to a ball game 'cause you want him to catch a foul ball, so you buy seats on the third baseline—only the batter is a leftie and he keeps pulling it down the first baseline. Hey, it's not your fault—you were in the right spot. The universe just missed, that's all."

Kemp rolled his eyes while Wes scribbled away.

"Here's another one," Biederman continued. "*Always bring your glove to the game.* The ball won't land in your lap; you've got to grab it away from some other guy's kid, and you're not gonna do that with your bare hands. *Always bring your glove to the game*, and the bigger the better—a first baseman's mitt if you've got one."

"I have season tickets with the Orioles," Tino said. "One time a foul ball hit me right between the eyes. What went wrong? Why did the ball hit me instead of the guy sitting beside me? I forgot to duck, that's all, and he remembered. There's a principle for you: *Don't forget to duck*. What happens when things go wrong in your life? The universe wasn't trying to hit you; it was probably trying to hit the guy beside you—you just forgot to duck."

"Can we get off of baseball?" Kemp groaned.

"What's wrong with baseball? Baseball is a metaphor for life."

"Oh, please."

The four men kept brainstorming until lunchtime and then decided to take a 'working lunch'—which meant that they worked at eating while pretending to think. The break didn't really hurt their momentum; none of them were used to doing serious thinking on a Saturday morning anyway and by lunchtime the ideas had slowed to a trickle. Loading their bellies with deli meat and potato chips didn't help matters, and the coffee was no longer strong enough to counteract the transfer of blood from their brains to their stomachs. Tino stared out the window, mesmerized by the cars passing by on Santa Monica Boulevard. Biederman had downed a Reuben with extra sauerkraut and within fifteen minutes he was stretched out on the sofa sound asleep—until Wes shook him awake and reminded him of the time. The abrupt rousing did nothing to improve Biederman's disposition, but that didn't really matter either; tempers were already short and patience had long ago worn thin.

The four men sat staring at the easel, saying nothing.

"What else?" Wes asked.

Kemp glared at him. "Is that your contribution to this process—sitting there asking 'What else?' while the rest of us do all the thinking?"

"At least I'm saying something. What's the last idea you came up with?"

"Let me think. Wait, I remember now—this whole thing was my idea."

Biederman interrupted. "You know, there's an old saying: 'In hell, it's always two o'clock.'"

"What's that supposed to mean?" Tino asked.

"It means we're tired and we won't get anywhere ripping out each other's throats, as enjoyable as that might sound right now. Has anybody got anything else? Any ideas at all? Bits, pieces—we'll take anything you got."

Nothing.

"I think the last suggestion was 'Cleanliness is next to godliness.'"

"That's not what I meant," Wes muttered. "It just came out that way."

"Can anybody do better than the Cub Scout motto? Because if we can't, we're obviously done here."

Nobody had anything.

"Then it's up to the angel," Biederman said, looking at Kemp. "Let's get some notes together so Kemp can get going."

Kemp leaned over to Tino and whispered, "I need to talk to you—in private."

They stepped out onto the balcony and Kemp pulled the sliding glass door shut behind them. "I've got a problem," he said.

"And why should this concern me?"

"Because it's your problem too."

"I'm listening."

"Hayden's neurologist is a guy named Smithson. I think he might be onto us—at least he might be soon."

"You told me that wasn't possible. You said there would be no evidence."

"There shouldn't be—I mean, there isn't. He's just guessing, really—but he's getting suspicious and he says he's going to start asking questions."

"About what?"

"About me. Last night Smithson told me he's going to put in a call to Johns Hopkins on Monday. He'll hear back from them in a couple of days—and when he does he'll know they don't have any record of a Kemp McAvoy there. How long will it be before Hopkins connects me with Bobby Foscoe? Then Smithson will blow the whistle for sure."

Tino said nothing.

"Well?"

"Why are you telling me this? Why aren't you including our other partners in this discussion?"

"C'mon, Tino, this is your line of work, not ours."

"I'm in the loan business, Bobby."

"And you have to protect your investments, right? Well, this one's about to go up in smoke—unless we do something first."

Tino studied him for a moment. "I'm faced with a difficult decision," he said. "I have a sizable investment in you, Bobby, but at some point the risks of an investment outweigh the rewards. I have a feeling I should walk away from this."

"If you do, you'll never get your money back. That's half a million you can kiss good-bye."

"True—but dealing with a problem like yours adds considerable risk. Why should I assume that risk?"

"For money—*more* money."

Tino paused. "How much more money are we talking about?"

"I don't know. I suppose maybe I could—"

"Another half million," Tino said. "That would make an even million you owe me—a nice round number."

Kemp looked stunned. "I—I need to think it over."

"No, you don't—we don't have time. Besides, you're in no position to bargain."

Kemp swallowed hard. "Okay—another half a million. When will you—you know . . ."

"Never mind. Just forget about it. You've got more important things to worry about—like paying me. And Bobby—that's something you don't want to forget."

23

*K*emp looked at the clock—it was nearly 3:30 a.m. He had dared to go an extra thirty minutes because he knew this was the angel's final opportunity to converse with his earthly apprentice—his last chance to convey anything to Liv Hayden that he wanted her to remember later on. This was the final installment in the "message from beyond." Tomorrow UCLA would begin to taper off the propofol and slowly bring her out of her coma and back to a fully conscious state—back to planet Earth.

He rolled the examination light into place and looked down at Hayden. It suddenly dawned on him that this would be his last face-to-face encounter with her. Granted, the conversations had been slightly one-sided—but he still felt that the two of them had somehow grown closer from the experience and he was going to miss these late night tête-à-têtes. Kemp bent a little closer and studied Hayden's face. *Man, that is one good-looking woman.* Most of the bruising around her eyes was already gone and her skin had more color in it; the day nurse had even brushed the tangles from her hair.

Sure, she was good-looking—but hey, he hadn't exactly hit every ugly branch falling out of a tree himself. That was another thing they had in common: sex appeal—the kind that sometimes attracted the wrong kind of people. But whose fault was that? You don't blame honey because it draws ants. As Kemp looked at her, he began to realize how many other traits they shared: intelligence, talent, ambition, drive, and that mystical combination of intangible qualities that made them both stand head and shoulders above their contemporaries.

The thought made him feel a little sad. She was so close—he could reach out and touch her face if he wanted to—and yet it was as if there were a sheet of glass between them, keeping them apart. Life was so unfair. Two truly compatible souls, isolated from each other by random fate into two separate worlds. What were the chances that they would ever meet again once she left the hospital? Even if they passed on the street, he knew he would be just another pretty face to her—how could she ever recognize all their commonalities with just a passing glance? Of all the men that she could choose from, how would she know the magic she could share with Kemp McAvoy? How would she know . . .

. . . *unless I tell her.*

He quickly checked the notes one last time to make sure he had covered everything that Wes and Biederman and Tino had written. Kemp looked at his watch. Yes—he still had a few minutes to spare.

"I think that's enough business for tonight," he said to Hayden. "Let's talk about something a little more down-to-earth now, shall we? Let's talk about love."

The expression on Hayden's face never changed.

"I know you haven't had the best of luck in that area," Kemp said. "How many husbands has it been now? Four? Five? I wouldn't blame you if you're feeling a little discouraged about love right about now—maybe even hopeless. Don't give up,

Liv—I'm going to tell you a secret that will change the rest of your life.

"You're going to wake up from your coma tomorrow. You're going to leave this hospital and return to your normal life—but your life will never be normal again, Liv. You've been entrusted with a life-changing message, and with great privilege comes great responsibility. It's your job to spread that message to the world. But I know you're only human, Liv. You're not just a messenger; you're a woman, and you have needs. You need a companion—a soul mate—someone who understands a woman like you, someone who appreciates the finer things in life just like you do.

"You know what I'm telling you is true. You've been search-ing for this man all your life, but you haven't found him yet. Who can blame you? There are almost seven billion people on your planet; what are the odds of finding the one man whose heart truly resonates with yours? Because of your human limi-tations you are forced to live in one time and one place, and that makes the task almost impossible—but I don't share those limitations, Liv. I am a cosmic being; I transcend all time and space, and I can see your entire world at once. I can see every man on your planet, and I have found the man you have been searching for all your life. He is your perfect soul mate; your heart's deepest desire; your one true love. I know who this man is—and I'm going to send him to you.

"I'm going to describe him to you so that you'll recognize him when you see him. He is very handsome, as you would expect. You could probably recognize him by his looks alone, but just to make sure there are no mistakes, I'll give you some-thing more—a 'password' you might call it, a way for you to know it's him and no one else. When he finds you and approaches you for the first time, he will look deep into your eyes and say these words: 'I don't believe in accidents—do you?' Remember those words, Liv. Burn them into your memory, because that is how you will know your one true love."

═══

Leah woke unexpectedly and sat up on the sofa. For a moment she didn't remember where she was; it was her fifth night sleeping in the nurses' break room, but the shadows still looked strange and unfamiliar. She felt a little frightened, though she didn't want to admit it to herself, and she knew that if she lay back down she wouldn't be able to fall back to sleep right away. She hated the idea of just lying there in the dark, staring at the shadows and listening to the unfamiliar sounds—so she threw back the flap on her sleeping bag and felt around on the floor for her slippers.

163

She looked at the door and saw light flooding in underneath. The light made a long, thin line, like the glowsticks she carried when she trick-or-treated on Halloween. She wondered if anyone would be in the hallway at this time of night, or if everyone would be in their rooms fast asleep; the light seemed to invite her to take a look. She remembered her mother's strict instructions not to leave the break room again—but it was only a look, and surely her mom didn't expect her to sit there in the dark all night long.

She walked to the door and opened it. Light flooded into the room; she squinted and covered her face with both hands. When her eyes had adjusted she looked down the hallway to the left—there was no one in sight, and though the doors were all open, most of the rooms were dark. She looked down the hallway to the right; those rooms were all dark too—except for one room at the very end of the hall. That door was closed—and light seemed to be pouring out from under it.

Why was that door closed? What was causing the light? She had to know, though she wasn't sure why.

She padded down the hallway toward the room; her slippers made almost no sound on the hard linoleum floor. When she reached the room she put her ear against the door—nothing. She twisted the knob and pushed the door open just enough to peek inside.

The room was filled with a light so brilliant and blinding that it washed the color out of everything in it. The walls, the draperies, even the woman lying faceup on the bed with her eyes half open—everything was a pale whitish-yellow. The light was so intense that it should have hurt her eyes and burned her face, but it didn't. She stared directly into the light without even blinking—and she had the strangest sensation that the light was looking back.

24

Natalie sat on the park bench and watched Leah dangling from the ancient playground equipment. The jungle gym was the same kind Natalie had played on when she was a little girl—not the molded plastic monstrosities found in more affluent areas, but a simple, stark birdcage of thick plumber's pipe painted green and showing bare metal wherever a child's hands had eventually worn through. Natalie actually preferred the old playground because it gave her a sense of security and continuity with the past, and those were qualities in short supply these days. She wished the park was in a better neighborhood, but at least it was easy walking distance from the house, and so it was their regular recreational destination every Sunday afternoon.

Three sides of the park were surrounded by chain-link fence, and the fourth was a salmon-colored cinder-block wall covered in cryptic spray-painted messages. The territorial claims of the local gangs seemed to be everywhere in LA—on every boxcar and overpass and retaining wall. They had become so familiar that to children they were nothing more than decorative artwork, but to grown-ups they served as a reminder that the possibility of violence was never far away. Natalie never looked away from Leah for more than a few seconds at a time, and she kept a wary eye on every childless adult in the park. That's why she had read the same paragraph of her *People* magazine four times—and that's why she spotted Matt while he was still fifty yards away.

She watched him as he approached. He walked directly toward her, and when he smiled and waved he didn't seem at all surprised to see her. *This is no coincidence*, she thought. She shoved her magazine into her purse and thought about reaching for her mirror, but it was too late for that. She ran a quick hand over her hair and turned to greet him.

"What a surprise," he said. "Imagine meeting you here."

"Liar."

He made a low whistle. "You don't let a guy get away with much, do you?"

"It's a lesson I've learned the hard way."

He pointed to the bench. "Do you mind?"

She shrugged, and he took a seat beside her.

"So," Natalie said. "What brings you here?"

"Well, I had this whole spiel worked out about how I just happened to be in the neighborhood and I saw this nice park and thought I'd cut across—but you blew that story. I'm not sure what to tell you now."

"The truth is always nice."

They watched as Leah attempted to swing from hand to hand on the monkey bars. She missed the second rung, dangled by one arm for a moment, then dropped to the sand.

"Leah's a terrific little girl," Matt said.

Natalie didn't reply.

Matt looked at her. "You missed your cue. You were supposed to say, 'Thank you, Matt, that's very kind of you.'"

"I'm waiting for the other shoe to drop," Natalie said. "Leah's a terrific little girl, *but*—"

"There's no *but*. I think Leah's terrific, that's all. She's bright, and imaginative, and—"

Natalie turned to face him. "Come on, Matt, this little meeting is no accident. You went out of your way to come by here today. Why are you here? What do you want?"

Matt paused. "I wanted to see you, Natalie—outside of school, since our last couple of meetings there haven't ended very well. Leah told me you two come to this park every Sunday afternoon, so I thought I might find you here."

"You asked my daughter where to find me?"

"I didn't have to ask," Matt said. "Leah volunteers a lot of information. You'd be surprised what I know about you."

Terrific, Natalie thought. "It's this 'angel' business—that's what you want to talk about, isn't it?"

"Yes, it is. I think the whole thing's getting blown out of proportion, and I wanted the chance to tell you that. I think we're losing sight of the fact that Leah is an outstanding little girl."

"So do I."

"She's very intelligent. Have you ever thought about moving her forward a grade?"

"She's already smaller than most kids her age," Natalie said. "Look at her—she can't even reach the monkey bars. I want her to fit in, Matt. That's what bothers me most about this whole thing—it makes her seem so different."

"She is different. She has her own gifts."

"Yeah—like the ability to see angels."

He didn't reply.

"Can I ask you something, Matt?"

"Sure."

"Do you believe in angels?"

"Wow—that's not an easy question."

"Why is it so difficult? Do I believe in dinosaurs? Yes. Do I believe in leprechauns? No. It's a simple yes or no question, Matt. Do you believe in angels or not?"

"I'm not really sure. Maybe they're more like dinosaurs than leprechauns."

"What does that mean?"

"Maybe they used to exist, but not anymore."

"What happened to them? Did they become extinct? Are we finding their bones in old tar pits?"

"I just mean—"

"I know what you mean—you mean maybe we've become too sophisticated to believe in them anymore. That's a little snooty, don't you think? Maybe we're not sophisticated at all. Maybe we've lost something along the way—the ability to see them the way people used to."

"What about you? Do you believe in angels?"

She paused. "I'm willing to believe."

"*Willing* to believe?"

"Mr. Armantrout—that self-important twit of a counselor—he keeps looking down his nose at what he calls 'religious mythology.' He's absolutely convinced that angels could never exist, so they never will—not for him. Do you see what I'm saying, Matt? You can't believe in something unless you're at least willing to believe it's possible—otherwise you'll never take a second look." She leaned closer and lowered her voice. "Have you ever considered the possibility that Leah has actually seen an angel?"

"Whoa. Natalie."

"Why is that so unthinkable? This universe looks pretty strange to me, and from what I read it keeps getting stranger all the time."

"An angel would definitely qualify as 'strange,'" Matt said.

"But not unthinkable."

"Maybe not. But let's be realistic, Natalie—Leah seeing real angels? We'd have to consider every other explanation before that one; we'd have to consider all other possibilities first."

"Not Armantrout—he'll consider all other possibilities *period*."

"So is that what you think? You think Leah is actually seeing angels?"

"I don't know," Natalie said. "I just want to give her the benefit of the doubt, that's all."

"So do I," Matt said. "Why do you think I'm here? Believe it or not, single men don't usually spend their Sunday afternoons cruising the neighborhood parks."

"No?"

"Not much action here. I have more luck crashing into women's shopping carts over at Costco."

They watched as Leah perched on one end of an old wooden seesaw and bounced a few inches into the air before crashing back to earth again.

"What do you know about me?" Natalie asked.

"What?"

"You said, 'You'd be surprised what I know about you.' What has Leah told you?"

"I know that you're seeing someone. I know that he lives with you, but you're not married. I know that Leah doesn't like him very much."

"She told you that?"

"Yes, she did. And based on the fact that I've never seen him at a school function or a parent-teacher meeting, I'd say he's either very busy or not very interested."

She frowned. "You have no right to say that."

"No, I don't," Matt said. "I just hate to see a girl like Leah struggling—and I hate to see a woman like you taken for granted."

Natalie looked at him. "Matt, I'm—I'm involved with someone."

Matt nodded. "I know—that's why I've held off saying anything as long as I have. Believe me, Natalie, if you were married I wouldn't get within a mile of you. But you're not married, and I never see this guy, so I have no way of knowing how 'involved' you are."

She said nothing.

"I know this is not the best timing," he said. "It sure would be nice if life would cooperate a little more—if every man who might be interested in you would just line up end to end so you could sort through them one at a time. 'No thanks, no way, next please, keep the line moving'—but it doesn't work like that, does it? You can go a long time without anyone on the horizon and then suddenly, guess what? You've got two men interested in you at the same time."

Natalie realized that her mouth was open a little and closed it. "I—I don't know what to say."

"I know, and that's okay. It's probably better that you don't say anything—especially something really humiliating, like 'I'm so flattered,' or 'You're such a good friend.' I know this isn't what you were expecting to hear today, and to tell you the truth, I wasn't really planning to say it."

"Then—why did you?"

"I guess it's like you said: you can't consider something until you think it might be possible. I just wanted you to know it's possible—at least from my end."

"Matt—"

"Just think it over. Give it time. I don't need any decision from you. I just wanted you to know you have options."

TIM DOWNS

They heard a sound and looked up. Leah was standing right in front of the bench, staring at Matt in disbelief. Neither one of them had heard her approach.

"Mr. Callahan!"

Matt smiled at her. "I know how you feel, Leah—I used to think the same way about my teachers. I thought they just locked themselves in the classroom all weekend and waited for us to come back on Monday. It's not true. They let us out from time to time, and when they do we always head straight for the park."

"We were just talking about you," Natalie said.

"That's right. I was just telling your mom how smart you are, and how good you are at reading and telling stories—"

"I saw another angel," Leah said, "at the hospital."

There was a stunned silence. "I know," Matt said. "You told me about it in class."

"No, I saw another one—just last night."

Natalie let out a weary sigh. "Oh, honey."

"Tell me about it," Matt said cheerfully. "Was it a boy angel or a girl angel this time?"

"It wasn't either," Leah said. "I was out in the hall 'cause I woke up and couldn't go back to sleep. Mom said not to look in the windows anymore 'cause people need their privacy, so I didn't—but the last room didn't have a window, and there was this light coming out from under the door. It was really bright, like maybe there was a fire in there, so I opened the door just a little and looked inside."

"What did you see, Leah?"

"The whole room was filled with light—the brightest light I ever saw, only it didn't hurt my eyes. I saw a man standing in the middle of the light, and he was glowing like he was on fire, only he didn't burn. He was talking to a woman in the bed. She

171

was looking right at him—the light didn't hurt her eyes either. I watched for a minute and then I closed the door."

Matt just looked at her.

Leah turned to her mother. "Do we have to go home now?"

"No," Natalie said, wiping her eyes. "We've still got a few minutes. You go and play."

"Bye, Mr. Callahan."

"So long, Leah. See you tomorrow."

Matt and Natalie watched as Leah turned and ran for the merry-go-round. Neither of them said anything for a few minutes.

"I know what you're thinking," Natalie finally said. "Go ahead and say it."

"Say what?"

"'Your daughter's a nutcase.' First it was a man, then a woman, and now a blinding light. What's next—flaming chariots in the sky?"

"That's not what I was thinking," Matt said, "and I told you before—I don't think Leah is a 'nutcase.'"

"Then what's happening to her, Matt? Please—I need to know."

"There could be a simple explanation," Matt said. "Leah's a clever storyteller; maybe she's just embellishing the story as she goes along. A man, a woman—now a blinding light."

"But she believes it. You can see it in her eyes."

"Yes, I think she does." He looked at her. "There's something I need to say to you, Natalie, and I don't think you're going to like it."

"Go ahead."

"I think you need to seriously consider that MRI."

"What? Why?"

"Whatever Leah is seeing, it seems to be progressing. You're a nurse, Natalie—think about it: a brilliant light that doesn't hurt her eyes. Isn't that exactly what you might experience if something was going on in your brain?"

"I thought you said she wasn't a nutcase."

"I'm talking about a physical abnormality—something that might be getting worse. I know you don't want to hear this, but Armantrout might be right on this point. Doesn't it make sense to get her checked out, if only to cross the possibility off the list?"

Natalie didn't reply.

Matt reached out and put a hand on her shoulder, but she pulled away.

He got up from the bench and looked down at her, but she refused to make eye contact. "Every time I see you it seems to end badly," he said. "I hope it's not always like this. Just think about what I said, okay? Please, Natalie—think about *everything* I said."

25

*B*iederman poked his head into the hospital room. "I'm looking for Sleeping Beauty," he said.

Liv Hayden set down her *Entertainment Weekly* and looked at him from her bed. "Yeah? Who wants her?"

"Who wouldn't?" He stepped into the room and produced a bouquet of flowers from behind his back with a dramatic flourish.

"That's it? Flowers? No handsome prince?"

"Princes you got," Biederman said. "Flowers don't want alimony." He laid the roses on the bed and bent over her, making a kissing motion in the air. "Sweetheart, you look terrific."

"Look at me, Morty—I've got two shiners. I look like I just went three rounds with my second husband—or is it two rounds with my third husband?"

"I see you've still got your sense of humor," Biederman said. "That's a good sign."

"When can I get out of here?"

"As soon as the doc signs off on you. How do you feel?"

"Good, all in all. A little stiff—sore in some places. Well rested, that's for sure. How long was I out?"

"Nine days. They wanted to make sure your head didn't swell."

"Give me an Oscar, my head will swell. They just wanted

to say they had a movie star here, that's all." She lowered her voice. "Nobody got any pictures, did they? I mean, look at me. I don't want to see this face on the cover of the *Enquirer*."

"No pictures—I made sure of it. This is a private room and you had your very own nurse. No visitors allowed."

"Thanks, Morty, I owe you—ten percent."

"You're a hundred percent welcome."

Liv picked up her magazine again and held it so Biederman could read the cover. The headline said: LIV HANDLER RETURNING FROM DEATH'S DOOR. "Nice work, Morty. You were right on top of things, as always."

"I wanted to create a sense of anticipation, you know? As if you were coming home from someplace far away. *Liv Hayden returns*—what will she be like? How will she be different? What did she bring us?"

"'What did she bring us?'"

"You know—like kids say when you get back from a business trip: 'What did you bring us?'"

"Oh, I get it."

Biederman paused. "So—what did you bring us?"

"Sorry, maybe next trip. There were no gift shops where I was."

"Are you sure about that?"

She dropped the magazine again. "What are you talking about, Morty?"

"Think about it, sweetheart. Things like this—tragedies, accidents—they're defining moments in a person's life. They make you stop and think; they make you reevaluate your life; they give you insights you maybe didn't have before. I don't think you're the same person you were before."

"What do you mean?"

"You seem—different somehow."

"I do?"

"Don't you feel any different?"

"Should I?"

"You were out for nine days. You never slept so long in your whole life."

"Sure I did—in those studio budget meetings."

"I'm being serious here. What was it like?"

"It was like being asleep. What did you think?"

"Was it?"

"Was it what?"

"Like being asleep? They gave you drugs, Liv. They knocked you out so deep that you didn't move. That's not how I sleep. I thrash around—I throw off all the covers. My wife has to sleep in another room sometimes."

"I recommend the drugs. See if they have takeout here."

"Did you dream?"

Liv hesitated. "Why?"

Biederman shrugged. "They knocked you out deeper than you've ever been before—like the headline says, 'at death's door.' I don't know—I figured maybe you might have dreamed deeper than ever before."

"Why are you asking me this?"

"Like I said: you seem different somehow. Just thought I'd ask."

"Well, it's the same old me, okay?"

"Good. Glad to have you back. I'll start getting your things together."

She watched in silence as he began to gather items from the drawers.

"You really think I seem different?" she asked.

"I don't know what it is, but it's definitely there. Maybe it's like you said—you just got a good night's sleep for a change."

"You know something, Morty? I feel a little different."

"You do? How so?"

"I don't know. Just—different."

Biederman stopped and looked at her. "Listen, this is a fresh start for you. This is a chance for you to redefine yourself. It was the old Liv Hayden who wrecked that car—it's the new Liv Hayden who's walking out of here. People will expect you to be different after something like this, and you can be anything you want. I just want you to know that I'll be there to support you, whatever you decide to be."

She paused. "Can I tell you something, Morty?"

"Anything, sweetheart."

"I did have a dream—and it was a doozy."

"No kidding." Biederman sat down on the edge of her bed. "Why don't you tell me all about it?"

26

*Y*ou boys need anything else?" the waitress asked.

"A little privacy would be nice," Kemp said without looking up from his plate.

Biederman gave the waitress a smile and a wink. "It's a business meeting, sweetheart—if you don't mind."

"You got it. Call me if you need me."

"I'll take the check," Tino said.

The waitress set the black vinyl folder in front of him and left.

"You don't have to do that," Wes said. "We can split it up."

"No problem," Tino said. "As I told you, I'm an investor—it's the least I can do. Besides, it's bad luck to split a check when you're doing business."

The four men sat in the back section of Jerry's Famous Deli on Beverly Boulevard, just across the street from Cedars-Sinai. Jerry's was a convenient choice for all of the men, since it was situated just a few miles from each of their offices as well as the medical center at UCLA.

Tino, unwilling to face another California entrée, went for the pastrami on rye with a double side of Russian dressing. Biederman, a Jerry's regular, had a bowl of yellowish broth with a single matzo ball the size of an orange. Wes chose the garden pizza with a simple side salad, while Kemp selected the priciest item on the menu—a New York steak, medium rare.

"I think this occasion deserves a toast," Biederman said, hoisting his Heineken into the air. "To *entrepreneurship*. May those who seize life by the horns get the best cut of beef—and the next time we meet, may we toast with champagne."

"Here here," Wes said, "and I'd like to add to that. To *vision*—and to the soon-to-be runaway international best seller, *It's All About You*."

Biederman cleared his throat. "Not to mention the film version, which I am mentioning now."

Tino slowly rose to his feet. "To *trust*, without which every business venture is doomed to failure—with sometimes painful consequences."

All three men now turned and looked at Kemp, who gradually felt the weight of their eyes and looked up. He slowly raised his own bottle into the air. "To the snobs at the Los Angeles Country Club," he said. "May I soon be among them." When none of the others seemed to comprehend he added, "To *money*—and all the possibilities it brings."

Biederman nodded approvingly. "As our angel would say: 'Amen.'"

Tino turned to Kemp. "How are things going at work?"

"What?"

"It must be a big relief now that you don't have to play angel night after night. There must be less pressure on you now. Is there less pressure?"

Kemp paused. "Oh—right. Yes, there's a lot less pressure."

Tino nodded. "I thought there might be."

"There'll be even less pressure once the money starts rolling in," Biederman said.

"Speaking of money," Kemp said, "how's everything progressing?"

"Like a well-oiled machine," Biederman said. "You wouldn't believe it."

"Why wouldn't I? Whose idea was this whole thing?"

"I must admit, my young friend, when you first presented this little plan of yours, I thought you were just another meshuggener. I know better now; I stand corrected."

"And how's our Chosen One doing?"

"Olivia's been in excellent spirits the last couple weeks—better than I've seen her in years. You know, I think this whole thing has been good for her. It's given her a new sense of purpose."

"How's her memory holding up?"

"I've been doing what you said—going over the story with her again and again, asking for more details. She seems to remember a little more each day. I think she'll eventually remember every last word Kemp told her. I can't say I'm surprised; Olivia is a first-class actress, after all—she's used to memorizing pages of script."

"It doesn't hurt to have it embedded in your subconscious," Kemp said.

"It's an eerie feeling, listening to her repeat back to me the things we wrote for her and pretending I'm hearing them for the first time. It's like déjà vu or something. I know her next words before she says them."

"How do you think she'll handle the interviews?"

"We're talking about Olivia Hayden," Biederman said. "The woman has done thousands of interviews. She comes alive in front of a camera."

Now Kemp turned to Wes. "How's the book going?"

"It's at the printer now," Wes said. "This has got to be the fastest release in the history of publishing. I had the manuscript practically finished before I even interviewed her. I just pasted in a few of her own words so she'd think it was hers. She couldn't believe I wrote the thing so fast—she thinks I'm some kind of genius. I told her I felt a spirit guiding me as I wrote—she loved that."

"When does it hit the bookstores—and more to the point, when will I see a check?"

"The official pub date is a week from Thursday. The orders have been pouring in—the presales look terrific, and that's for a hardcover. If the sell-through looks anything like the sell-in, we won't have to go to trade paper for years. We'll make a killing."

"The check, Wes—what about the check?"

"Be patient," Wes said. "We'll issue royalty statements at the end of every quarter; you'll get your first check about six weeks after that. But remember, Vision Press has to recoup its production and promotion costs before the three of us start making any profit—we agreed on that. And then there's the matter of the advance—that has to be recovered too."

"What 'advance'?"

"An author always gets paid an advance. It's sort of like a down payment or a signing bonus. The author gets a nice fat check up front, but she has to pay it back out of her future royalties. We had to offer Liv Hayden a sizable advance. She'll pay it back over time, but we had to come up with the cash up front."

"How much cash are we talking about?"

"Two million."

Kemp blinked. "Two *million*?"

Biederman stepped in. "I encouraged Olivia to publish with Vision Press, but I had to give her a reason. After all, why Vision Press? Why not Random House or Simon & Schuster? I told her that Vision Press had the most experience with this type of book, but Olivia is a very shrewd businesswoman. She knows the book will be big and she knows it deserves a big advance. Vision Press had to make an offer that would be competitive with other publishers. Two million was barely enough to do the trick."

"Wait a minute," Kemp said. "As her agent, are you getting a percentage of this advance?"

Biederman lowered his voice. "You understand, I'm not at liberty to discuss the details of a financial arrangement with my client."

Kemp looked at Wes. "Vision Press is in debt up to its ears. Who in the world would loan you two million bucks?"

Wes nodded to Tino.

Tino made a modest shrug. "I was happy to be able to help in time of need."

"I'll just bet you were," Kemp said. "And what were the terms of this little 'short-term loan'?"

Wes hesitated. "Fifty percent. Two years."

"*What?* Are you telling me we'll have to pay this shylock *three* million bucks before I'm going to see any profit?"

"It was a bargain, considering," Biederman said. "Who else would have loaned us that kind of money? And without the money, why would Olivia have chosen Vision Press? What if she went with a different publisher—then where would we be?"

"I think Bobby understands," Tino said. "His emotions are clouding his judgment right now, that's all. He knows what it's like to need money right away."

Kemp glared at the three men. "Why didn't somebody ask me about this 'loan' idea?"

"We didn't think you had that kind of money."

"He doesn't," Tino said. "Trust me."

"That's not what I meant. Why didn't anybody bother

to run this idea by me? Why didn't you ask for my approval first?"

"It was a business item," Wes said. "No offense, Kemp, but you're not exactly a businessman. The three of us figured you were handling the technical side of things. We decided not to bother you with it."

Kemp looked at each of the men. "Let me see if I understand all this. Biederman convinces Liv Hayden to go with Vision Press, but only if she gets an advance of two million bucks first. So Hayden gets two million, and Biederman takes a percentage of that. To pay the two million, Wes has to take out a loan from Tino here, so Tino makes a quick million himself. In the meantime, the book comes out and Wes's company starts raking in money—and someday in the distant future, after the loan is repaid and all the expenses are finally recovered, my check will finally arrive in the mail." Kemp narrowed his eyes. "Is it just my imagination, or do I seem to be the only one not getting paid around here?"

"Stop being paranoid," Wes said. "Nobody's gotten paid anything yet. You'll get your money, Kemp—we all will. We just have to be patient."

"How patient?"

"A few months maybe. That's all."

"But the money is coming, right?"

"Haven't you been listening? Everything's going according to plan."

"Speaking of money," Biederman interrupted, "we need to talk about the movie rights. Columbia Tri-Star is showing strong interest; so is Sony, but they both want to see some sales numbers first. The three of us had a meeting with Liv last week, and—"

"Wait a minute," Kemp said. "The *three* of you met with Liv?"

183

"That's right."

Kemp looked at Tino.

"Charming woman," Tino said. "Lovely home in the Hollywood Hills. We had a very nice lunch."

"What were you doing there?"

"I was there as a potential investor—in the movie."

"Now you're getting a piece of the movie?"

"What's the problem?" Biederman asked.

"What's the problem? The three of you met with Liv Hayden—that's another meeting I wasn't in on. This was supposed to be a threesome, and *he* wasn't supposed to be part of it."

"What are you, crazy?" Biederman said. "You can't meet with Liv Hayden."

"Why not?"

"Has it ever occurred to you that you might look slightly familiar? You bear a striking resemblance to an angel she once met. What if she recognized you?"

Kemp stopped to consider that. "I just think I should be included more," he grumbled. "I'm getting everything after the fact. All the decisions are being made without me, and I don't like it."

"What's the matter?" Tino asked. "Don't you trust us?"

Kemp frowned at him but didn't reply. He kept imagining himself stretched out on a chaise lounge beside Liv Hayden's pool, gazing out over the infinity edge at Beverly Hills and West Hollywood below.

"I have something that might cheer us all up," Wes announced. "I was saving this news for later, but maybe this is a good time. I just heard from our marketing department this morning: Oprah Winfrey has agreed to do a weeklong series of live interviews with Liv Hayden right here in LA, followed by a

184

big book signing on Saturday over at that new mall in Glendale to kick off the release of the book. We're talking about Oprah's Book Club; we're talking about a featured link on Oprah.com; we're talking about a week of exposure to fifty million viewers, most of them women—and women are the ones who buy books. Brace yourselves, boys—we're about to be Oprahfied."

27

*H*ello? Yes, I'm still holding—I've been holding for the last ten minutes. No, I understand. That's okay. Look, I'm trying to schedule an MRI for my daughter—I've been trying to get an appointment for weeks."

Outside the house, a car horn was bellowing every few seconds. Natalie pressed the phone tighter against her ear.

"She needs a cranial MRI. No, there's no referring physician. My daughter's name is Pelton—that's 'P' as in 'Patrick.' Leah—L-e-a-h—Leah Pelton. She's six years old. What? No, she's never had an MRI before."

The car horn continued to blare.

"I'm sorry, could you repeat that? I think somebody's car alarm is going off. Yes, I hate that too—I feel like grabbing a baseball bat. What? You've got an opening? Is that a Thursday? Great, that would work for me. Sorry? Oh—Blue Cross."

Now the car horn began to make short, intermittent blasts.

"Yes, I know where you're located—I work at UCLA too. What? Yes, I heard about that. Has anyone seen him yet? Smithson—he's a neurologist. I used to see him all the time and he just vanished a couple of weeks ago. Was he married? I know, it's kind of scary—I can't help thinking about it every time I walk out to that parking deck at night."

The horn made a long, insistent wail . . .

"Fine, I'll have her there thirty minutes early. Is there any-thing else I need to know—anything I should bring? Okay then, thanks. Bye."

The car horn began to emit a codelike signal—short taps fol-lowed by longer bursts. Natalie slammed down the phone and charged into the kitchen. She threw open the door and shouted at the street, "Hey! Do you mind? People are trying to—"

"Man, it's hard to get your attention. What were you doing in there, taking a nap?"

Natalie's mouth dropped open. Kemp was standing at the curb, grinning at her and leaning against the hood of a gleam-ing new car.

He tipped down his sunglasses and winked at her. "Like it?"

187

Natalie stepped out onto the sidewalk. "Kemp—what is that?"

"I believe they call it an 'automobile.'"

"I know what it is. Where did you get it?"

"I bought it."

"You *bought* it?"

"Leased it, actually, but I expect to pay it off soon. The Mercedes CL65 AMG: 604 horsepower, biturbo V-12 engine, 5-speed driver-adaptive automatic with sport suspension—hottest production coupe on the road. What do you think, babe? Does this thing look good on me or what?"

"What do I *think*? I think you're out of your mind! We can't afford something like this—that thing must cost a hundred thousand dollars."

"Closer to two."

Natalie threw up her hands in desperation. "Kemp—what were you thinking?"

"I was thinking it's about time I did something for myself. Why shouldn't I? I think I deserve it."

"But—where did you get the money?"

"Forget the money, Natalie. Our ship is about to come in."

"What are you talking about?"

"I've been working on a little business venture that's about to pay off—big-time."

"What business venture?"

"The one that kept me from getting any sleep for a few days. You know, a couple of weeks ago—the thing you got all worked up about. Now aren't you glad I didn't come home on time?"

"Kemp, I'm not stupid. You can't make that kind of money in a few days—not legally."

He ran his hand over the side of the car. "Apparently you can."

"What kind of a deal was this? I need to know."

"Now there you go again—always looking for the downside."

"I just don't want you to get us into any trouble. I have a daughter to look out for, you know."

"Yeah, you keep reminding me."

"Exactly how much did you make on this 'deal'?"

"Don't worry, babe, there'll be plenty when the deal pays off in a few months."

"Wait a minute—are you telling me that you don't actually have this money?"

"Not yet—but it's a sure thing."

"Oh, Kemp."

"Hey, it's not like I'm waiting for some horse to come in—this is a legitimate investment. It just takes a few months to pay off, that's all. Stop worrying."

"Kemp, you spent money we don't even have. You should have waited."

"I'm always waiting, Natalie—waiting to have a decent car, waiting for that place near the beach in Santa Monica, waiting for two lousy weeks of vacation so I can finally do something I want to do. Well, I'm sick of waiting. I had an idea—a brilliant idea, a real stroke of genius—and it's working, Natalie, it's about to pay off. After all these years of waiting, I am finally going to get to do what I want and buy what I want and go wherever I please."

Natalie waited. "Don't you mean, 'we'?"

"Sure. Of course—we."

She glared at him. "I'm sick of waiting too, Kemp. I'm sick of waiting for you to grow up—for you to stop acting like a spoiled teenager and take some responsibility around here. All you do is whine about how your life didn't turn out the way you wanted it to. Well, neither did mine, but I've still got responsibilities and so do you. Leah needs an MRI, Kemp— she's still having these visions, and her teacher and counselor think there might be something wrong with her. Do you know what an MRI costs? Do you even know what the deductible on our health insurance is? Two thousand dollars—that's the part we'll have to pay. I don't have two thousand dollars lying around, and unless you've been keeping something from me, neither do you. Do you understand what I'm saying to you? *Leah needs an MRI and we don't have the money*—but you just went out and leased a two-hundred-thousand-dollar car."

"We'll get the money," Kemp said. "It might be a little tight for a couple of months, but—"

"What's the lease payment on this car?"

He hesitated. "Thirty-three hundred a month."

"*What?* Where in the world is that supposed to come from?"

"It doesn't matter, Natalie. We'll put it on the MasterCard—it's only for a couple of months."

"Just until your deal comes through."

"Exactly. We'll have all the money we need then—enough for the MRI, enough for the place in Santa Monica, enough for everything."

"And what if your deal falls through?"

Kemp shook his head in disdain. "What does it take to make you happy, Natalie? If I do nothing, you complain that I'm not carrying my weight around here. If I show some initiative and grab a once-in-a-lifetime business opportunity, you complain that it might fall through. There's no pleasing you, is there? That's the difference between you and me, babe—you like to worry, and I like to enjoy life."

He took the keys from his pocket and dangled them in front of her. "I came by here to show you my new car—and to take you for a drive. Maybe that's not such a good idea. I might drive too fast. I might wreck the car, and where would we get the money to repair it? I tell you what—why don't I go for a drive, and you can stay here and worry about it."

"Kemp—"

He climbed into the car and roared off.

28

mmet guided the floor polisher into the custodian's closet and coiled the thick black extension cord around the silver handle. He took a toilet brush and a pair of rubber gloves from a shelf and picked up a corroded metal pail; he held it under the spigot of a fifty-five-gallon drum and pumped the handle until a thick, sweet-scented liquid spurted into the bottom of the bucket.

He heard the door close behind him. He turned and looked.

"Hey," Kemp said simply.

"Hey yourself."

"I thought maybe we could talk."

"In the janitor's closet?"

"There's not a lot of privacy around here."

"In other words, you don't want nobody to see you talkin' to me."

"Something like that, yeah."

Emmet set down the bucket. "Well, go ahead and talk."

"A couple of weeks ago, when that movie star was here. Olivia Hayden—remember her?"

"I remember. The woman seems to be in the news a lot lately."

"She was my patient."

"I remember that too."

"You . . . walked in on me one night. Do you remember that?"

"Sorta hard to forget."

"You didn't say anything at the time—you just turned around and walked out again."

"Didn't quite know what to say. In my experience, when a man don't know what to say it's best not to say anything."

"I was just wondering . . . what you think you saw."

Emmet paused. "Now that's an odd question."

"I mean, it probably looked a little strange."

"Strange in what way?"

"Well, that's what I'm asking. Did it look strange to you?"

"Mr. Kemp, I been around here a long time. I seen all kinds of things—things a man with my background can't even begin to understand."

Kemp seemed to relax a little. "That's true—some of these procedures are very technical and they must look pretty strange. That's all it was, of course—just a standard procedure."

"What sort of procedure?"

"I beg your pardon?"

"The thing you were doin' when I walked in. What sort of procedure was that?"

"Well—"

"I remember a big light with you standin' right in front of it. I remember you dressed up like a doctor—in a white coat instead of your usual scrubs. I remember the woman starin' up at you even though she was supposed to be sound asleep. And if I'm not mistaken you were talkin' to the lady, though I had the feelin' I interrupted when I poked my head in."

Kemp said nothing.

"Now that you mention it, it did all seem a bit odd—never

saw anything quite like it. What sort of procedure was that, anyway?"

"It was just—an examination, that's all. That's what I needed the light for."

"You know, you might get a better look if you step to the side a little—you seemed to be blockin' the light."

"I—didn't want the light to hurt her eyes."

"Funny they were open right about then."

"Well, that's why I was examining her. Patients can grow resistant to anesthesia over time—we have to constantly regulate it. I saw her coming out of it a little so I thought I'd better check."

"And the white coat?"

"Oh, right, the coat. See, when a patient comes out of sedation too quickly they can experience anxiety and agitation. I thought it might have a calming effect if I looked more like a doctor than a nurse."

"So you were talkin' to the woman just to calm her down a bit."

"That's right—just to reassure her."

"Well, that makes perfect sense then. That explains all of it—except for one thing."

"What's that?"

"If it was all just a standard procedure, how come we're talkin' in a closet?"

Kemp's eyes began to dart like gnats.

"Like I told you, Mr. Kemp, I been around here a long time, and I seen all kinds of things. I seen patients come runnin' out of their rooms buck naked and nurses runnin' right after 'em. I seen people who were supposed to die walk right out of here, and people who came in with nary a scratch pass on. I thought I seen just about everything—but I got to admit, I never saw a man pretend to be an angel before."

193

"Now, wait a minute—"

"You're good, Mr. Kemp—good at lyin' I mean. You're just about the best I ever seen. You're light on your toes—you think on your feet. I can't say I admire the quality, but I truly am impressed. Please don't take that as a compliment."

"You've got it all wrong," Kemp said.

"Do I? You once asked me what the janitors are reading these days; let me show you what I been reading of late." From a shelf beside the door he took a copy of *Star* magazine and showed Kemp the cover. "Have you seen this? Somehow I got a feelin' you have."

The cover headline announced: LIV AWAKES! MOVIE STAR MEETS HEAVENLY HOST—BRINGS DYING CAREER BACK FROM DEAD.

"It's not my usual fare," Emmet said, "but I found it in the waiting room and the headline caught my eye. Interesting story—let me read you part of it." He opened to the first page and read:

> Most people in comas spend their days and nights in a deep and dreamless slumber. Not movie star Liv Hayden—she passed her time in conversation with an angel, dispatched to her bedside with what Hayden calls "a life-changing message of hope and renewal." Hayden, seriously injured in a recent automobile accident, was kept in a coma at UCLA Medical Center for more than a week. Upon awakening, Hayden immediately reported her heavenly visitation—and announced a change in career. "Something precious has been entrusted to me," Hayden said in an exclusive interview with *Star* magazine. "I feel responsible to pass it on." Hayden apparently intends to "pass it on" by publishing her story with Vision Press, well known for the international

best seller *Lattes with God*. Industry insiders tell *Star* that if Hayden's book is anywhere near as successful as *Lattes*, the angels won't be the only ones rejoicing.

Emmet closed the magazine and returned it to the shelf. "Sorta makes you wonder, doesn't it?"

"What do you mean?"

"The woman's supposed to be in a coma, but she comes out of it just a little. When she opens her eyes she sees a man standing over her—a man dressed in white. The next thing you know she thinks she's seen an angel. That's quite a coincidence."

"You think she confused me with an angel?"

"Not by accident."

Kemp lowered his voice to a whisper. "Look, Emmet—"

"You know my name. I wasn't sure."

"The whole thing was just a harmless prank."

"Does that seem harmless to you? You put words in an angel's mouth—that's a mighty bold thing to do. You're foolin' with things you don't understand, Mr. Kemp. An angel's just a messenger; that means you put words in the mouth of the Almighty, and that's a fearful thing to do."

"I don't believe in angels—or the bogeyman."

"Your daughter does."

"My girlfriend's daughter is a loon. Bad genes, I suppose."

"Then let me put it to you another way: You're foolin' with words. Folks are gonna read those words, and some folks are gonna believe 'em. Words are some of the most powerful things in the world, Mr. Kemp. Not a terrible thing's been done in this world that didn't start off with words. Words matter—a smart man like you should know that."

"Skip the sermon," Kemp said. "What is it you want?"

"I just came in here to fetch a bucket. How 'bout you?"

"I want you to keep your mouth shut."

"And why should I do that?"

Kemp paused. "I can pay you. There's money in this—a lot of it. I stand to make . . . thousands on this deal, and I'm willing to give you a share."

Emmet shook his head. "You make fun of my name, you speak to me with contempt, you treat me like I'm somethin' you'd scrape off your shoes—but this is the first time you really insulted me. You think I'm like you, and I'm not."

"There are powerful people involved in this," Kemp said. "Trust me, you don't want to cross them."

"Now you're threatening me."

"A word to the wise—that's all I'm saying."

"Now that's funny," Emmet said. "A word to the wise from a fool."

"You don't believe me?"

"I believe you—I'm just not afraid of you."

"Then I'll give you another reason to keep your mouth shut."

"What's that?"

"Natalie. You like Natalie, don't you? I know she likes you. So does Leah—she talks about you all the time."

Emmet paused. "What's Natalie got to do with this?"

"Nothing—and everything. We're both nurses; we work in the same ICU in the same hospital; we even work the same shift. I live with Natalie—we share everything. If you go public with this, do you really think anybody will believe she had nothing to do with it? It would mean her job. It would mean her career—no hospital would touch her after this. She'd end up doing home visitations for shut-ins."

Emmet slowly cocked his head to one side. "Mr. Kemp, I believe I'm seein' you in a whole new light."

"Glad you've seen the light," Kemp said. "So—can I count on you?"

There was a long silence as Emmet considered.

"It was harmless," Kemp assured him. "Just a little scam to pick up a few bucks on the side. So a washed-up movie star writes a book—so what? Books like this one come and go all the time—a year from now nobody will even remember what it said. Everybody profits; nobody loses. What's the harm?"

Another pause.

"C'mon—for Natalie. For Leah."

Emmet reluctantly nodded. "There's just one thing I'd like to know. How did a fine woman like Natalie ever get hooked up with a good-for-nothin' like you?"

"Just lucky, I guess. So—we're okay?"

"We are definitely not okay—but I'll do it for Natalie's sake. I won't say anything, Mr. Kemp, but I won't lie for you either. That's a different thing entirely."

"Fair enough. And don't forget, there'll be a few bucks in it for you. You can buy yourself a new mop."

When Kemp reached for the doorknob, Emmet said to him, "You know, you'd do well to take your own advice."

Kemp looked back. "How's that?"

"I'd be careful if I were you."

29

Natalie heard the bedroom door open and looked up from the TV; a moment later Kemp came bounding into the living room like a wet retriever.

"Are you watching this?" He plopped down on the sofa beside her and pried the remote from her hands.

"Apparently I'm not. Please, help yourself."

Kemp began to eagerly flip through the channels.

"There are two of us living here, Kemp. Don't you get enough golf and Sports Center on the weekends? I sit down to watch a few minutes of TV before I pick up Leah from school—"

"Would you shut up? I can't hear anything. What channel is she on?"

"Who?"

"Oprah."

Natalie stared at him in disbelief—then took back the remote and punched in the number 7 for KABC. A commercial for auto insurance was airing.

Kemp checked his watch. "Shoot—it's after three. I might have missed part of it."

"Part of what?"

"Watch—you're in for a surprise."

When the commercial ended and the show returned, Oprah was seated beside a strangely familiar face—it was

Olivia Hayden, propping up a book on her thigh titled *It's All About You*.

"What a surprise," Natalie said with a groan. "You know, if all you want to do is ogle your girlfriend, why don't you just go rent one of her—"

"Do you mind? 'Talk show' means *they* talk."

Kemp took the remote back and turned up the volume.

"*It's All About You*," Oprah announced. "That's the title of the astonishing new book by my old friend Liv Hayden, and let me tell you all something: this is a book that could change everything."

The audience erupted in applause.

"Liv, we've known each other for a long time—ever since I was filming *The Color Purple* and you were shooting *See You in Your Dreams*. So I'm going to ask you a hard question, because that's what friends do." She reached over and took Hayden by the hand. "You were kept in a coma because of a possible injury to your brain. A brain injury, Liv—that could explain a lot. How do you know this angel was real?"

"Is this that angel thing?" Natalie asked. "I saw this in the paper."

"Shut up!" Kemp leaned closer to the screen.

"I know there are doubters out there," Hayden said confidently. "Some people think I made the whole thing up, but I could never have invented a message like this—it could only have come from a superhuman intelligence."

"You got that right," Kemp said with a smirk.

"Kemp—I'm trying to listen."

"I'll tell you how I know it was real: the same way I know you're real—that you're flesh and blood and not just some figment of my imagination." She held up Oprah's hand and shook it as if to demonstrate.

The audience applauded again.

"Did you ever actually touch the angel?" Oprah asked.

"No—I was afraid. But somehow I think he wanted me to."

Kemp winked at the screen. "Right again."

Natalie gave him an elbow. "Will you be quiet? *They* talk, remember?"

"Describe the scene for us—tell us all what you saw."

Hayden reached into the air in front of her and began to make small sweeping gestures, as if she were painting a picture on a canvas that only she could see. "It's as if I was floating in a great darkness, when all of a sudden I saw a pinpoint of light. The light began to grow larger—closer—as if I was rushing through space toward a distant star. I finally arrived—who can say where—and all the darkness was suddenly gone. There was nothing but blinding white light all around me—light so bright that I could barely look into it. And in the middle of the light was a man—a man like no man I've ever seen before."

"And you've seen some good ones," Oprah said.

The audience laughed; so did Hayden.

"You bet I have—that's how I knew that this was no ordinary mortal."

"What did the angel say to you? What were his very first words?"

Hayden shook her head. "You'd never believe me."

"Try me."

"Seriously—it's too 'out there.'"

"Come on now, Liv. Most of us will never get a chance to meet a real angel. What did he say?"

"Well—he said . . ."

Kemp grinned. "Greetings, earthling!"

" . . . he said, 'Greetings, earthling!'"

Natalie looked at Kemp. "Hey—how did you know that?"

Kemp shrugged. "Lucky guess."

Oprah looked at Hayden doubtfully. "You're pulling my leg. This angel had a sense of humor?"

"You need a sense of humor to survive in this world—I think that's what he was telling me."

The audience applauded gratefully.

Oprah leaned closer to her guest. "Did you get the impression that the angel knew you—I mean, knew who you are? What you do for a living?"

"Yes, I did. In fact—"

"What?"

"No, this is too weird."

"Go ahead, say it."

Kemp spoke first: "He said, 'I've seen most of your pictures.'"

Hayden was just a beat behind him: "He told me that he'd seen most of my pictures."

The audience broke into laughter.

Oprah said, "I wonder if he watches my show. Did he say anything about that?"

Natalie grabbed the remote and switched off the TV.

"Hey! Turn that back on!"

"Kemp—what's going on?"

"At least record it so I can watch it later."

Natalie aimed the remote at the DVR and pushed the red Record button, then stuffed the remote down between the seat cushions. "Now what's going on? I want to know."

"I don't know what you're talking about."

"Why the sudden interest in Oprah? You've never watched her show before—never."

"It's Olivia Hayden—I heard she was going to be on, that's

all. She's been in the news lately. She was my patient. What's the big deal?"

"This is a live show, Kemp—it's not a rerun. How come you seem to know what Olivia Hayden's going to say before she says it?"

"It seemed obvious to me. All you had to do was listen."

"'Greetings, earthling'—you call that obvious? I was listening, and I never would have thought of that."

"Maybe I'm a better guesser than you are."

"Stop treating me like an idiot. You've been meeting with her, haven't you?"

"What? That's ridiculous."

"Is it? I tried to look the other way when you had your little emotional fling with her in the hospital. Don't deny it—all the nurses noticed it. You practically bit my head off when I interrupted one evening. I thought it was just a silly infatuation, but you've obviously been talking with her."

"The woman's never said a single word to me—I swear it."

"It's the only possible explanation and you know it. How else could you know what she's going to say next?"

"You might be surprised."

"Are you cheating on me?"

"Hey, let's not get crazy here."

"I want to know what's going on. I have a right to know."

Kemp slowly broke into a grin. "Aw, why not? I've been dying to tell somebody anyway."

"What are you talking about?"

"You know that business deal I've been telling you about? Well, you might say Liv Hayden is a part of it—a big part of it, in fact. It's like this . . ."

Fifteen minutes later Natalie found herself staring at Kemp in utter disbelief.

"Kemp—it isn't possible."

"Brilliant, isn't it? Like the woman said—it could only have come from a superhuman intelligence."

"What were you thinking? What you did was completely unethical—it was illegal! You violated a doctor's orders. You adjusted a patient's medication. Even if you have your MD, you don't have hospital privileges at UCLA—that's malpractice! What if somebody finds out about this? What if Liv Hayden finds out? She'll sue you—she could sue the whole hospital."

"Calm down," Kemp said. "Nobody's going to find out. How could they? There's nothing to find—no evidence of any kind. I backed off on her anesthesia a little, that's all. They were only keeping her sedated as a precaution—she was never in any danger. And all I did was talk to her. It was perfect."

"It was *wrong*. Can't you see that? I'm a nurse, Kemp. I know that doesn't mean anything to you, but it still means something to me. Nurses help people—we serve people—we don't use them."

"See, this is why I didn't tell you before," Kemp said. "You have no imagination—no vision."

"I have *morals*," Natalie said, "something you apparently lack. Kemp, you can't go around putting ideas in other people's heads—it's just not right."

"Why? People do it all the time—parents, teachers, politicians . . ."

"That's different. You pretended to be somebody you're not."

"So what? Suppose a man walks up to you on the street and says, 'You don't look so good—you should go to a hospital.' You'd ignore the guy—you might even think he was nuts. But suppose he was dressed like a doctor—then you might take him seriously. I just applied the same principle: A message gets

203

more attention when it comes from an authority figure. I figured, who's got more authority than an angel?"

"You need to put a stop to this—right now, before it goes any further."

"How am I supposed to do that—by admitting what I did? That's exactly what you're worried about: someone finding out."

"Kemp—find a way to stop this before it's too late."

"It's already too late, Natalie. It's a done deal. That's another reason I didn't tell you before—I knew you'd try to talk me out of it. Look at the TV. Liv Hayden is doing a week of live interviews on *Oprah*, right here in LA. There's no stopping it now."

"I don't want any part of this."

"Are you sure about that? The book comes out on Thursday, and people will start flocking to Borders and Books-a-Million to shell out $24.99 for a shiny new hardcover. The book will sell millions of copies, and I get one-third of the publisher's take. That'll be *millions*, Natalie—enough to get that place in Santa Monica; enough to buy a new car every time one runs out of gas; enough to buy Leah all the MRIs she ever needs. Babe, this is what we've been waiting for."

"That doesn't change the fact that it's wrong."

"Look, every year the state of California swindles people out of billions by encouraging them to play a lottery they can never win. Isn't that wrong? What am I doing that's so different? So some sucker wants to shell out twenty-five bucks to read a story by a has-been movie star. If he can't afford the money, he won't buy it—and if he's got twenty-five bucks to waste, I'm more than happy to take it from him. Hey, we can even throw a few bucks to the schools if it makes you feel any better—just like the lottery does."

"This is insane," she said. "I don't know what to do."

"Don't do anything, Natalie. Just pretend you don't know. Just sit tight and wait for the money to roll in. You'll feel different then."

"No, I won't. Wrong is still wrong."

"And rich is still rich. I can live with that."

"Kemp—I want to ask you something, and I need you to give me an honest answer." She searched his eyes as she asked the question. "Do you know what happened to Dr. Smithson?"

"What? Now how would I know that?"

"That's not an answer."

He paused. "I have no idea what happened to Smithson, okay? The guy's a doctor. He's got money. Who knows? Maybe he got a sudden urge to run off to Cozumel or something. He can do that if he wants to—and so can we in just a couple of months if you'll just keep your mouth shut."

205

Natalie continued to study his eyes. "You should have told me, Kemp. You should have asked me first. You've put Leah and me at risk. You know what I'm talking about—if this thing goes wrong, it'll come back on us too. You had no right to do that."

"I was thinking of you, babe. You'll see that in a few months."

"I know you, Kemp. I know what money means to you. I have a daughter to think about. I don't like pretending, and there are limits to what I'll do for you. You'd better remember that."

She got up and walked out of the room.

30

*O*prah smiled at the camera. "We're talking again today with actress Liv Hayden. As those of you who've been watching the show already know, we're broadcasting this week from Los Angeles, California. For those of you who haven't been watching the show—shame on you."

The audience loved it.

"We're talking with my good friend Liv Hayden, an Oscar-nominated actress who's playing a different kind of role these days. Liv, welcome back."

Hayden's reply was drowned out by the audience's enthusiastic applause.

"Hey, turn this up!" Kemp shouted to a waitress.

It was midafternoon and the lunch crowd had long since departed, but there were still enough lingerers in the sports bar to make it difficult to hear the flat-screen TV. Kemp could have watched the show at home, but that would have just led to another run-in with Natalie. Besides, there was something about seeing it on the big screen; it was almost like being there himself.

When the waitress increased the volume, one of the other patrons let out a groan. "C'mon, put a ball game on. I can watch *Oprah* at home on the nineteen-inch."

"You can watch a ball game anytime," Kemp replied. "This

woman has an amazing story to tell. Watch—you might learn something."

Oprah's mellow voice carried across the bar. "Liv Hayden has played a lot of roles in her life: actress, producer, model . . . Now she has another role to add to her list of accomplishments: author. This is her brand-new book, just about to be released—here, let me hold it up for you—*It's All About You*, the story of Liv's encounter with an unexpected visitor—an angel."

A moan from a skeptic across the bar. "You gotta be kidding."

"For those who don't know," Oprah said, "Liv Hayden was recently in a terrible automobile accident—an accident that left her in a coma for more than a week. While she was in that coma, an angel appeared to her night after night. The angel had a message for her—a message for all of us."

207

"Sounds like some serious drugs to me," the skeptic chided. "I took too many Darvon once—I saw angels too."

"Hold it down," Kemp shouted back. "Some of us are trying to listen."

"We all saw the news photos of the accident," Oprah said. "Your car was completely demolished, Liv—it looked like Princess Diana's. It's a miracle you survived at all."

"There are no accidents," Hayden said. "That's what the angel told me."

"Why you?" Oprah asked. "Why do you think the angel chose you to receive this message?"

Hayden made a humble shrug. "I don't feel worthy, that's for sure. I can only tell you what the angel told me: He said I was 'special' somehow—I don't know what he meant by that. He said my mind is especially 'receptive to new ideas' . . ."

Kemp grinned. "She's spiritually attuned."

"The angel said I'm 'spiritually attuned,' whatever that means."

A woman sitting at the table next to Kemp's turned and looked at him. "Hey—how did you know she'd say that?"

Kemp gave her a wink. "I must be 'spiritually attuned' too."

"What did the angel tell you?" Oprah asked. "The book doesn't come out for another two days—give us a little preview."

"The angel taught me a series of profound principles," Hayden said. "Principles that describe how life really works and how we should all live together."

"For example."

"He told me that you can't make others happy if you aren't happy yourself."

208

"What did he mean by that?"

"I think he was talking about the power of your attitude. If you're an unhappy person you project that onto others; if you're happy you project that too. I think he was saying that we don't place a high enough priority on our own happiness. We're always working out of a vacuum; we're trying to give other people what we don't possess ourselves."

The audience nodded their approval.

Hayden smiled. "He even had a cute name for this principle. He called it—"

"*Get yours first*," Kemp said.

"*—get yours first*," Hayden followed.

Half the people in the bar turned and looked at Kemp.

"Who are you?" someone asked him.

"Just a fellow seeker of truth," Kemp replied.

"*Get yours first*," Oprah repeated. "That is kind of clever."

"I think he was trying to make it memorable," Hayden said.

"Sounds like it worked. You seem to remember everything clearly even though the message came to you while you were in a coma."

"Not everything," Hayden said. "There are parts of it that are still coming back to me—I remember something new every day. The doctor told me that's not unusual—he says my brain is still recovering from the trauma."

"Did the angel speak English? Did he use actual words to communicate with you, or was it more like a telepathic kind of thing?"

"There's no way to say for sure. I couldn't speak to him, of course—I was in a coma. All I could do was stare up into that majestic face."

"Majestic," Kemp said. "Not bad."

"But however he did it, he got through to me."

"What else did the angel tell you? Give us another principle."

"The angel said we expect too much from ourselves. A size fourteen expects to be a size two overnight; a forty-year-old expects to look twenty."

Kemp predicted her next words. "We choose unattainable role models."

"He said we choose unattainable role models, and that just leads to disappointment and frustration."

Another bar patron leaned out from his chair and looked at Kemp. "How do you know all this? I thought this show was live."

"It is," Kemp said. "Live from right here in Los Angeles."

"Then how come you know?"

"Maybe I'm an angel too," Kemp said.

"Yeah, and I'm the pope."

"You never know. Stranger things have happened."

The man looked Kemp over. "I doubt it."

Hayden went on with her explanation. "The angel said we need to choose more realistic role models. Instead of focusing on some unattainable ideal, he said we should aspire to be like the people who are standing right beside us every day. Ordinary people—but people who might be just a little bit better at something than we are."

"That really is profound," Oprah said. "Did he have a clever name for this principle too?"

"Yes, he did," Hayden said. "He called it—"

"*Look at the next guy in line*," Kemp announced with a grin.

"*—look at the next guy in line*," Hayden said.

Now everyone in the bar was looking back and forth between Kemp and the flat-screen TV.

"What can I tell you?" Kemp said. "Great minds think alike."

Hayden continued. "Then the angel said something else, and this is a little bit fuzzy—I'm not sure I understand it yet. He said you need to be careful when your role model is the next guy in line, because that guy is only imitating the guy next to him. He said what you really need to ask is, 'Who's the *first* guy in line?'"

Kemp blinked. "Hey—I never said that."

"That sounds almost contradictory," Oprah said.

"I know," Hayden said. "Maybe it's some kind of paradox. What I just told you isn't even in the book—I just remembered it."

"You mean right now?"

"The whole encounter is kind of an unfolding thing for me," Hayden explained. "There are things I'm just now remembering—parts of the conversation I couldn't recall before."

"Sounds like a sequel to me," Oprah said.

The audience laughed and applauded.

"An 'unfolding thing,'" Kemp grumbled. "Unbelievable! Who does the woman think she is, anyway?" He took out a twenty and slapped it down on top of his check, then hurried for the door.

"What's the problem?" the skeptic said as he passed. "One of your psychic predictions didn't come true?"

"Kiss off, bozo."

"Now is that any way for an angel to talk?"

31

Kemp switched off the DVD player and turned to face the three men. He waited, but there was no response.

"So what?" Biederman finally said. "I don't see the problem."

Kemp did a dramatic double take. "Are you out of your mind? Didn't you hear her? Oprah asked Hayden about 'Look at the next guy in line,' and Hayden said, 'Look at the *first* guy in line.' That's not what she was supposed to say—she was supposed to say 'the *next* guy.' That's the right answer; that's what I told her to say; that's the line we wrote for her."

"I'm with Biederman," Wes said. "What's the big deal?"

"What's the big deal? She's ad-libbing, that's what—she's ignoring the script we gave her and making it up as she goes."

"I have to agree with our partners," Tino said with a shrug. "It seems like a minor departure to me."

"It's minor now, maybe, but what about later on? It's like bowling—if you set the ball down just an inch or two off track, it'll be a mile off when it reaches the pins."

"This isn't a bowling alley, McAvoy. You're getting upset over nothing."

"Nothing? It could be a catastrophe! Did you hear what she told Oprah? 'This whole encounter is kind of an unfolding thing for me.' She said, 'There are things I'm just now remembering.' Translation: 'I'm planning to make this up as I go along.'"

"She's an actress," Biederman said. "What did you expect? Liv Hayden never stuck to a screenplay in her life—her script departures are legendary in Hollywood. Writers have shot themselves because of her; directors have threatened to shoot her. Did you ever see *The Kresbach Constancy*? Liv kept changing her lines so often that Brad Pitt couldn't remember his cues—he just sat there shaking his head. They had to keep reshooting; they went over budget. Now *that* was a catastrophe."

"It's not the same thing," Kemp said. "You're talking about a memorized script; I'm talking about a message we implanted in her subconscious mind. She can't be 'just now remembering things' unless we told them to her. Where's she coming up with this stuff, anyway?"

"An actress is trained to improvise," Biederman said. "So what?"

"But this is supposed to be a message from an angel—where does she get off throwing her two cents' worth in? Moses didn't say, 'Here are the Ten Commandments—and while we're on the subject, let me throw in a couple of my own.'"

Wes frowned at him. "Is that what's eating you? She's changing *your* message? Lighten up, Kemp—you're taking this angel thing too seriously."

"That's not it at all."

"Besides, it's not your message. The three of us contributed just as much as you did. You don't see us getting upset, do you?"

"You guys don't get it," Kemp said. "We gave her a message so we could write a book. Now the book is about to come out, and she's doing interviews to promote the book. Don't you see? Her story is supposed to match the story in the book. She can't go around contradicting herself. What will people think?"

"They'll think it's an 'unfolding thing,' just like she said."

"These slight departures of hers may even be profitable," Tino added. "We've all considered the possibility of a second book; the three of us had enough trouble coming up with the first one. Ms. Hayden may be writing the second one for us. Like Oprah said: 'It sounds like a sequel to me.'"

"These 'slight departures' could be disaster," Kemp replied. "You said it yourself, Tino—we had enough trouble coming up with the first book, and there were three of us working on it. What's she going to come up with all on her own?" He looked at Biederman. "Tell the truth, Biederman. When Liv was 'improvising' on those movie scripts—was the stuff she came up with better than what the writers wrote for her? Was she improving the movie or just changing it? What if she just 'improvised' the whole thing—then what would you have had? Because that's what we're going to have if we just let her keep talking off the top of her head."

The group paused to consider this.

"What are you suggesting we do?" Wes asked.

"We need to go talk to her," Kemp said.

"No," Wes said. "*We* need to go talk to her. Not you, Kemp—remember? I want to remind you again that you can never, ever meet Liv Hayden face-to-face. Are we absolutely clear on that?"

"Fine, whatever. You and Biederman can talk to her. You're her agent, Biederman—you must have had this conversation with her before. And you, Wes—you're her publisher. You're just taking an interest in the success of the book—she can't get mad at you for that."

Biederman looked as if he had just swallowed sour milk.

"What's the problem, Biederman?"

"You're right, I have had this conversation with Olivia before—and I'm not looking forward to doing it again."

"Just tell her to stick to the script," Kemp said. "I'll give you guys a call later. I need to get back to work." He popped the DVD out of the player and headed for the door.

The three men watched Kemp until the door closed behind him.

Tino turned to the other two men. "Does Bobby seem a bit edgy to you gentlemen?"

"The book comes out tomorrow," Wes replied. "We've all been under a lot of pressure lately."

Tino smiled. "I'd like to think that accounts for it."

"Accounts for what?"

"I've known Bobby for several years. He's very intelligent, but also very foolish. He makes decisions without considering the end result—that makes him a very bad business partner."

"But we're stuck with him."

"Are we?" Tino held up the check for the waitress. "That's something to think about, now, isn't it?"

32

The elevator opened onto the rooftop pool at the Thompson Beverly Hills. Wes Kalamar and Mort Biederman stepped into the bright sun and quickly slipped on their sunglasses. The pool was a tiny rectangle of perfect turquoise surrounded by lounge chairs draped with generously oiled bodies glistening in the sun; beyond the lounge chairs was a spectacular 360-degree view of the city of Los Angeles—though no one seemed particularly interested. The pool deck was made of teak like the deck of a ship, and the white canvas sunshades that surrounded the pool looked like cocktail umbrellas in some exotic drink.

Wes nudged Biederman and pointed to the far side of the pool where a row of private cabanas stood like tents gently flapping in the breeze. In front of one of them, Liv Hayden lay stretched out, baking under the midday sun.

"Follow my lead," Biederman said. "I know how to handle her."

They worked their way around the pool deck to the cabanas. "Sweetheart," Biederman called out as they approached.

Liv rolled her head to one side and tipped her sunglasses down. "Morty. Wesley. You boys are overdressed."

"I didn't bring my swimsuit," Biederman said. "Something we should all be thankful for."

Liv turned her face back to the sun. "What's new in the world of publishing, Wes?"

"It's all good news," Wes said. "Things couldn't be better."

"That's what I like to hear. The book's on schedule then?"

"Absolutely—it hits bookstores tomorrow. Don't forget the grand opening and book signing Saturday at the Americana at Brand over in Glendale."

"Let's cancel that. I've been under a lot of stress lately."

Wes turned to Biederman with a look of panic.

"It's very important, sweetheart," Biederman said. "I wouldn't bother you with it if it wasn't. We've got a big event all planned— lots of press coverage. Think of it like a premiere."

"Send a car, will you, Morty? I'm not driving all the way to Glendale."

"Of course, sweetheart, whatever you want."

217

"Have you boys been following me on *Oprah*?"

"Every day. Wouldn't miss it."

"Be honest now—tell me how good I've been."

"You've been terrific," Biederman gushed. "I knew you'd hit it out of the park, and you haven't let me down."

"Have I ever?"

"Not in twenty years. You were personable, you were profound—you were funny too."

"I was funny, wasn't I? I think that's a new part of me."

"You're blossoming like a flower right before our eyes."

There was a brief pause here and Wes took advantage of the opportunity. "We do have one small suggestion," he said.

There seemed to be a sudden chill in the air. Liv lowered her sunglasses and stared at him.

"It's just a little thing," Wes fumbled, "so little I really hate to even mention it."

"Stop sucking up," Liv said. "That's what Morty gets paid for. What's on your mind, Wes?"

Biederman tried to intervene. "It's just a small suggestion regarding content, sweetheart. We were just thinking—"

"I'm talking to Wes. Do you mind?"

Wes swallowed hard. "Well, it's just that—"

"Spit it out. I'm losing the sun."

"It's just that the book is so perfect. The story is so beautifully crafted—the plot, the pacing, the dialogue, the transitions."

"So?"

"I hate to mess with perfection—that's all."

"What are you talking about?"

"In your interviews with Oprah—yesterday and today— you've been introducing story elements that aren't even in the book. New thoughts, new ideas—conversations with the angel you never mentioned before."

"I didn't remember them before. They're just coming back to me now. Every day I seem to wake up and remember something else. What am I supposed to tell Oprah, 'Sorry, I can't talk about that—it's not in the book'?"

Biederman took over. "We just don't want to confuse people, that's all. It's like showing a scene in a trailer that doesn't appear in the movie. People get upset—they feel cheated. They think, 'Hey, what happened? I loved that scene—that's why I bought a ticket.' Same thing here, Liv. You tell Oprah something new, something you just remembered, the viewer thinks, 'I love that—I'm gonna buy that book.' But when she buys the book, it's not in there. How's she going to feel?"

"She should feel lucky," Liv said. "It's like bonus material at the end of a DVD. She gets the book and I throw in a little something extra free of charge."

Wes tried again. "But these new things you're remembering. Sometimes they sound sort of—well—"

"What?"

"Contradictory. First the angel says one thing, then he disagrees with himself. It's like he can't make up his mind."

"Maybe he couldn't make up his mind. Maybe it's too deep—you know, one of those puzzles wrapped in a mystery inside an enigma. Something like that."

Wes finally lost patience. "We just think it might be better if you stuck to the book. Okay?"

Biederman gave Wes a quick sideways glance. "What he means is—"

"I know what he means. I speak English."

Liv got up from her lounge chair and stood face-to-face with Wes. She pulled off her sunglasses and began to study his face as if she were searching for a hair in her linguini. "You need to have a talk with your boy here, Morty—you need to tell him about me. Tell him what an actress is and what we do for a living. Tell him how we take some moron's empty words and bring them to life—how we interpret them the way *we* think they should read. Tell him how I fired three directors and divorced two husbands for committing the unforgivable sin: *overdirecting*. You tell him all that, and then maybe we'll try talking again."

Wes just stood there, blinking, trying to think of some response. Fortunately, nothing came to mind.

She looked at both men now. "Let me make something clear to you two: This is not a movie, and this is not a book—this is something that happened to me. An angel appeared to me and entrusted me with a message—can you get that through your thick heads? This is my story, and I'm not about to change it just to satisfy some anal-retentive editor. I'm a messenger, okay? My job is to pass this message on just the way I got it. Find it a little confusing? Too bad—take it up with God. And it's not about money—not this time. That's your job, and I don't want to bother with it. I have a calling here; I've got something important to do for a change, and guess what? *I like it.* Now get out of here and leave me alone."

She gave Wes one last searing stare and then snatched up her towel and charged off toward the elevator.

The two men stood staring even after the elevator doors had closed—then Biederman turned to Wes. "I think that went well," he said. "Let's ask Kemp if he's got any more bright ideas."

33

Natalie begged to be in the procedure room with her daughter during the MRI. She tried every appeal she could think of—as a nurse, as a mother, as a fellow UCLA employee—she even volunteered to undergo a strip search to prove she had no metal on her body that could damage the enormous electromagnet. But it was strictly against hospital policy, and she was politely but flatly refused and consigned to the waiting room outside.

The waiting room felt small, cramped, like everything at UCLA. Everyone said it would be so much better when they finally moved across the street to the new million-square-foot Ronald Reagan UCLA Medical Center, but until then everyone just had to squeeze in, and the MRI department was no exception. The waiting room was neat, even pleasant, but the looming walls seemed to echo and amplify Natalie's anxiety and she felt suffocated and claustrophobic. She couldn't imagine what Leah must be feeling inside the narrow tunnel of the massive magnetic resonance imaging machine. There was nothing to do in the tiny waiting room but wait—that was the worst part of all. Natalie divided her time between praying, staring at the clock, and checking her cell phone for messages. There were none.

She looked at her watch again.

Kemp knew about the MRI; he knew the day and the time. They'd been talking about it all week—at least, she had. Natalie had mentioned it every time there was a lull in the conversation just to make sure he knew. She even wrote it in big letters on the calendar on the refrigerator: MRI—THURSDAY, 3 PM. Kemp was still asleep when she left with Leah for UCLA, but she didn't wake him. Why should she have to? She had told him a dozen times, and she wasn't going to beg. He knew about the MRI and he knew what it meant to her. He knew, all right, and if he didn't bother to come it was because he just didn't care.

The door to the waiting room suddenly opened and Natalie jumped. She turned and saw Emmet's smiling face in the doorway.

"Are visitors welcome?" he asked.

Natalie let out a breath. "It's an MRI, Emmet—Leah can't have visitors."

"She's got all kinds of company in there," Emmet said. "I came to visit you."

There were two rows of chairs on opposite walls but Emmet took the seat right beside her so that their legs were almost touching. Natalie expected to be annoyed but instead felt relieved and reassured by his nearness.

"Thanks for coming," Natalie said. "It was sweet of you to think of it."

"You asked me to come," Emmet said.

Natalie blinked. "I did? I don't remember."

"Asked me plain as day."

"I guess I've had a lot on my mind lately. At least you remembered. I'm glad you did."

"Brought you a gift," Emmet said, hoisting a brightly colored bag and setting it upright on his lap.

"For me? Leah's the one who deserves a gift."

Emmet shook his head. "Let me tell you something I learned a long time ago: it's easier to suffer yourself than to watch someone you love go through it instead. Am I right or am I right?"

Natalie nodded. "I'd trade places with her in a minute if I could."

"'Course you would. That's why I figured you might need something to cheer you up a bit." He held out the bag to her and smiled.

Natalie took the bag and peeked inside, then reached in and pulled out the gift. It was a glossy hardcover book. She turned it over and looked at the cover, where huge embossed letters proclaimed, *It's All About You.*

Natalie groaned.

"Just came out today," Emmet said. "Had to wait in line to get it for you."

"It was very thoughtful of you," she said, sliding the book back into the bag.

"Have you heard about this book? It's in all the papers."

"Yes, I've heard about it."

"Olivia Hayden—she's that movie star who came in with the head injury a few weeks back. Remember her?"

"I remember."

"You'd never in a million years guess what happened to that woman right here in our hospital—right there on our floor. Seems while she was in that coma, an angel of the Lord appeared to her—stood right over her bed and spoke to her plain as day. Now how 'bout that?"

"Yeah," Natalie said. "How about that?"

"She was Mr. Kemp's patient, as I recall."

"That's right."

"I remember he took real good care of her. I noticed he spent a lot of time with her night after night."

Natalie said nothing.

"I suppose you noticed that too."

She just shrugged.

"That ever bother you?"

"Why should it?"

"Just asking. Mind if I ask you something else?"

"Go ahead."

He paused. "Do you know what an angel is?"

She glanced at him. "Excuse me?"

"An angel—do you know what that is?"

"I guess I . . . I'm not really—"

"An angel is a messenger—nothing more, nothing less. He goes where he's told to go and he says what he's told to say. He has no words of his own—he's only a messenger. That means you won't find an angel comin' up with a whole lot of nonsense—like you find in that book. Not a real angel, anyway."

Natalie could feel him watching her, but she kept her eyes fixed on the gift bag in her lap.

"I'd like to ask you something," he said softly. "It's a bit personal."

"Okay." Her voice seemed too high and the word sounded childish.

"Why does a fine woman like you share a roof with a man she doesn't love?"

Natalie turned and looked at him, and tears began to well up in her eyes. "You wouldn't understand."

"You might be surprised what I understand."

She wiped the corners of her eyes.

"Maybe you felt alone in the world," Emmet said. "Maybe

you felt old and tired and afraid about the future. Your husband didn't love you anymore, and maybe you wondered if another man ever would. Then Mr. Kemp came along; he paid attention to you; he made you feel wanted, and that felt real good. It wasn't love—you knew that—but it was the best you could find. Only now it's not enough anymore. It never was, but now you know better."

She winced. "It sounds so pathetic when you say it."

"Sounds pretty human to me. Foolish, but human—the two often go together."

Natalie watched his eyes as he spoke; they were clear and dark and as penetrating as ice picks—but there was no coldness or meanness in them. "Emmet, I want to tell you something," she blurted out, much to her own surprise—but there was something about his eyes that seemed to draw the words out of her. "That book—it's a fake."

"I know that."

"There was no angel. Kemp did it. He made the whole thing up."

"I know that too."

"You know? Then why—"

"I wanted to know if you'd tell me. I'm glad you did."

"I had nothing to do with it, Emmet—I swear it. I only found out a few days ago, and by then it was too late. I wanted to tell someone, but Kemp said if I told anyone they'd think I was part of it too."

"And he'd probably let 'em think it. The man has the conscience of a jackal."

"It would mean my job—my whole career. I have Leah to think about, especially now. I feel like such a coward. I'm so sorry, Emmet."

"Why apologize to me?"

225

"I don't know. I had to apologize to somebody. I guess I just wanted to hear you say, 'It's all right.'"

"It's not all right—but it's not your fault either."

"What should I do?"

"Well, I can tell you one thing: I'd get as far away from that man as I could if I were you—and I'd be sure and take my daughter with me."

Natalie said nothing.

"What's the matter?" Emmet asked.

"I can't pay the rent without him. I can't even pay the deductible on this MRI."

"Is that the problem here? Is that what's holdin' you back? Money?"

She didn't answer.

Emmet rested a hand on her forearm and whispered, "It's a hard thing to walk away from a man when you don't see another one on the horizon. It's hard to take the right path when you don't know where it might lead you."

"Thanks," she said. "That's not much help, but it's good advice."

"You don't need advice, Natalie—you just need a little more self-respect."

Just then the door to the procedure room opened and a nurse stepped into the waiting room. "Natalie Pelton?"

Natalie snapped to her feet. "Here."

The nurse smiled warmly. "Leah did just fine—she's a real trouper. We're just letting her rest for a few minutes—we want to let the sedative wear off a little before we release her."

"What about the MRI? Has the radiologist read it yet?"

"We sent it to the radiologist and he's already reviewed it."

"And?"

"He forwarded it on to one of our staff neurologists."

She stiffened. "Why? What's wrong?"

"The neurologist would like to see you."

"Why? Tell me!"

"I don't have that information, Ms. Pelton. You'll have to speak to the neurologist."

"All right," she stammered. "I'll make an appointment for next week."

The nurse put a hand on her shoulder. "No, Ms. Pelton—now."

34

"Welcome back on this fine Thursday," Oprah said as the applause died down and the camera moved in for a tight shot of the host and her guest. "This is our fourth conversation with writer and movie star Liv Hayden, author of the new book *It's All About You*. Liv, thanks for joining us again."

"It's a privilege, really," Hayden said. Then she turned to the audience and asked, "Is this a wonderful woman or what?"

The audience poured out their appreciation.

Kemp aimed the remote at the TV and turned up the volume a little. He took a quick glance at his watch—what time was that MRI again? Three, three thirty, something like that . . . He had time to catch part of the show. Shoot, they'd probably have to spend at least an hour filling out paperwork and insurance forms anyway—no sense rushing over there just to sit like a lump in some waiting room. Sure, he could TiVo the show and watch it later, but when? Not when Natalie was around—that would just lead to another fight, and he didn't need the grief right now. Besides, the show was live; his brilliant plan was coming to fruition right before his eyes, and he deserved the chance to watch it happen in real time.

He settled back on the sofa.

Oprah looked out at the audience. "Folks, Liv Hayden's colossal new book *It's All About You* was just released today—it's officially in bookstores right now. Liv, do you think you're ready?"

"I think so. We're doing a big book signing over at the—"

"I mean are you ready for the new platform? Are you ready for the influence?"

"I'm not really sure," Hayden admitted humbly. "It feels like such an awesome responsibility. I didn't ask to be a messenger—I didn't want this role—it was just given to me."

"And I'm the one who gave it to you," Kemp said to the TV. "So why don't you just stick to the message the way I wrote it?"

"Tell us what else we can expect from the book," Oprah said. "What else did the angel say to you? Come on, Liv—whet our appetites."

Hayden wiggled her eyebrows. "Well—we talked about love."

Someone shouted "Woo!" from the back of the audience and a wave of eager laughter rippled across the studio.

Kemp sat up a little straighter.

"You're kidding," Oprah said. "An angel talked with you about your love life?"

"About my lack of a love life," Hayden corrected.

"Excuse me? You're Liv Hayden—you've had more men than any three women I know."

"Quantity isn't quality," Hayden said. "I think the angel knew that. He told me I was lonely."

"Are you?"

"At the risk of sounding pathetic—yes, I'll admit it. I've

been busy—my film career has demanded my complete attention for years. A career can be hard on relationships."

"I know something about that," Oprah said.

So did the audience—they applauded in agreement.

"The angel told me that I've been searching for a special man all my life, but I haven't found him yet. He told me he would help me find him."

Encouraging applause from the crowd.

Kemp grinned. "Don't thank me, ladies—it's the least I can do."

"Did the angel tell you how you'll recognize this man when you meet him?"

"As a matter of fact, he did. The angel told me exactly what he looks like—he even told me what he'll say."

Oprah leaned closer.

Hayden shook her head. "And that's all I'm going to tell you."

The audience let out a disappointed groan.

Hayden turned to the audience. "C'mon now—if I describe this man on national television, I'll have every look-alike in America knocking on my door. I don't need that kind of distraction; I have to find this guy."

"Do you want to find him? Are you ready for a new relationship?"

"I think it's time," Hayden said. "There's only so much a career can give you. Besides, the angel said this will be the perfect man for me—my one true love. How often does a girl get a tip like that?"

Kemp was grinning from ear to ear. It was perfect—everything he had told her was locked into her memory, right down to the description and password. *You beautiful genius*, he said to himself. He was a true visionary—that's what set him apart from the other partners. The other three couldn't see past Hayden's money; Kemp was the only one clever enough to realize that he could have Hayden herself.

"I understand," Oprah said, "so I won't press you for any more details. Good luck finding this perfect man, Liv—you deserve him. Okay, let's change the subject. What else did the angel tell you—when you weren't discussing your love life, that is?"

"Well—he told me that it's very important to love yourself."

"Good girl," Kemp said. "That was in the script—keep going."

"The angel said that by loving yourself, you demonstrate to other people that you're a lovable person. In some mysterious way, by loving yourself you give other people permission to love you."

The audience responded with a solemn "Hmmm."

Kemp nodded with satisfaction. "Almost verbatim—now that's more like it."

Then Hayden looked thoughtfully into the air above Oprah's head. "But now that I think about it, there was something else."

Kemp stiffened.

"The angel said that it actually works the other way around. He said that when someone loves you, it proves to you that you're lovable—and that frees you to love someone else. He said that the more you feel loved, the more loving you become."

Kemp jumped to his feet. He hurled a sofa pillow at the TV and knocked a potted philodendron to the floor with a crash. "There you go again! Stop ad-libbing, woman! Just tell it the way I told you!"

231

Oprah paused. "That sounds like another one of those paradoxes."

"You're right," Hayden said, "it does."

"*She's* the paradox!" Kemp shouted. "She's supposed to be an actress, but she's got a memory like a third grader at a spelling bee!"

"You know," Oprah said, "those thoughts seem so different that they almost sound like two voices."

"It's funny you should mention that," Hayden said. "There was a second voice."

Kemp's jaw dropped.

"I just remembered something this morning, and I wasn't sure I should tell anyone."

"Remembered what?" Oprah asked.

232

Kemp sank back down on the sofa. "Yeah—remembered what?"

"It just came back to me—there was a second angel."

Oprah blinked at her. "*Two* angels?"

"Oh no," Kemp moaned. "What now?"

"There were two of them," Hayden said. "It was all jumbled together at first, but now it's becoming clear to me. It was just one voice at first; then there were two voices; then two faces."

Kemp shook his head in disbelief. "Where's she going with this?"

"Did the voices sound different?" Oprah asked.

"One of them sounded deeper, I think."

"Older, maybe?"

"Maybe. I'm not sure."

"Are angels different ages?" Oprah looked at the audience for an answer, but no one seemed to have one.

"I don't know," Hayden said. "I never thought about it before."

"What about their faces?"

"I couldn't see them clearly. They were mostly silhouettes—it was like staring into the sun. But I did notice one thing."

"What's that?"

"One of them was white—the other one was black."

35

mmet returned the mop to the wall hook and draped his pair of yellow rubber gloves over the edge of the pail. All of a sudden the custodian's closet grew dark and he heard the door click shut behind him. He turned in the darkness and looked down at the floor; he could see the silhouette of two shoes dividing the sliver of light below the door into a dash-dot-dash. A moment later there was the click of a light switch and a single overhead bulb illuminated the face of a very angry man.

"You," the man growled in a guttural tone.

"Mr. Kemp," Emmet said. "We got to stop meeting like this, you and me. Folks will start to talk."

"It was you, wasn't it?"

"Beg pardon?"

"The second angel—the black one—it was you. It had to be."

Emmet slowly smiled.

"How dare you," Kemp sputtered. "You had no right to go poking your nose where it didn't belong."

"Talk about the pot calling the kettle black," Emmet said.

"I had a plan. You weren't part of it."

"Seems to me that movie star could say the same to you."

"You knew what I was doing, didn't you? You figured it

out that night when you walked in on me. When I upped her medication again—when I went on my break to let it take effect—you came in after I left. You put on the white gown— you stood in front of the light—you put your own two cents' worth in before she had time to go back into her coma. I'll bet you did it every night."

"I thought the woman could use a second opinion. It's a hospital, after all."

"You idiot! Do you have any idea what you've done?"

"I believe I do. Do you?"

"My plan was perfect and you almost ruined it."

"You call that 'perfect'? Feeding the woman a lot of non-sense and makin' her believe a messenger of the Lord told it to her?"

"Nobody asked you."

"Nobody asked you either, but you jumped right in feet-first—so I did too."

"You sly old fox," Kemp said. "Wandering around the ICU night after night, pushing your little mop and bucket like a doddering old fool, pretending to be just some half-wit trying to make enough money for bus fare back to East LA."

"Pushing a mop and bucket is what I do," Emmet said. "It's honest work, and that's nothing to be ashamed of—you should try it sometime. And as for 'pretending to be a half-wit,' I did no such thing. You thought me a half-wit because of my age and my job—maybe even the color of my skin. That makes you the half-wit in my book."

Kemp shook his head in disgust. "A *janitor*. Who would have thought?"

"You're confusing what a man *is* with what a man *does*— big mistake, Mr. Kemp. You don't know me; you don't know who I am or where I'm from or what I can do."

"I guess I underestimated you."

"You looked right through me, that's what you did. Happens to folks like me all the time—the invisible man."

"Believe me, it won't happen again."

"We'll see."

Kemp looked him over carefully. "What is it you want, old man?"

"No more than I'm entitled to."

"You're not entitled to anything."

"I don't see it that way. We both gave that woman a message; you just figured out a way to get that message published. The way I see it, part of that message belongs to me."

"But the whole thing was my idea."

"Take your idea to the bank and see if they'll cash it for you. Folks will be payin' for the message, not for your bright idea. Half that message is mine."

"Half? Are you kidding? Hayden barely even remembers you. She's been on *Oprah* for four days, and she just mentioned you for the first time."

"Give the woman time. It'll come back to her."

"Besides, your message didn't even make it into the book, and the book is where the money comes from. Why should we pay you?"

Emmet arched one eyebrow. "'We'?"

Kemp hesitated. "The partners."

"I wondered about that. I didn't think you could manage to pull off something like this all by yourself. Tell me, who are these partners of yours—or should I say, 'partners of ours'?"

"They're my partners, and it's none of your business."

"I say it is."

"How much do you want, Emmet? I figure five percent tops, maybe less when you consider—"

"I was thinkin' half."

Kemp's mouth dropped open. "Are you out of your mind? There's no way on earth you're getting half!"

"Seems fair to me. Maybe I was too late to make it into the first book, but everything I told Ms. Hayden'll make it into the next one—the 'sequel' I think they call it. Think it over, Mr. Kemp: I did you and your partners a big favor. You gave her enough for one book, but I gave her enough for another—and that one's bound to make even more money than the first. I think that's worth half, don't you?"

"Look—you can't—there's no way—"

"There's no point in arguing with you. I want to talk to the partners—all of them."

"The partners? Why?"

"Because you don't negotiate with a middleman—that's a waste of time."

"I'm not a 'middleman.'"

"Are you the one who writes the checks?"

Kemp didn't reply.

Emmet nodded. "I want to talk to the partners."

"Well, they don't want to talk to you," Kemp said.

"Yes, they do—they just don't know it yet. When they find out who I am—that I know what you did and I know how you did it—they'll talk to me. They'll talk to me because they want to keep me happy—'cause if I'm not happy, I just might tell somebody what I know."

"Is that a threat?"

"I'm just negotiating—that's what you wanted, isn't it? 'Negotiating' just means making sure everybody's happy. You want me to be happy, don't you, Mr. Kemp? Then let me talk to your partners—we'll work out something that'll make all of us happy. I promise."

"What if I refuse?"

"Then I won't be happy. You don't want that."

"What if they refuse to meet with you?"

"Why take that chance? Let's surprise 'em. They might not like the idea at first, but once we all have a chance to sit down and talk, I'm sure we'll get along just fine."

Kemp paused. "When?"

"The sooner the better. Tonight works for me."

"Tonight? Impossible."

"The sooner the better, Mr. Kemp—once your boys hear what I have to say, I think they'll agree. Why not give 'em a call? Tell 'em you got some emergency. Just make somethin' up—you're good at that. The sooner we get this thing worked out, the sooner we can all rest easy."

Kemp stared at the wall above Emmet's head . . .

"Well?"

"Take your lunch break at one," Kemp said. "Meet me in the lobby."

"I'll be there," Emmet said. "You know, I believe I feel happier already."

36

*I*t was just after one a.m. when Kemp and Emmet stepped into O'Hara's Bar on Gayley Avenue in the heart of Westwood Village, just three blocks south of UCLA Medical Center. The bouncer at the door let them pass without a second look; he was busy explaining the legal drinking age to a belligerent young man with a phony ID. When the door opened, blinding neon light from the Fox Theater across the street poured into the room ahead of them. The bar was impossibly crowded despite the late hour, with UCLA students jammed around every table and packing every corner. The ceiling seemed low and the room looked dingy and worn. The walls were covered with black-framed photographs of famous patrons and celebrities and UCLA luminaries from years past, and a dozen plasma-screen TVs presented obscure sporting events from all over the globe. The noise was almost overwhelming—a deafening din of laughter and catcalls accompanied by a sound track of classic rock anthems and forgettable '80s tunes. No one in the bar seemed to mind the noise. No one noticed anything beyond their immediate circle of friends—so no one noticed as Kemp and Emmet worked their way toward a table where three other older men were already seated.

Emmet leaned over to Kemp. "It smells like feet in here."

"College bar," Kemp shouted back. "They always do."

Biederman, Wes, and Tino Gambatti sat at a table in the corner of the room. They seemed to hunch over the table slightly, as if they were huddling around a campfire for warmth. They all looked at Kemp as he approached the table—then all eyes immediately shifted to Emmet.

No one said a word.

"Guys, this is Emmet," Kemp said simply.

Emmet nodded a polite greeting but offered no explanation for his presence; he simply pulled out a chair and sat down. Kemp did the same.

All three men turned to Kemp for an explanation, but Kemp was busy trying to get the attention of a waitress.

Biederman tried to ignore the old man. "Is this your idea of a meeting place, McAvoy?"

240

"I don't have much time," Kemp said. "This place is walking distance from the Med Center. It's one of the only places in Westwood open this late."

"My shoes are sticking to the floor."

"O'Hara's is a Bruins hangout. All the kids come here."

"I can see that." Biederman turned and looked behind him; a young woman was dancing enthusiastically, though no one seemed to be dancing with her.

"We can talk here," Kemp said. "There's less chance of being overheard than there is on the street."

"I believe you," Biederman said. "I can't even hear myself."

An attractive young waitress sidled up to their table and set a check down in front of Kemp. "Hey, fellas, how you doing tonight? What can I bring you?"

"What's good?" Kemp asked for the group.

"We've got Miller Lite on the cheap tonight—eight bucks for two liters. The Irish nachos are good too—great combination."

"It was a great combination forty years ago," Biederman replied. "Today it would eat through my stomach like battery acid. Can I get a glass of white wine, sweetheart?"

She grinned. "You're kidding, right?"

"Just bring us some beer and glasses," Kemp said. "Clean ones if you've got any."

The waitress winked and waded back into the sea of bodies.

Wes finally addressed the issue of the unexpected visitor. "Who's your friend, Kemp? When you called this emergency meeting, I assumed it would be private. No offense, sir."

"None taken," Emmet said. "You must be Mr. Kalamar, since you're the youngest of the three. That would make you the publisher."

Wes didn't reply.

Emmet turned to Biederman. "And you must be Mr. Biederman—the talent agent, Mr. Kemp said. Is that right?"

Biederman just looked at Kemp.

Last of all Emmet turned to Tino, who had said nothing so far. "That would make you the man from Baltimore—Mr. Gambatti, is it? The investor—the man with the pocketbook."

Tino kept his eyes fixed coldly on Emmet. "That's odd. You seem to know all about us, but we don't know anything about you."

Wes glared at Kemp. "You know, this is the second time you've expanded our membership without asking us."

"I can explain," Kemp said. "Emmet works at the hospital—on the same floor I do. He's not a nurse, he's just a janitor. A couple of weeks ago, when we were working on—you know—our little project? Well, Emmet happened to—he sort of—"

"I walked in on him," Emmet said with a smile. "A man pretending to be an angel—never saw anything like it in all my born days. I remember seeing you a few days later, Mr. Biederman, come to pay a visit the moment that poor woman came out of her coma. Right nice of you, I remember thinking. A soul needs a friend at a moment like that—someone to lend a guiding hand when your mind is all muddy and confused."

Biederman looked as if he'd swallowed those Irish nachos.

Emmet turned to Wes now. "And you, Mr. Kalamar. What a lucky man you must be—blessed, I'd call it. I heard about the new book coming out, and in record time—almost like you wrote it before it even happened."

Wes opened his mouth to speak, but nothing came out.

Emmet looked at Tino last of all. "And Mr. Gambatti—I don't know exactly what part you play in all this, but you sure know a good investment when you see one. Hookin' up with these three—what a bargain that was."

"Emmet's the second angel," Kemp explained. "You know, the black one—the one Liv Hayden told Oprah about this afternoon. Hayden wasn't just making it up, guys. Emmet figured out what we were doing—he came into Hayden's room each night after I was finished and before she went back into her coma. He—he sort of—"

"I threw in a few thoughts of my own," Emmet said. "Sort of a closing comment, you might say—a different take on things."

Wes Kalamar looked at him indignantly. "You did *what*? Who do you think you are?"

"Beg pardon?"

"Are you a writer? Have you ever published anything? Do you have any concept of character development or plot or pacing? Do you have any idea how to—"

Emmet interrupted. "Can you tell me how to get to Valencia?"

242

"What?"

"Valencia—can you give me directions?"

"No," Wes stammered. "I've never been to Valencia."

"Then I best get directions elsewhere," Emmet said. "You don't give directions to a place you never been."

"We're wasting time," Kemp said. "The point is, he *knows*—and he wanted to meet with all of you right away."

Tino glared at Kemp. "And you agreed."

"I had no choice—he threatened to tell if I didn't. What difference does it make? He knows—he figured it out."

"He figured it out. All by himself."

"That's right."

"Did he figure out our names all by himself?"

Kemp just stared.

Emmet leaned across the table. "Mr. Kemp was nice enough to brief me on your names earlier this evening—just so's I'd know who's who."

"That was very thoughtful of him—and very bad for us."

"What's the difference?" Kemp said impatiently. "He knows!"

Tino slowly shook his head. "Bobby, you are a very stupid man."

"Huh?"

"Why do you think this man wanted to meet the rest of us? Because he only knew about your involvement; he didn't know about the rest of us until you told him. If he had tried to blackmail you, I could have easily killed him—after all, he could only have exposed you, and why would I care about that? But thanks to your stupidity, now he can expose all of us. You've practically made him a partner, you fool."

Kemp looked at Emmet.

Emmet nodded. "That's about the size of it."

243

Kemp tried his best to drum up some justification for his actions but could think of nothing.

Tino ignored him and focused on Emmet instead. "Why did you want to meet with us, old man?"

Emmet cleared his throat. "First of all, I wanted the chance to say to each and every one of you: shame on you."

"Excuse me?"

"Shame on you—shame on each of you—for taking advantage of a poor young woman, and for putting words in the mouth of the Almighty. You ought to be ashamed—and fearful too, though I imagine you're all too thickheaded to know it."

"That's all you wanted? To slap our hands?"

Emmet paused. "No. I want in."

Tino smiled. "Of course you do. Why should a little shame cause you to miss out on a business opportunity like this?"

"I like to think some good can still come from all this," Emmet said.

"Why not? A new car, maybe—or a couple of weeks in Vegas."

"The point is, I know who you are and I know your whole plan, and that makes me practically a partner—you said it yourself. Like it or not, a part of this 'message' belongs to me—and I think that entitles me to something. Fair is fair."

"And what do you consider fair—exactly?"

"I'm a reasonable man with reasonable needs. I been thinkin' it over. I don't want to make it too hard on you boys. I was thinking maybe . . . ten thousand dollars."

Kemp looked at him in disbelief. "Ten *thousand*? Is that all you—"

Tino quickly held up a hand and silenced him. "Ten thousand dollars," he said. "That's a lot of money."

Emmet shrugged. "Fair is fair."

At that moment Kemp's pager went off; he unclipped it from his belt and checked it. "It's an emergency code," he said. "I have to get back."

"You go on ahead," Emmet told him. "I'm sure the four of us can wrap things up without you. You go on—they need you at the hospital. I can fill you in later."

Kemp looked around the table and slowly got up from his chair. "I'll go with whatever you guys decide," he said.

Tino nodded. "Yes, you will."

Kemp quickly disappeared into the crowd.

Emmet watched until he saw the door open and close again—then he turned back to the rest of the partners. "Now down to business," he said. "I want one million dollars—not a penny less."

Biederman stared at him in astonishment. "A *million dollars*? What happened to ten thousand? Did I miss something?"

"I think you boys know I just said that for Mr. Kemp's sake. He never would have left without some kind of offer on the table. I figured ten thousand would be just little enough to set his mind at ease."

"It set my mind at ease too," Wes said. "What's this nonsense about a million dollars?"

"I want a cashier's check," Emmet said. "Make it out to cash."

Tino nodded admiringly. "Bobby didn't really have to go back to the hospital, did he?"

"You mean Mr. Kemp? Is that his real name?"

"That's right—Bobby Foscoe."

"I can see why he changed it. I wouldn't do that to a dog."

"Did you arrange the page?"

Emmet nodded once. "Thought it might give the rest of us a chance to talk business."

"Fair enough. What's on your mind?"

"I told you—a million dollars."

"In exchange for what?"

"The chance to keep doin' what you're doin'—that's about all, really. See, when Mr. Kemp told me your names this evening, I wrote 'em all down right away—I wrote down everything I saw and what I figure each of you did. I dropped that letter in a mailbox on the way down here—addressed it to a lawyer friend of mine. I told him that if anything should happen to me, he should mail that letter to the police."

"That was good thinking," Tino said.

"But a million dollars is out of the question," Wes complained. "You have to be reasonable. The book's barely out—there's no revenue yet. There's no way on earth we can—"

"When do you want it?" Tino asked Emmet.

"Saturday morning," Emmet said calmly. "That'll give you all day tomorrow."

"I appreciate that. Where? When?"

"The lobby of UCLA Medical Center. My shift ends around seven; I like to tidy up a bit and grab a bite in the cafeteria. Meet me about nine."

"Done."

Wes and Biederman sat frozen in their chairs.

"You—you just gave away a million dollars," Wes said.

"A million dollars of *our money*," Biederman added.

Emmet shook his head. "Mr. Kemp's money."

"What?"

"Why should you boys be out a million dollars? This is all Mr. Kemp's fault—why shouldn't he pick up the check?"

Tino smiled.

"I think Mr. Gambatti here already had that figured out," Emmet said. "That's why he's sittin' there grinnin' like an old tomcat. He's not out a million dollars—neither are you boys. Mr. Kemp is."

"How do we explain that to Kemp?" Wes asked.

"We don't," Tino said. "We just tell him: his mistake, his money. Fair is fair—isn't that right, Emmet?"

"It is in my book. We have an understanding, then?"

"We do—but there's something I want you to understand."

"What's that?"

"I'll meet you in the lobby—I'll bring your money—but after that I don't expect to see you again. Don't come back to us in six months and tell us your 'reasonable needs' have increased. That would make me very, very upset. Do we understand each other?"

Emmet nodded.

"You're a very smart man, Emmet. It was a pleasure doing business with you—though I doubt Bobby will feel the same. You know, I believe you're about as clever as your friend is stupid."

"He's not my friend," Emmet said.

"He's not mine either. You can pick your friends, but you can't always pick the people you have to do business with."

"True enough." Emmet rose from his chair and took a last look at each of the men. "Shame on you all," he said again.

"Shame on all of us," Tino replied.

Emmet squeezed between two students and vanished into the crowd.

247

37

*N*atalie sat on the edge of Leah's bed and gently stroked the hair back from her eyes. It was almost eight in the morning; she had stopped in to check on her daughter hours ago and never left. In the half-light of the bedroom Leah's face looked pale and wan; Natalie held the back of her hand up to Leah's nose and mouth to feel the reassuring warmth of her breath. *Six years old*, she thought. *It's not fair—no one should have to go through what she's been through when you're only six years old. The shouting, the fighting, the stupid and senseless divorce—and now this. It's just not fair.*

She looked at the side of Leah's head and wondered what it would look like without hair; she imagined the horseshoe-shaped scar where the plate of bone would be removed to allow the surgeon access to her brain. She wondered if Leah would need radiation; she wondered if the hair would ever grow back on that spot. *What's wrong with me? My daughter has a tumor that could take her life, and I'm worried about whether she'll have pretty hair. It's not important*, she told herself. *It just doesn't matter.*

But somehow it did.

She heard the doorknob slowly turn and heard the hinges make a shrill squeak; she turned just in time to see Kemp poke his head into the room. When he opened his mouth to speak, she quickly raised one stern finger to her lips, then eased her aching body from the bed and followed Kemp into the hallway. She quietly closed the door behind her.

"I just got home," Kemp said. "I couldn't find you. I looked everywhere."

"It's a two-bedroom house," Natalie said. "How hard did you have to look?"

"Sounds like somebody had a bad night."

Natalie glared at him. "Leah had her MRI yesterday—or don't you remember?"

"Yeah, sorry I couldn't make it. I was about to, but something came up last minute. How'd it go?"

"Fine. Thank you for your interest."

"C'mon, it was just an MRI. No big deal."

"Not to you, maybe. We work in a hospital, Kemp; we're immune to all this stuff—all the needles and drugs and equipment. Leah is six years old—can you even remember that far back? She was afraid of the machine; they had to place an IV to sedate her a little. The nurse couldn't find the vein in the back of her hand—it took her three tries. Leah was in tears."

"You're a nurse—you could have done better than that. Why didn't you do it yourself?"

"Because I don't like to cause my daughter pain. Does that make any sense to you at all?"

"Not much. If you could do it on the first try, that's less pain for Leah."

"I didn't expect you to understand. I never expect you to understand anymore."

"Pardon me for making a practical suggestion."

"I don't want practical suggestions—I wanted you to be there. I wanted you to sit beside me and hold my hand and tell me everything would be all right."

"What good would that do?"

"If you don't know the answer to that, you'll never understand anything."

"Look, I didn't know this was so important to you. Why didn't you tell me?"

"I shouldn't have to tell you. You should have known."

"I don't read minds, Natalie."

"Is that what I'm asking you to do—read my mind? Do you have to be a mind reader just to notice when I'm worried or anxious or afraid?"

"Okay, okay."

"Why didn't you come yesterday?"

"I told you, something came up last minute—I've got a lot going on right now."

"Your 'business deal.'"

"*Our* business deal."

"The one that's going to save us from all our problems."

"Wait and see."

"You know, Kemp, I'm trying to believe you. I'm desperately trying to believe that all these extra hours and time away from me and Leah are because you're trying to provide for our family—and not just because you're a selfish, heartless jerk."

"Now wait just a—"

"She has a tumor."

"What?"

"Leah has a brain tumor. Her MRI showed a grape-sized tumor in the hippocampus of her brain. It's putting pressure on the medial temporal lobe—they think it's creating a condition called temporal lobe epilepsy."

"Epilepsy? But she's never had a seizure."

"Maybe she has. They call them simple partial seizures—they don't affect consciousness. The neurologist thinks that might be why Leah's been seeing angels; people with temporal lobe epilepsy sometimes experience paranormal sensations. They sometimes see bright lights or hear voices; it's possible they could even see angels."

"So what's the prognosis?"

"I talked to a neurosurgeon right after the MRI—he says the tumor's operable, but it needs to come out right away. He can't tell if it's malignant until he removes it and they do a biopsy."

"Wow, that's tough. Babe, I'm so sorry." Kemp wrapped his arms around her and pulled her in close.

Natalie rested her hands lightly on his hips. "Her surgery is Saturday."

Kemp pulled away and looked at her. "Tomorrow? What time tomorrow?"

Natalie gave him a smoldering look. "Why?"

"I've got this thing. It's part of that deal."

"Change it. Reschedule. Cancel."

"I can't. It's important."

"It's *important*," Natalie repeated slowly.

"Look, you have to understand—"

"No—I *don't* have to understand. I spent the whole afternoon imagining what you might say when I told you this news, and there's only one thing I wanted to hear: 'Of course I'll be there, sweetheart—nothing on earth could keep me away.' That's what I wanted to hear from you, Kemp. That's the only acceptable response—nothing else even comes close."

"What time is her surgery tomorrow? Maybe I can squeeze it in."

"Forget it. I don't want to be 'squeezed in' to your precious schedule. Just once I was hoping to hear that Leah and I would come first—that you'd drop everything else to be there for us. I should have known better. Get out."

251

"What?"

"Get out—right now. Take everything you can cram into that ridiculous car of yours, then come back and get the rest. I want you and everything you own out of this house by the end of the day."

"Where am I supposed to sleep?"

"Where have you been sleeping? Start packing—right now. If I come back from that surgery tomorrow and find anything of yours left in this house, I swear I'll take it out in the front yard, soak it with gasoline, and set it on fire."

"Calm down, babe. Let's not get crazy here."

"I'm way past crazy, Kemp—I'm fed up and I'm terrified. My daughter could die, and she's the only thing I have in this world. I sure don't have you; I must have been out of my mind to ever think I did."

"This is nuts! You're letting your emotions get the best of you. Tomorrow is the kickoff of this whole deal—it's like opening day for a new business. I can't miss that—there's no way. I can't help it if both things happen to take place on the same day. I didn't schedule Leah's surgery, you did—if you'd bothered to check with me first we might have avoided this whole thing."

"Are you going to start packing or do I start throwing stuff out onto the sidewalk?"

"You're out of your mind! You're out of your freaking mind!" Kemp stormed into their bedroom and slammed the door behind him.

Natalie placed two fingers on her left carotid and felt; it was pulsing like a fire hose. She opened Leah's door a crack to look in on her; somehow the poor thing had managed to sleep through the entire argument—or at least pretended to. *No more*, Natalie swore to herself. *No more shouting matches in front of my daughter. No more men who love money more than family—no more men who love themselves more than they love us. No more, Natalie. Never again.*

She went to the kitchen and opened the refrigerator; she found a half-empty bottle of cranberry juice cocktail and took it out. She checked the pantry, hoping to find something stronger to add to it, but found nothing. She poured herself a cup of coffee instead and sat down at the table; she lifted the cup with trembling hands.

A few minutes later Kemp walked quietly into the kitchen and leaned against the counter. "I'm sorry," he said.

She shook her head. "Too late."

"I know that. I'm not asking you to forgive me. I'll move out, like you said. I just wanted to tell you something."

She just stared down at her cup.

"This deal I've been working on—it really was for both of us. And it still is—that's what I wanted to tell you. Even though you're kicking me out, I won't back out on you. A promise is a promise. You and Leah need this money, and I'll make sure you get it."

Natalie slowly turned and looked at him. "Why, you miserable little weasel."

"What?"

"I know what you're doing. You told me what you did to Liv Hayden, and now you're worried—if I kick you out, what's to keep me from turning you in? I could do it too—I could tell the authorities that I just found out what you did and that's why I threw you out. The only guarantee you have that I won't tell is if I take money from you—then I'm part of it too."

"Why do you have to twist everything? I try to do something nice for you and—"

"Forget it, Kemp. I don't want your money."

"Be reasonable, Natalie. You don't even earn enough to pay the rent by yourself."

"Leah and I will get by somehow—we always have. And as for turning you in, well—you'll just have to wonder. There's no telling what I might do in the mood I'm in."

"That would be a big mistake," Kemp said.

"It wouldn't be the first one I've made with you. Now—don't you have some packing to do?"

38

The three men quietly sipped their afternoon coffees around an outdoor table at the Starbucks on North Robertson in Beverly Hills. Wes Kalamar had ordered a triple caramel macchiato, while the more senior Mort Biederman made a calorie-conscious selection: coffee, black, no sugar. Tino sipped an espresso from a tiny porcelain cup; when he lifted the cup his gold-ringed pinky finger pointed into the air like a cell phone antenna.

"This place sure beats O'Hara's," Wes said. "What a bad choice that was."

"There's less vomiting," Biederman said. "It improves the ambience."

"Speaking of bad choices, where's Kemp this morning? Doesn't he get off at seven? He's late."

"He isn't coming," Tino said. "I didn't invite him."

"Why not?"

"Because I think it's time the three of us had a talk—privately." He pulled an envelope from his blazer pocket and laid it on the table.

"What's that?"

"A cashier's check for a million dollars—I'll be dropping it off to our friend at UCLA tomorrow morning. Take a look if you like; you don't see a check that big very often."

Biederman slipped two fingers into the envelope and peeked inside. "How in the world did you manage to come up with a million in just twelve hours?"

"I made a few calls. I know people."

Wes lowered his voice. "Do you think we can trust that Emmet character?"

"Of course not. But he won't tell."

"How do you know?"

"Because he's smart and he knows when he should be satisfied—unlike Bobby. Forget the old man—he's not our problem. Bobby is our problem."

"What do you mean?"

"Bobby has become more of a liability than an asset to us. He's undisciplined; he has no mind for business; he doesn't think through the consequences of his actions. Now he's put the rest of us at risk. We need to do something about that."

"What can we do?"

"We can let him go."

"You mean . . . *fire* him?"

"The man who starts a business is not necessarily the best qualified to run it. Bobby's entire contribution to this venture was on the front end—he possessed technical expertise. He's like a man who constructs a factory for you; once the factory is completed, you send him on his way. You don't keep him on to run the operation—that's not his gift."

"But this whole thing was his idea."

"The sources who loaned me that million will want their money back—with substantial interest—and they will not accept excuses or delays. I obtained this money at great personal risk because we had no choice and because I believe in the profitability of our venture. But I am now at risk; *we* are now at risk. Do you understand what I'm telling you?"

Both men nodded.

"Bobby owes me a great deal of money already, and he's been very poor about repaying his debts in the past. Have you seen his new car? Bobby loves the good life; at the rate he's going he'll probably spend his entire portion of the profits before he's even earned them. The three of us will have to do better; we need to do whatever we can to ensure timely repayment of our debt."

"What do you suggest?"

"Bobby owns a one-third interest in this business venture of ours. I think it might be time for the three of us to redistribute our capital."

"You mean—cut him out?"

"Yes."

"And what happens to his third?" Biederman asked.

"First it will go to repay our two-million-dollar debt; after that it will go to repay what Bobby owes me."

"*Two* million? You only borrowed one to pay off the old man."

"Interest, gentlemen. You don't get a million dollars overnight for nothing."

"Wow," Wes whispered, and a long silence followed. Then: "Okay, two million plus Kemp's debt to you. But after we pay off the debt—what happens to the rest of Kemp's third?"

"It belongs to me."

"But that could be millions more," Wes said. "Why should we just hand it over to you?"

"Because you owe me." He picked up the envelope. "If I tear up this check, you'll both go to prison."

"So will you."

"Exactly. We're in this together now, and that makes me more than just an investor—that makes me a full partner. I'm taking my share of the risk; I want my share of the rewards."

"But a *third*?"

"*Bobby's* third. Bobby has added a great deal of unnecessary expense to this venture; shouldn't he bear that burden alone? Why should we split the remaining profits four ways when we can split three?"

"But—what will Kemp say?"

"It doesn't matter."

"But there's no telling what he might do."

"Yes—that is a problem."

"But how will you tell him? What will you say?"

"I'll stop by his house and have a talk with him. You two have so much on your plates already—you don't need another problem right now. Let me worry about Bobby. As our angel would say—*forget about it.*"

39

*H*ey, Charlie, have you got a minute?"

Charles Armantrout looked up from his desk to find Matt Callahan standing in his office doorway. He turned around to his window and parted the venetian blinds that he always kept shut to keep the afternoon sun from turning his tiny office into an oven; he saw the thinning carpool line and the last of the children slinging backpacks into cars that quickly and silently pulled away. "School's out already? How time flies when you're having fun."

Matt pulled out a chair and sat down. "I get the feeling you're not too crazy about this job."

"You have to be a little crazy to take a job like this," Armantrout replied. "The work is menial, the hours are impossible, and the pay is downright insulting."

"Then why did you take it?"

Armantrout sank a little lower in his chair. "I have a bachelor's in psychology. Need I say more?"

"My undergrad's in philosophy. Tell me about it."

"So you're stuck here too."

"Not me—I always wanted to be a teacher."

Armantrout looked bewildered. "You're pulling my leg, right?"

"Nope. I had a couple of teachers who made a big impact

on my life. I wanted the chance to do the same for someone else."

"And the hours? The pay?"

Matt shrugged. "Some jobs you do because you love them. Some jobs are just worth doing."

"An idealist," Armantrout said. "What's that old saying? 'If you're not an idealist when you're twenty, you have no heart. If you're still an idealist when you're forty, you have no mind.'"

Matt smiled. "I take it you're not an idealist then."

Armantrout groaned. "I lost my illusions a long time ago, thank you very much. I consider myself a realist."

"A 'realist,'" Matt said. "What does that mean exactly?"

"It means I see life as it is—not as I wish it was."

"Not the way people see it around here."

Armantrout just smiled.

"I'm curious about something," Matt said. "Don't you find it a little awkward being a realist around all these idealists? It's an Episcopal school, after all; these are people of faith."

"I find it a bit suffocating at times," Armantrout said, "but I do what I can to introduce a more balanced perspective."

"A more realistic perspective," Matt said.

"Exactly."

"A perspective on life as it really is."

"As I said."

"On life as *you* think it is."

"What about you, Callahan? You have to be around some of these 'people of faith' too. Are you one of them? Are you a believer?"

Matt paused. "I'm not sure yet. I'm still working on that one."

Armantrout made an obvious glance at the clock. "Did you just drop by for a philosophical discussion, Mr. Callahan? Because it's getting late. Maybe another time."

"I wanted to talk to you about Leah Pelton."

"What about her?"

"I'm not sure we're approaching her the right way. I'm not sure we're being fair."

"We? Or me?"

"I got together with her mom a couple Sundays ago. We met at a park near her house. She said something that's been bothering me ever since. She asked me a question—sort of like the one you just did, only a little different. She asked me if I was *willing* to believe."

"Willing to believe what?"

"That's just it—it doesn't matter what. She said you have to at least be *willing* to believe something before you can actually believe it—you have to at least be open to the possibility of an idea or you'll never even consider it. It reminded me of something from one of my philosophy courses—something they called 'defeater beliefs.' We all hold certain beliefs we assume to be true—beliefs that make it impossible for us to believe in other things. They *defeat* other beliefs."

"For example?"

"Suppose I plan to do research on UFOs—but suppose I'm convinced in advance that there can't be life on any other planet. What am I going to conclude when I look at all the evidence? That UFOs are all optical illusions or secret government projects—but under no circumstances will I ever consider that they might be visitors from another planet. I can't consider that—my defeater belief makes it impossible."

"When there could, in fact, be life on other planets."

"Exactly. The question to ask is, 'Where did I get my defeater belief—and can I be sure it's true?' Because if it's wrong, it'll keep me from considering other things that might be true."

Armantrout slowly smiled. "Fascinating—but are we talking about UFOs here?"

Matt paused. "No. We're talking about Leah Pelton."

"I had a feeling. Go on."

"Leah thinks she saw an angel—and we automatically think she has an emotional problem or a brain disorder. Why is that?"

"Because those are the only logical possibilities."

"Are they? Isn't there another possibility we might be overlooking?"

"Such as?"

"Isn't it possible that Leah actually did see an angel?"

Armantrout tipped his head forward and peered at Matt over the top of his glasses. "An angel. A chubby little cherub with rosy cheeks and curly blond hair in a diaper. The kind you see on Valentine's cards."

"C'mon, Charlie, that's just a caricature. I'm talking about a real angel here—some sort of divine being—a messenger from God. Isn't it possible?"

"No. It's not."

"Why not?"

"Because there is no God. No God, no messenger—it's that simple."

"But that's your defeater belief—don't you see? What if there is a God? What if you're wrong about that?"

Armantrout shook his head. "I appreciate the lesson in philosophy; now let me give you one from my own field— psychology. Freud said that people have a tendency to project their wishes onto the real world until their wishes become confused with reality. In other words, people believe what they believe largely because they want to."

"And you think I want to believe in angels?"

"No—I think you want to believe in Natalie Pelton."

Matt didn't reply.

"You said you met with Ms. Pelton on a Sunday—in a park—near her home. Do you often meet with parents on weekends, Mr. Callahan? That sounds a bit like a social call if you ask me. Not that I blame you; Natalie Pelton is a very attractive woman—though I believe she's currently involved with someone, if I remember correctly."

Matt felt his face flush a little. "What are you saying, Charlie?"

"I'm simply asking a question: Are you attracted to Natalie Pelton?"

Matt hesitated. "Yes. I am. But that doesn't mean—"

"It means your emotions are clouding your better judgment. That's not a criticism—it's just human nature. Natalie Pelton desperately wants to believe that there's nothing wrong with her child. Who can blame her for that? She's willing to believe anything right now—even the ridiculous notion that her child has actually seen an angel."

"And me?"

"You want to support Natalie in her belief. That makes you willing to entertain ideas that you know deep down are absurd."

"Do I?"

"Yes—when you're thinking clearly."

"When I'm thinking like you."

"When you're thinking realistically."

"Maybe you're right," Matt said. "Maybe Freud was right. Maybe people do believe what they want to believe deep down inside—maybe that's what faith is. But if that's true, Charlie, it's true for you too."

"What do you mean?"

263

"Maybe you don't believe because you don't want to. Maybe you can't believe because you're not willing. Did you ever consider that?"

Armantrout picked up a piece of paper from his desk. "That reminds me—I got a call from Ms. Pelton today. She wanted to notify the school that Leah will be absent for the next week or two."

"Why?"

"It seems she took my advice after all—she got that MRI. It turns out Leah has a tumor in her brain. Ms. Pelton seemed hesitant to offer many details, but I pressed her a little and took a few notes. Yes, here it is . . . the tumor is putting pressure on the 'medial temporal lobe.' The neurologist told her this sort of thing has been known to cause auras—even visions. Who would have guessed?"

Matt was stunned. "What are they going to do?"

"They can't tell if the tumor is malignant or benign until they do a biopsy, so they want to remove it right away. She's having surgery at UCLA tomorrow. Poor kid; somebody should send flowers."

Matt immediately stood and headed for the door. He stopped in the doorway and looked back. "You know, Charlie, there are people all over the world who believe in God, and there are people who think they've seen angels—smart people, educated people, and they don't all have brain tumors. Either I'm beginning to see something that's not really there, or you can't see something that is. One of us is blind, Charlie; I'm just not sure yet which one of us it is."

Armantrout smiled. "If you want my opinion, stop by anytime."

Matt disappeared down the hall.

40

Tino yawned and looked at his watch: it was almost nine a.m. Saturday morning and Bobby had not returned to his house. Bobby's shift had ended at the hospital at seven; he should have been home before this. His girlfriend and her daughter had returned an hour ago, but Kemp's pricey new Mercedes was nowhere in sight.

Tino caught a glimpse of Bobby's girlfriend when she walked from the car to the house. *Pretty woman*, Tino thought. *Nice little girl too. If I had a family like that I wouldn't be out riding around*. The house had been quiet for an hour now; there was no sign of activity except for the glow of a TV. The woman was probably in bed asleep—which is exactly where Bobby should have been.

But Bobby wasn't there.

So much for making it look like a robbery, he thought. *Too bad—it would have been nice to do it while he was asleep*. Tino considered the hospital again. It was impossible—UCLA was enormous and there were people everywhere. No, it had to happen away from the hospital—and soon. There was no way around it: Bobby was a loose cannon, and there was no telling what he might do next—unless Tino got to him first.

Tino needed to find him. A great deal of money was riding on this—and if anything went wrong, maybe even Tino's life. *My life for Bobby's,* he thought. *Sounds like a good trade to me.*

He started the car and drove off.

⇒≡≡⇐

Fifteen minutes later Tino was standing in the center of the lobby of UCLA Medical Center. Straight ahead of him was an information desk manned by two elderly volunteers with stooped backs and welcoming smiles. On the left was a gift shop filled with all the forgotten sundries a patient or an overnight visitor could ever need. On the right was a glass-encased vending machine stocked with vases of roses and daisies—instant comfort or consolation, whatever the occasion called for. The ceiling was high and the floor was covered in a slick, glistening stone that seemed to muffle all the footsteps. Though it was only the hospital's lobby, the air already had a slight smell of disinfectant that imparted a vague sense of dread. And there were people—some talking, some laughing, some seated on vinyl sofas consoling weeping friends. There were people everywhere; Tino wondered if the lobby was ever empty. *The old man's no fool,* he thought.

"You lookin' for me?"

Tino turned. There was Emmet, staring at him coldly with his open hand already outstretched.

"You like to get right down to business, don't you?"

"This ain't no social call. You got somethin' for me or don't you?"

Tino took the envelope from his blazer and held it out. "A cashier's check made out to cash, just as you asked. Feel free to verify the amount."

"No need. A man like you don't make mistakes like that."

"Thank you."

"It's not a compliment. I just figure you're the smart one in the group—though I can't say you got much competition."

When Emmet took hold of the envelope, Tino held on to the other end. "This is a great deal of money," he said. "What do you plan to do with it?"

"I'll find a use for it," Emmet said, tugging the envelope free. "The thing with money is, you don't want to let it stick to your fingers."

"Very wise. Mind if I give you a piece of advice?"

"I can't stop you."

"Don't deposit that in your checking account. Most people would, just to see the nice fat account balance—but if you do, you'll have a federal agent knocking on your door within the week. They keep an eye out for large cash deposits; it smells like drug money."

267

"I'll keep that in mind."

"I'm just looking out for myself. A man in your line of work would have a difficult time explaining where he managed to come up with an extra million dollars. I don't want you pointing your finger at me—that would be bad for both of us."

"I'll remember."

"You do that. By the way, have you seen Bobby today? I didn't see his car in the parking lot."

"It's Saturday—might be his day off. Did you try his house?"

"He didn't come home this morning."

"Can't say I'm surprised—the man's too dumb to stay where he belongs. No tellin' where he's been—but I can tell you where he's bound to be later on."

"Where?"

"Don't you read the papers? Figured you'd know all about it. That book of yours—there's a big book signing over at that new mall in Glendale. Olivia Hayden's set to be there, and if she's there I don't believe Mr. Kemp will be far away."

"Thanks for the tip."

"Just lookin' out for myself."

Tino smiled. "You're a very smart man, Emmet—a lot smarter than Bobby."

"Like I said—not much competition."

Tino turned without further word and headed for the exit.

⟫⟪

Emmet watched him until he left the building, then walked around the corner and found an old wood-paneled phone booth. He pulled the door shut behind him and dialed a three-digit number. When the emergency operator answered, he said, "Is this where I find the police? No, ma'am, it's not an emergency exactly, but it's sort of important so I thought you wouldn't mind. Can you put me through? Thank you—you have a good day now.

"Yes, hello—is this the police? Well, if you don't mind, I'd rather not tell you my name—but I have some information I think you'd like to know. Remember that doctor over at UCLA—the one who just up and disappeared a couple weeks back? Smithson, I believe his name was. Well, I believe I know the man responsible for that—and I can tell you right where to find him. You know that new mall over in Glendale?"

41

Kemp stretched up on his tiptoes and peered down the line of people. The line must have been fifty yards long, winding like a river down the long pedestrian walkway at the new $400 million Americana at Brand. The outdoor mall was the ideal setting for a book rollout and signing of this magnitude; no single bookstore could have ever contained the crowd. From where he stood Kemp couldn't even see the front of the line, but he knew where it had to be because the location was marked by thousands of multicolored balloons bound together in a gigantic rainbow arch stretching across the pavilion. At one end of the arch was a wall-sized rendering of our own Milky Way galaxy; at the opposite end was an enormous photograph of a beaming Liv Hayden holding a glossy hardcover book. The crowd prevented Kemp from seeing beneath the arch, but he knew what he would find there when he eventually reached the front of the line. Directly beneath the arch would be a table, and seated at that table would be none other than Liv Hayden herself, smiling mechanically and jotting inane greetings to total strangers inside the cover of her just-released and soon-to-be-best-selling book: *It's All About You*.

Kemp could almost hear the sound: *ka-ching, ka-ching, ka-ching . . .*

He turned around and looked; there were as many people behind him as there were in front of him, and more were arriving all the time. Buses pulled up to the curb and dropped off people in droves, shuttled in from other malls across the city. He tried to take a head count of the people in front of him but it was impossible; there were people of all shapes and sizes, some alone and some in groups, some standing at attention like soldiers while others wandered in and out of line with food and drinks. There was no way to tell how many of them were actually buying books and waiting for them to be signed, so there was no way to estimate how long he would be stuck in this seemingly endless line.

To make matters even worse, Kemp's line wasn't the only one. There were two lines running parallel to each other about twenty yards apart, converging like train tracks at a point beneath the rainbow bridge. The people in each line eyed their counterparts in the opposite line warily, measuring the relative progress of each column, grumbling and complaining when either line seemed to be moving faster than the other. *What's the difference?* Kemp thought. *Two long lines or one gigantic one—either way we'll be here all day. Suckers—at least I'm getting paid for this.*

Kemp knew he should be thrilled by the size of the crowd—it was exactly what Kalamar and Biederman had predicted. Every autograph meant a book purchase, and every book purchase meant a third of the publisher's take for him. He should have been ecstatic—but he wasn't. In fact, the longer he stood in line the angrier he became. Why did he have to wait in line like everybody else? This whole thing was his idea. The book, the autograph session, even the stupid balloons—none of it would have happened if it wasn't for him. He shouldn't be standing in line like all these other peons—he should be sitting

270

at the table beside Liv Hayden, laughing and flirting with her like the costar of one of her movies. He should be signing books too—*Best Wishes, the Angel.*

The entire scheme was his inspiration; he alone was responsible; it was his flash of genius that was behind it all. The thought should have given him a sense of pride and satisfaction, but it didn't. It stuck in his craw like a jagged sliver of bone—because nobody knew it but him.

≥≈

Tino Gambatti also looked down the line of people, but he wasn't counting heads—he was searching for one particular face. There was something sticking in his craw too, but it had nothing to do with whose idea the whole thing was or who was getting credit for it now. Tino didn't care about who got the credit; he only cared about who got the money. He was a businessman, an investor, and he had a great deal of money invested in this project—money that had been borrowed from others. He knew these people; they were businessmen, too, and they had no interest in apologies or excuses. They simply wanted their money back—on time, to the dollar, with interest. In Tino's line of work there was a simple rule of thumb: if you want forgiveness, you go to a priest; if you want to live, you repay your debts.

It's just business, Tino thought. A man who risks his money must do whatever he can to protect his investment—and right now Bobby Foscoe was looking like a very bad investment. This idea of his, it was pure genius; but Bobby himself was a fool, and now he was allowing his own vanity to endanger the entire project—a project that Tino was heavily invested in. Bobby was free to destroy himself, but he had no right to take the other partners down with him. It was time to end their

271

partnership—and if Bobby wanted to destroy himself, Tino would be only too glad to help.

There he is.

He spotted Bobby in the opposite line about fifteen yards back. Bobby seemed agitated, impatient—no surprise there. Tino stepped out of line and started across the open space toward him.

⇒⇐

The line inched forward again but Kemp found the progress maddeningly slow. *What's taking so long?* he wondered. *How long does it take the woman to sign her name?* He went up on his tiptoes once again, searching the pavilion for any sign of Biederman or Kalamar or Tino. They were the last ones he wanted to meet here—they were the ones who had warned him that he could never, ever come face-to-face with Liv Hayden. But they were wrong. Hayden would never recognize him—not at first, anyway. Each time he had played the angel he had been careful to position himself directly in front of the brilliant examination light. His face should have been completely silhouetted—just a dark shadow against a blinding aura of light. How much detail could she have made out? Besides, he had to meet Hayden face-to-face. He had something he wanted to tell her.

He thought again about the words he had implanted in Liv Hayden's mind while she was still in that semiconscious state—how the "angel" had told her she would find true love, that the man of her dreams would soon come to her and that she would know him the instant she saw him. He had described himself to her in exhaustive detail: his handsome, chiseled features; his sinewy jaw; the deep cleft of his chin; his aquiline nose with the sexy flaring nostrils; his penetrating eyes the color of plush sable; and his black hair so thick that fingers could get lost in it. Who else could that describe but Kemp? How could she possibly miss him? What did the woman need, a map?

Kemp imagined for the hundredth time how his first encounter with Liv Hayden would go. When he reached the front of the line he would slowly extend his book for her to autograph; when she took hold of the book he would refuse to let go, forcing her to look up and make eye contact. Then he would slip off his sunglasses and flash his most engaging smile, turning his head slightly from side to side to give her a thorough look. And then he would say it—the "password" that would identify him as her unmistakable one true love: "I don't believe in accidents—do you?"

After that he would just let the old McAvoy instincts take over, and who knew what might happen next? *I just hope she doesn't do anything embarrassing*, he thought.

He briefly thought about Natalie again; when he did he felt a surge of anger and resentment. What was the woman's problem, anyway? Kicking him out of the house without even a day's notice, making him spend the night in some cheap hotel. He should have been furious, but he wasn't. It just made things easier in the long run. No awkward breakup, no tearful good-byes—this way the whole thing was her idea. *Natalie's a good woman, but that daughter of hers . . . Who needs the grief? A kid who sees angels—what's she been smoking? And she's not even a teenager yet. Better to cut bait before the kid goes off the deep end completely.*

273

≈

＝≈

Tino was only halfway across the pavilion when two men in blazers and sunglasses stepped in front of him.

"Tino Gambatti?" one of them said.

Tino looked at him. "Who are you?"

The man flashed a badge. "Detectives Isaacson and Garibaldi, Los Angeles Homicide. Are you Mr. Tino Gambatti from Baltimore, Maryland?"

"Maybe. Maybe not."

"Look, pal, I got a whole list of questions for you and that's the easiest one. Now are you Tino Gambatti or not?"

"Okay, I'm Tino Gambatti. What about it?"

"We have some questions we'd like to ask you, Mr. Gambatti. Would you come with us, please?"

Tino glanced over at Kemp. "This is not a good time."

"Well, it's a dandy time for us. Now are you coming with us or do we have to arrest you?"

Gambatti took one last look at Kemp, then reluctantly turned and followed the detectives to a waiting car.

=≡=

"Hey, do you mind? Stop pushing."

Kemp looked down. The voice came from a squat-bodied woman standing in line in front of him. "Are you talking to me?" he said.

"You're the one pushing. Who else would I be talking to?"

"I'm not pushing, lady. It's a little crowded, okay?"

"Pushing, shoving, call it what you want. It's not your line, you know. Wait your turn like everybody else."

Kemp glared at her. "Oh yeah? Well, suppose I told you it is my line."

She sneered at him. "Who do you think you are?"

"I happen to be a personal friend of Liv Hayden."

"You know Liv Hayden."

"As a matter of fact I do."

"You're friends."

"Close friends."

"And as a personal favor, she asked you to wait in the back of the line with everybody else."

People around them began to snicker.

Kemp was about to give a stinging reply when something caught his attention from the corner of his eye. He looked and saw three big men standing together near the center of the pavilion. They seemed somehow out of place; two of them were dressed in business attire and wore dark glasses, as if they were security guards. They suddenly turned and headed toward the exit together, and when they did Kemp could see the third man clearly—it was Tino Gambatti. What was Tino doing here? More important, where was he going—and who were the two men with him? Then he noticed that one of the men was leading Tino by the arm.

Kemp felt a sudden wave of panic and began to frantically search the area.

275

⌇

≈≡

Emmet watched as the two homicide detectives led Tino Gambatti away, then looked across the pavilion at Kemp. He waited for Kemp's frantic gaze to pass close to his position— then he raised his hand and waved. When he saw Kemp's eyes lock onto his own he smiled back, and when he did he saw a look of astonished recognition flash across Kemp's face, as if the two men were high-voltage wires that had suddenly crossed.

≈≡

Emmet! What's that old fart doing here?

The instant Kemp's mind formed the question he also

knew the answer. Emmet must have been there for the same reason Kemp was—he wanted to meet Liv Hayden face-to-face. But the old man had no romantic interest—he was the other angel, and he just wanted to see if Hayden would recognize him. But what if she did? That would be disaster—then she might figure out the whole thing! How could the old man take a chance like that? Kemp knew the answer to that question too: The old man had nothing to lose. If Hayden wanted to make trouble, Emmet would just point the finger at Kemp. And if she didn't want to make trouble—if she kept her sense of humor—the old man might even take credit for the whole idea!

Then an even more sickening thought occurred to Kemp: If Hayden recognized Emmet, she'd know the entire message was phony—including the part about the man of her dreams.

Kemp looked at his line, then over at Emmet's. He knew he had to get to Liv Hayden before the old man did.

≡≡

Emmet turned to a young man standing in line in front of him. "Warm day," he said.

"Hotter'n blazes if you ask me," the man replied. "That's LA for you."

Emmet nodded. "Must be almost noon—that ol' sun's about straight overhead. But I suppose a strapping young fella like you can bear the heat a mite better than an old man can."

"You feelin' okay, mister?"

"Don't like to complain," Emmet said. "A man could get a bit light-headed under a sun like this, that's all. Never you mind."

"Here, why don't you go ahead of me?"

"I couldn't. It wouldn't be fair."

"No, I insist. Here." He stepped aside and allowed Emmet to take his place—then he turned to the next person in line, a man about his own age. "Hey, we got an old man here, and the sun's getting to him. How about we let him go ahead of us—that okay with you?"

"No problem," said the other man, who then turned to the next person in line and made the same request. Within minutes Emmet had moved forward eight positions.

Emmet looked over at Kemp and grinned.

⇒⇐

Kemp panicked. He turned to the squat-bodied woman in front of him. "Fronts?"

"What?"

277

"Fronts? Mind if I go ahead of you?"

"What is this, recess? Wait your turn like everybody else."

"Look, this is important. I'm in a big hurry."

"And your time's more important than mine?"

Kemp pulled out his wallet. "I'll give you ten bucks if you'll switch places with me."

She looked at his wallet. "This must be important to you."

"Very important."

"Then make it twenty."

"Twenty! Forget it!"

She turned away. "Have a nice wait. I think I might get *two* books."

Kemp pulled out a twenty. "This is blackmail."

"You're breaking my heart."

Kemp stepped in front of her and tapped the shoulder of the man next in line. "Hey—ten bucks if you'll switch places with me."

The squat-bodied woman leaned out from behind him. "He gave me twenty."

Kemp stepped to the left and blocked her out. "Ten bucks, buddy—here you go."

The man frowned. "How come she gets twenty and I only get ten?"

"Because you're a nice guy and she's a bloodsucking leech. C'mon, how about it?"

The man narrowed his eyes at Kemp. "Did you just call my wife a bloodsucking leech?"

⇒⇐

"How long you been waiting?" Emmet asked the next woman in line.

"About two hours," she said. "How about you?"

"'Bout the same. How much longer you think it'll be?"

"Hard to say. It could take another hour."

Emmet let out a sigh. "Just hope I can wait around that long."

"Why? What do you mean?"

"I'm a working man. This is my day off—got a lot of things I need to take care of."

"Here, go ahead of me."

"Oh, now, I couldn't do that."

"No, please. I insist."

Another ten positions. Another smile at Kemp.

⇒⇐

Kemp was frantic. He looked at his empty wallet and all the people still ahead of him. They sure wouldn't take credit cards, and even if they would he didn't have time to fool with them anyway—Emmet was way ahead of him, almost halfway to the front. Kemp jumped out of line and hurried forward until he was a few positions ahead of the old man—then he looked for the friendliest female face he could find and approached.

"Hey!" he said with a big smile. "Nice to see you again!"

She looked at him awkwardly. "Um . . ."

"It's me—Kemp McAvoy. Don't you remember?"

She tried.

"We met awhile back—at the place—with what's-his-name."

"I'm sorry, I don't think I—"

Kemp felt a tap on his shoulder. The man who was next in line said, "That's really low."

Kemp looked at him indignantly. "What is?"

"Hitting on a woman just to move up in line."

"I happen to know this woman," Kemp said. "I'm just blanking on her name right now."

"Teresa," the woman offered.

"Right, Teresa—I remember now. This is my friend Teresa. How are you, Teresa?"

The woman glared back at him. "My name is Paula. Get out of here, you scumbag."

Kemp spun around and looked for Emmet—he was only ten people from the front of his line now. Kemp hurried forward again and searched for another sympathetic face—but word about the scumbag who was trying to cheat his way into line had spread like wildfire, and every man, woman, and child had mentally locked arms against him. There was no way he was cutting in line.

He looked at the table and could see Liv Hayden plain as day.

"This is incredible," Biederman said. "Better than we could have even hoped for."

"Even *Lattes* didn't have a kickoff like this," Wes said with a grin. "We're off to a fantastic start. See that camera team over there? That's CNN, my friend."

The two men paced back and forth behind the signing table, watching the two lines roll steadily toward them like twin conveyor belts—conveyor belts lined with cash. *It's a money factory*, Wes thought, *a freaking money factory*. Each eager reader stepped to the front of the line and extended a book, grinning from ear to ear as Liv Hayden illegibly scribbled her famous name, some buyers taking the opportunity to snap a quick photo while others tried to somehow touch her fingers as she handed the book back.

"She's a real trouper," Biederman said, smiling admiringly at his client's shapely back. "You know, she hates this kind of thing. Despises it."

"It wouldn't have worked without her," Wes replied. "People don't line up just to buy a book—they're here to get a piece of Liv Hayden. I don't think they—"

He suddenly stopped.

Biederman looked at him. "What's the matter?"

Wes pointed to the line on the left. There seemed to be some kind of disturbance near the front of the line—people were pushing and arguing. Wes stepped closer to get a better look . . .

He saw Kemp McAvoy trying to force his way into line.

≕≍

"It's an emergency!" Kemp shouted, trying to squeeze in front of a pregnant woman.

Two men hurled insults at him while a small boy kicked at his shins.

Biederman and Kalamar grabbed Kemp by the shoulders and dragged him out of line.

"What do you think you're doing?" Wes whispered angrily in Kemp's ear.

"I'm just trying to get an autograph," Kemp whispered back. "What does it look like?"

"Are you out of your mind?" Biederman said. "Get out of here, McAvoy. She can't see you—you'll ruin everything!"

"This whole thing was my idea!" Kemp said, raising his voice. "Why am I standing in line with the rest of these morons?"

Biederman grabbed the book from his hand. "Give me the book, you fool—I'll get it signed for you."

Kemp snatched the book back. "No! I have to meet her myself—I have to get to her before *he* does!"

Kemp looked over at Emmet. The old man was next in line now; in a few more seconds it would be too late.

In frantic desperation Kemp twisted out of Biederman's and Kalamar's grips and hurtled toward the front of the line. Each of the people ahead of him in line did his or her level best to block Kemp's path or at least slow his progress, but Kemp plunged ahead through the gauntlet of hands and arms until he finally shoved the last man aside and reached the front of the line—but the table was closer than he had estimated, and he was running with such reckless abandon that he couldn't stop himself in time.

Liv Hayden looked up just as Kemp crashed into the table and slid across it onto her, sending books flying everywhere and tipping her chair over backward until she slammed against the ground with Kemp on top of her.

281

Kemp raised himself up and stared down at her face six inches below. He whipped off his sunglasses and flashed his best smile.

Liv Hayden found herself staring up into a strangely familiar face—a face that was silhouetted against the noontime sun.

"I don't believe in accidents," Kemp said. "Do you?"

42

$\mathcal{M}$att Callahan looked through the window of the surgical waiting room and saw Natalie sitting by herself. She looked exhausted; her shoulders were rounded and there were dark circles under her eyes. Matt leaned closer to the glass and looked around the room; she seemed to be all alone. He straightened the flowers in his simple bouquet and opened the door.

Natalie looked up as he entered.

Before she could speak he held up one hand. "I don't want to interrupt—you'd probably like to be alone. I know Leah has her surgery today, and I just wanted to drop these off." He set the vase of flowers on a table in front of her and gave her a quick wave good-bye.

"Do you have to go?" Natalie asked.

Matt stopped. "I wasn't sure I'd be welcome."

"I could use some company." She patted the sofa beside her.

Matt walked over and sat down. "How are you holding up?"

"I've been better."

"Any word yet?"

"There never is. Surgeons don't like to give preliminary reports—it just gets your hopes up when things could still go wrong. That makes the bad news worse."

"Nothing will go wrong," Matt said. "Leah will be fine."

"Promise? I work here, don't forget. I've made that promise to families a thousand times—sometimes I was right, sometimes I was wrong."

They sat together in silence for a few minutes.

"I'm sorry," Natalie whispered.

He looked at her. "Sorry for what?"

"You were right, Matt—Leah did need an MRI. I didn't want to hear that. I just wanted to hear that everything was all right. Weird, isn't it? I wanted my daughter to be all right so much that I almost killed her."

"Don't talk like that," Matt said. "You wanted the best for her, that's all, and nobody knew what the best thing was. We were all just guessing."

"Armantrout knew. He suggested the MRI right away. If I hadn't agreed to that MRI, they never would have found her tumor. Who knows how big it would have gotten before we found it some other way? By then it might have been too late. Armantrout was right. You know something, Matt? I think that bothers me more than anything else—he was right. He was arrogant, and rude, and heartless—but he was right. He may have saved Leah's life."

"He didn't save Leah's life," Matt said. "An angel did."

"What?"

"I've been thinking about it a lot, Natalie—I was up most of the night. Armantrout recommended the MRI, but the only reason he recommended an MRI was because Leah thought she was seeing angels. Do you see what I'm getting at? If it wasn't for what she saw, none of this would have happened."

"But what if it was all in her head?"

"When I couldn't sleep last night, I looked up *temporal lobe epilepsy* . . . It's true, sometimes it makes people see auras or bright lights, but they're usually just vague sensations. Leah saw a man and a woman, and both of them were doing something very specific—holding out their hands like this, remember?" He held out his hand palm-down. "Does that sound like a 'vague sensation' to you? Are we supposed to believe that a tumor pressing against a bunch of neurons would cause her to hallucinate in that kind of detail—twice?"

"But what about the third time—the blinding light?"

Matt shrugged. "I don't know. I can't explain that. I'm just saying there's another possibility, that's all. Maybe Leah actually saw something—something that was really there."

"An angel?"

"Why not? People have seen them before—at least, they thought so. And aren't angels supposed to do good deeds? If these really were angels, they started a series of events that helped you find that tumor before it was too late. That sounds like a good deed to me."

"You really believe Leah saw an angel?"

"I'm not sure if I believe it or not. But you know what? *I'm willing to*. Maybe Armantrout didn't save Leah's life—maybe an angel did."

Another hour passed—still no word from the surgeon.

"Can I get you anything?" Matt asked.

"No, thanks," Natalie said. "I don't want to keep you. Don't you have school today?"

"It's Saturday."

"Oh, right. I keep forgetting."

"It doesn't matter. If it was a school day I'd be here anyway. Hey, my star pupil is out sick—what's the point?"

She hooked her arm through his.

"To tell you the truth, Natalie, I was surprised to find you here alone. Where's your—you know—"

"My boyfriend? My significant other? My domestic partner? There's no good name for a man who won't commit to you. His name is Kemp, and he won't be here. He's never been there—not when I needed him."

"Sorry."

"I'm not. I threw him out—I told him to pack his bags and get out and never come back. To tell you the truth, I don't know what took me so long. That's why I'm here alone."

Matt patted her hand. "Who's alone?"

Natalie looked into his eyes and smiled.

43

Leah opened her eyes and looked up at the recovery room ceiling. It seemed to be spinning a little—the way the sky looked when she jumped off the merry-go-round and lay on her back in the grass. Everything was a little fuzzy; she blinked her eyes and tried to focus better, but it didn't seem to help. Her head ached terribly, and she could feel the bandages pressing her ears against her head like a winter cap. The worst pain seemed to come from the right side; she lifted her hand to touch the spot, but when she did she heard a voice:

"Now, don't do that."

A wrinkled old face smiled down at her.

"Emmet—what are you doing here?"

"Your momma asked me to look in on you. How you doin', girl?"

"My head hurts."

"They got it wrapped up real good. You look like a big Q-Tip."

She smiled and it hurt a little more.

"Brought you somethin.'" He held up a Little Debbie cupcake wrapped in plastic; he jiggled it so that it made a crinkling sound. "You take one of these every day and you'll be feelin' up to snuff in no time—doctor's orders. I know you can't eat this just yet, so I'll set it over here." He set the cupcake beside her on the nightstand.

"I guess I won't be seeing angels anymore," Leah said.

"No? Why not?"

"They took out part of my head—the part that sees angels."

"The part that sees angels—what part is that?"

"I don't know. I'm not sure."

"Don't be silly," Emmet said. "They didn't take out part of your head, sweetheart—they just took out somethin' that wasn't supposed to be there."

Leah rested her eyes for a moment. "Where's Mom?"

"You know where she is—where else would she be? Right out there in the waiting room worryin' her heart out and waitin' for you to wake up."

"Is Kemp with her?"

"I have a feelin' you won't be seein' Mr. Kemp for a while." He paused. "That okay with you?"

"Yeah. That's okay."

"Don't you be worryin' about your mom now. She'll be just fine—matter of fact, I saw a very nice man holding her hand when I passed by. Handsome fella too."

"Who?"

"I'll let you find that out for yourself. I should go now—I can see you need your rest. Just thought I'd stop by and lift your spirits a bit."

"Emmet."

"Yes?"

"You think I'll still see angels?"

"You never can tell. If you do, I wouldn't be ashamed to say so."

"Maybe I wasn't supposed to tell," Leah said. "The angels told me to *shhh*."

"Maybe they were just tryin' to warn you," Emmet said. "Life's not easy for folks who see angels these days—I doubt it ever was."

"Will you come and see me again?"

"Anytime you want. All you got to do is ask."

"Thanks," she whispered, and almost before the word left her lips she fell asleep.

44

Olivia Hayden stared out the floor-to-ceiling window of Wes Kalamar's office at Vision Press. Behind her, Biederman, Kalamar, and Kemp McAvoy sat three-in-a-row on a sofa with their sorry heads hung low. No one had said anything for a long, long time; none of the men had the courage to speak first.

"Nice office," Hayden said without turning around. "A little shabby, but it's got a decent view. I've got a house up there in the hills, you know." She glanced back over her shoulder, daring anyone to reply.

They all stared at the floor.

She turned and planted herself with her fists on her hips like a drill sergeant, staring at the tops of their heads one at a time. "Let me see if I understand all this," she said in a low and even tone. "There never was an angel. No vision—no message from beyond—no 'chosen one'—no special calling."

"I think you're very special," Biederman said. "I've always said so."

"Shut up, Morty."

"Whatever you say, sweetheart."

"So my 'vision'—the three of you just made the whole thing up. You manufactured it out of thin air."

"We put in some long nights," Biederman said. "Wes is very good at—"

"Shut *up*, Morty."

"Sorry."

She stepped in front of Kemp. "You—you're the one who came up with this whole idea. What are you, anyway, some kind of Nazi doctor?"

"I'm not a doctor," Kemp mumbled. "I'm a nurse."

"A *nurse*? What did you think you were doing screwing around with my head?"

Kemp didn't answer.

She stepped in front of Wes Kalamar next. "And you're the publisher. No wonder you got the book done so fast. I thought you must be some kind of boy wonder, but you just had a cheat sheet—you got the notes in advance."

Then it was Biederman's turn.

"And you, you little parasite. I guess I shouldn't be surprised at you. You've been sucking my blood for twenty years—why should you change now? A vulture doesn't turn vegetarian overnight."

When she turned away Biederman quietly rose to his feet and cleared his throat. "I'd like to say something, if I may."

Kemp and Wes stared up at him in disbelief.

"I know you're upset, sweetheart, and believe me, none of us blame you. You've called me a parasite, and a lesser man might be offended at this. But the truth is, that's precisely what an agent is—a parasite. I live off of you. If you succeed, I succeed; if you starve, I starve. As you so colorfully put it, I suck your blood. If someone cuts me, I bleed—but remember, sweetheart, when I bleed it's *your* blood I bleed."

"Morty, can I interrupt?"

"Of course, sweetheart."

291

"Are you out of your freaking mind? What are you babbling about?"

"I took advantage of you, agreed—we all did. But you need to remember that I did it for your own good."

"For *my* good!"

"I saw a business opportunity here—an opportunity for you to take on a role you might not otherwise consider."

"Yeah—like the alcoholic mother in *Lips of Fury*."

"On the contrary—this role had dignity, it had stature. Now tell the truth: haven't you enjoyed playing the role of visionary, of prophetess, of spiritual mentor to an entire generation? You had a conversation with an angel—now everyone wants to know what you think."

"But it didn't happen, Morty. It was all just a role."

"Is that so different for you?"

She looked at him. "What are you getting at?"

"You're an actress, sweetheart. You're paid to play a role; you play the role, and when you go home at night you set the role aside. It's what you've been doing for twenty years. Is this role really so different? Harrison Ford did a fourth Indiana Jones movie at the age of sixty-five. Why? Because he enjoys the role, and because he couldn't afford not to—the franchise is a gold mine. Your situation is no different. You have a very profitable role here; do you really want to give it up?"

She paused. "You're saying I should keep playing this role?"

"The question isn't whether the vision really happened or not. The question is, 'Do you enjoy this role?' and 'Is it profitable?'"

"You mean profitable for you."

"I don't eat unless you eat. I'm a parasite, remember?"

Wes saw where Biederman was headed and joined in. "Biederman's got a point, Ms. Hayden. I apologize for the past, but let's look to the future. It's already done—the book, the publicity campaign, even your own promotional tour. The question isn't whether you want to play the role; the question is, 'Why shouldn't I get paid for a role I already played?' There's money in this—big money—if we all just keep our heads here."

Hayden seemed lost in thought. "Prophetess. Visionary. I could get used to that. No more crash diets; no more tummy tucks; no more push-up bras from the Spanish Inquisition." She looked over at Wes's desk. "Is that an Interstuhl Silver?"

"It sure is," Wes replied. "Have a seat—give it a try."

She did, slowly rocking back and forth and caressing the arms. She looked up at Biederman. "What about the fiasco at that book signing yesterday—when this moron tried to do a swan dive on top of me? That made the evening news."

293

Biederman shrugged. "An avid fan tries to touch the prophetess. That was terrific publicity, sweetheart—we should have planned it."

Now Wes rose to his feet, too, his enthusiasm growing. "What Biederman is saying is that everything's still going according to plan. We can pick up right where we left off." He paused. "That is, if you say so."

Biederman smiled. "Think about it, Liv. A second book— maybe a third. And let's not forget the movie."

Hayden swiveled back and forth in her chair. "You really think you can sell the film rights to this?"

"Studios are calling *me*, sweetheart. They're hungry."

"I would star, of course."

"Whatever you say."

She looked at Wes. "This second book—would I have to write it?"

"I can handle everything. Production, editing, cover design—you wouldn't have to lift a finger. All you'd have to do is sit down for a chat with Oprah from time to time."

"I like Oprah," Hayden said thoughtfully. "I think we've bonded."

"What do you say, sweetheart?"

Hayden's expression abruptly hardened. "I say we need to renegotiate the finances—that's what I say. I'm feeling a little left out, if you know what I mean. What was I getting out of this deal—just the author's measly cut while you three walked away with the lion's share?"

"A minor oversight, easily corrected," Biederman said apologetically. "I'm sure we can easily come to terms that everyone will find amenable."

"Good. Let's do it now."

Wes blinked. "Now? Wouldn't you like to think about it first?"

"Why? I know what I want and I know what I deserve. Okay, here's my offer: I take everything—you boys get nothing."

The room became suddenly quiet.

"How's that again?" Wes asked feebly.

"Sweetheart, that's a little one-sided, don't you think?"

"You're right, Morty, that did sound a little selfish. I mean, what's in it for you three? I didn't make that clear, did I? Okay, let me put it another way: I take everything, and you boys don't have to spend the next ten years in prison. How's that?"

No one replied.

Hayden stood up. "I could sue all three of you morons—I could take you for everything you've got. I could sue that hospital; I could take this publishing company; and I could put all three of you in prison for a very long time. But why should I do that when you can all work for me—for nothing?"

Now Kemp spoke up for the first time. "That's not exactly fair, Liv. After all, we're the ones who—"

Hayden turned on him. "Excuse me. Who are you?"

Kemp blinked. "I'm the nurse, remember? This whole thing was my idea. I'm the one who—"

"That's who you *were*," Hayden corrected. "Who are you now? You're nobody, that's who. Morty can handle the film rights; the boy wonder here can write me another book. What do I need you for?"

Kemp had no answer.

Hayden stepped forward until she was almost nose-to-nose with him. "I've known a lot of men like you," she said. "I even married a couple. You're the worst kind of parasite of all—at least Morty feeds me before he sucks my blood. But you—you're the kind who takes everything and gives nothing back. Consider yourself lucky, nurse—these other two are going to be working for me for nothing. All I want from you is for you to get out of my sight."

Then she stepped in even closer and lowered her voice to a whisper. "Oh, and one more thing. I might forgive you for messing with my head, but don't you *ever* mess with a woman's heart—you got that? My 'one true love'—how desperate do you think I am? Now get out of here."

Kemp turned without a word and slunk toward the exit. At the door he looked back at Biederman and Wes; he put his hand to his head in an "I'll call you" gesture, but neither man would make eye contact with him. He left and closed the door behind him.

Hayden took a seat on the Interstuhl again and slowly crossed her legs. "I always wanted one of these," she said. "Okay, you parasites—let's get to work."

295

Kemp stepped out onto the sidewalk and stopped. Parked directly in front of the building was his very own Mercedes CL65, and leaning against the passenger door with his trunklike arms folded across his chest was a glowering Tino Gambatti.

"Hello, Bobby."

"Tino—what are you doing here?"

"I came to see you. We're partners, remember? I was concerned about you."

"Me? What about you? I saw you at the book signing—who were those guys who took you away?"

"Police. Homicide detectives, to be specific."

"What did they want?"

"I think you know."

"What does that mean?"

"They had questions about the disappearance of a certain neurologist from UCLA. I had no answers for them, and fortunately they had no evidence—so they were forced to release me. Why do you think they wanted to question me, Bobby? No one knows me here—I'm from out of town. Someone must have tipped them off."

"Well, it sure wasn't me," Kemp said.

"I'm glad to hear that," Tino said. "We're partners, after all."

Kemp swallowed hard. "About our deal. I'm afraid there might be a small—delay."

Tino smiled thinly. "Yes—I saw it on the evening news. You just had to see her, didn't you? You couldn't leave well enough alone."

"I didn't think she'd recognize me."

"You didn't think. You never think—that's your problem,

Bobby. I followed you here this morning, you and Biederman and Kalamar—and Ms. Hayden, of course. I know the four of you just had a meeting, and I'm sure by now you've told her everything—once she recognized you, what choice did you have? I've done business with Ms. Hayden before, remember? I have great respect for her as a businesswoman—she's very shrewd, very practical. Judging by the fact that you're out here on the sidewalk while our fellow partners are still inside, my guess is that she's found some use for them but you've been sacked. Am I right?"

Kemp nodded.

"That's too bad. If she doesn't need you, she won't want my money anymore either. Once a woman begins to clean house, it's difficult to stop her."

Kemp said nothing.

"That's unfortunate for both of us," Tino said. "If you're out of the partnership, you have no way to repay me—and if I'm out of the partnership, I have no way to repay the people I owe."

"Take the car," Kemp suggested. "It's yours."

"It's a lease," Tino said. "I already checked." He stepped aside and opened the passenger door. "Take a ride with me. Let's put our heads together. Let's figure something out."

Kemp suddenly bolted and started running frantically down the sidewalk—but he could hear Tino's voice calling calmly behind him.

"It won't do you any good, Bobby—you have to settle your debts. It's just business, Bobby. It's just business."

297

45

"Why do I have to ride in a wheelchair?" Leah grumbled.

"Stop whining," Natalie said. "It's hospital rules—everybody has to do it. Ask Shanice if you don't believe me."

The nurse nodded. "Your mom is right. We don't want our patients falling down on the way out the door. After you get outside we don't care anymore—you can fall down all you want to."

Leah reluctantly lowered herself into the wheelchair; painted across the back were the words UCLA MED CENTER in stenciled block letters. Natalie lowered the foot pedals for her daughter and Leah tried to place a foot on each of them, but her legs weren't quite long enough and they were left dangling from the slung leather seat.

"Have you got everything?" Natalie asked. "Your books? Your iPod?"

Leah nodded and they started rolling toward the hall.

Shanice held the door for them. "Bye, Leah. Come back and visit us, okay?"

"No way."

As the wheelchair rolled through the doorway, Shanice put a hand on Natalie's arm. "You gonna be okay?"

"We'll get by," Natalie said. "We're headed in the right direction now; the rest will take care of itself."

In the hallway Leah turned and asked, "Where's Mr. Callahan?"

"You can call him 'Matt' when you're not in school, honey. He's pulling the car around."

Leah began to look left and right down the long corridor. It was late morning, and the hallway was crowded with doctors and nurses and visitors searching for patients' rooms.

"Who are you looking for?" Natalie asked.

"Emmet," Leah said.

"Emmet works nights, honey. He won't be here this morning."

Leah tried to stamp her foot but missed the pedal. "I wanted to thank him."

"For what?"

"For coming to see me after my operation."

Natalie squatted down beside the wheelchair and looked at her daughter. "When did Emmet come to see you, honey?"

"I told you—after my operation. He said you asked him to."

Natalie frowned. "I did?"

"Well, he came anyway."

"After your operation? When they brought you back to your room?"

"No, before that."

"Before that? In the recovery room?"

"Right—when I first woke up."

Natalie stroked her daughter's hair. "Visitors aren't allowed in the recovery room, honey—that's a hospital rule too."

"He was there, Mom. He said he walked right by you."

"If he did I would have seen him. I was in the waiting room every minute—I never left."

"Maybe he knows a back way."

Natalie smiled. "There's no 'back way' into the recovery room, honey. I should know—I've worked here for ten years."

Leah was losing her patience. "He was there. I saw him. I talked to him."

"Okay. But you need to understand something about anesthesia—the medicine they give you to make you fall asleep. When you wake up you can feel a little fuzzy-headed. Did you notice that? Things can look different; people might sound funny; sometimes you can even imagine things that aren't really there."

"He was *there*."

"Okay, honey—whatever you say."

Natalie turned the wheelchair toward the elevators—but just as they started down the hallway, the door to Leah's room opened again and Shanice stepped out.

"Natalie—good, you're still here. You forgot something." She handed Natalie an envelope with her name handwritten on the front.

"What's this?"

"I don't know. It was under Leah's pillow. Looks like a card to me."

Natalie opened the envelope and took out the card. On the front of the card it simply said, "Wishing You a Speedy Recovery." She opened the card and looked inside—it was unsigned. A slip of paper fell out of the card and drifted silently to the floor. She picked it up and looked at it.

It was a cashier's check for a million dollars.

Her mouth dropped open.

"You forgot something too," the nurse said to Leah. "They found it in the recovery room a week ago, right after your operation. They said it must be yours."

The nurse handed her a small brown cupcake wrapped in plastic.

Leah broke into a huge smile and held the cupcake up to show her ashen-faced mother—but just as she was about to speak she saw something from the corner of her eye.

She saw Emmet standing at the end of the long hallway, leaning on his mop and smiling at her.

He raised one finger to his lips and went, *Shhh*.

Epilogue

I've told this story a hundred times; some people believe it and some people don't. Funny thing is, I tell it the same way every time, so the difference can't be me. I guess some people are ready to believe and some people just aren't.

I suppose some people think they're too smart for this kind of thing; they've got the universe all figured out and things like this just don't fit in. Even God doesn't fit in—they've got him all explained away too. The way I look at it, it's a really weird universe out there, and you'd better be careful when you start talking about what can and can't happen.

But what do I know? I'm just a girl who sees angels.

Acknowledgments

I would like to thank the following individuals for their assistance in my research for this book: Barbara Anderson, RN, Neuroscience/Trauma Unit Director, UCLA Medical Center; Susan Baillie, PhD, Director of Graduate Medical Education, David Geffen School of Medicine at UCLA; Judy Glover, Certified Registered Nurse Anesthetist, Raleigh, North Carolina; Peggy Patrick Medberry, Literary Manager, Patrick-Medberry Associates, Valencia, California; Drs. Chip and Ann Smithson, Cary, North Carolina; Sheila Trivedi, Beverlywood Realty, Los Angeles; and the helpful nurses of UCLA Medical Center who were kind enough to interrupt their lunch breaks to speak with an unknown novelist in the UCLA cafeteria.

Thanks to all the others who contributed to the creation of this book: my literary agent and friend, Lee Hough of Alive Communications; my beautiful wife, Joy, for reading my chapters each day and lending so many valuable insights; story editor Amanda Bostic for her helpful suggestions on timeline and plot; copy editor Deborah Wiseman for her unerring red pen; my publisher, Allen Arnold; and the rest of the staff at Thomas Nelson for their dedication, hard work, and patience with demanding writers.

Mea Culpa

I apologize profusely if any of my readers are tempted to suspect that Kemp McAvoy's derogatory comments about the nursing profession reflect my own opinions as well. Allow me to remind you that Kemp is a complete scumbag, whereas I am a very nice guy. Both my wife and I are ardent fans of nurses and the nursing profession as a whole; this book was co-dedicated to two wonderful nurses who have been especially important to our family. We sincerely believe that nurses contribute just as much as doctors to the process of healing—sometimes more. May God bless them for lending a compassionate face to the sometimes formidable and bewildering field of medicine.

Those familiar with UCLA Medical Center may not recognize some of my descriptions of the facility. That's because I visited UCLA to do my background research in January of 2008, five months before the doctors, nurses, and angels of UCLA made their move to the beautiful new Ronald Reagan UCLA Medical Center just across the street.

A special word of thanks to my publisher and my agent, who were forced to endure a novel wherein a publisher is portrayed as desperate and incompetent and an agent is described as a "bloodsucking parasite." I know better—and please note that in chapter 1 writers are described as "basically pond scum." Thanks for all your work, guys.

TIM DOWNS

first
the
DEad

A BUG MAN NOVEL

"Since *Shoofly Pie* the Bug man novels have progressively developed to become some of the best suspense reading on the market. *Less Than Dead* is the best of the bunch."

—www.TitleTrakk.com

TIM DOWNS

A BUG MAN NOVEL

LESS THAN DEAD

"The Christy Award-winning author's latest forensic
thriller is intelligent and thought-provoking and should
especially appeal to male fans of the genre."

—*Library Journal*

TIM DOWNS

A BUGMAN NOVEL

ENDS
OF THE
EARTH

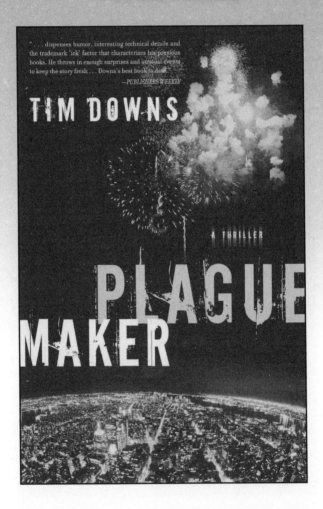

" . . . dispenses humor, interesting technical details and the trademark 'ick' factor that characterizes his previous books. He throws in enough surprises and unusual events to keep the story fresh . . . Downs's best book to date."

—Publishers Weekly

TIM DOWNS

A THRILLER

PLAGUE MAKER

"(B)rilliant! A must read that
takes the psychological thriller
to a new level!"
—Ed Rouse, Major, US Army Retired

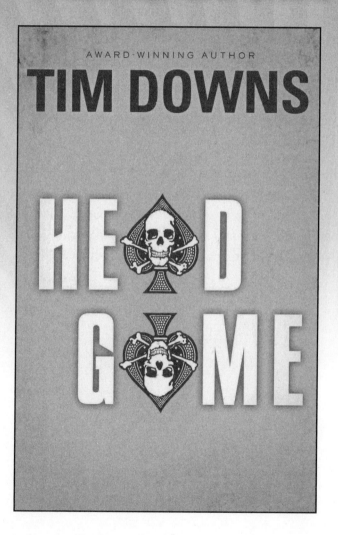

AWARD-WINNING AUTHOR
TIM DOWNS

HEAD
GAME

About the Author

TIM DOWNS has received high acclaim for his novels, such as a Christy award for *PlagueMaker*. He is also the author of the Bug Man novels *(Shoofly Pie, Chop Shop, First the Dead, Less than Dead,* and *Ends of the Earth)* and *Head Game*. Tim lives in North Carolina with his wife and three children.

visit TimDowns.com